MURDER
IN THE SNOW

MURDER
IN THE SNOW

VERITY BRIGHT

bookouture

Published by Bookouture in 2020

An imprint of Storyfire Ltd.
Carmelite House
50 Victoria Embankment
London EC4Y 0DZ

www.bookouture.com

ISBN: 978-1-80019-071-9
eBook ISBN: 978-1-80019-070-2

To Miren and Michael for championing Eleanor and Clifford, and, of course, Gladstone.

'It matters not how a man dies, but how he lives.'
– Samuel Johnson

CHAPTER 1

'Botheration!'

Despite weeks of meticulous planning, one small, but crucial detail had been overlooked.

Staring up at the cream-stone country mansion, Lady Eleanor Swift was, however, quite unable to fathom what it was. All three floors and both narrow towers that flanked the entrance were decked out in shimmering festive splendour. Inside, the finishing touches for the villagers' Christmas Eve lunch were being efficiently ticked off by her meticulous butler and hard-working staff. *So what was it?*

She walked inside looking around the impressive marbled entrance hall with her piercing green eyes. And then she remembered.

'Gladstone!' She clutched her mop of red curls. 'What on earth are you doing?'

The stumpy tail furiously wagging under the Christmas tree froze.

She strode over and tapped his back. 'Come out immediately!'

The elderly bulldog she'd inherited from her late uncle, Lord Byron Henley, backed out reluctantly and stared up at her. A green Christmas bauble swung from one of his bottom front teeth.

'Oops! I thought I'd made sure they were all too high for you to reach.' She relieved Gladstone of his prize and dropped to all fours, shuffling under the broad lower branches to check there were no more hiding. The bulldog joined her, covering them both in pine needles.

The tree had been planted in an enormous container filled with earth and she now saw, dotted around the base, the telltale signs of bulldog burial.

'Gladstone! You've been burying all the baubles the staff spent so long putting up.'

He gave a loud woof in reply and spun in a stiff-legged circle, which made the whole tree lurch dangerously.

She flinched at the sound of more decorations falling to the polished oak floor and then clutched her cheek. 'Ouch!' She held her breath. 'Shh! We need to sort out this mess before Clifford finds out.'

A polite cough came from behind her.

'Too late,' she whispered in the bulldog's ear. 'Double bother-ation!'

She crawled back out and straightened her dress against her slender frame. 'Ah, Clifford, there you are. The tree looks absolutely wonderful.'

Her impeccably turned-out butler cast a disapproving eye over her muddy hands, the nest of pine needles in her hair and the gash on her cheek. 'Most perceptive of you to crawl all the way underneath to fully appreciate it, my lady.'

His tone was reminiscent of the way he'd spoken to her as the little girl who used to spend rare summers at the Hall during holidays from her boarding school.

'Very funny. Gladstone and I were—'

He pointed a white-gloved finger at the cream damask-uphol-stered settle streaked with muddy dog prints.

She winced. 'Okay, I was just trying to cover up the fact he's been un-decorating the tree before you noticed.'

'A plan unlikely to have succeeded, my lady, seeing as I was hanging onto the tree from the first-floor landing to save it from falling on your, and Master Gladstone's, head.'

'Ah! Thank you.'

'Regrettably, I appear not to have totally preserved you from injury.' He pulled a pristine handkerchief from his pocket. 'That cut needs attending to.'

She put a tentative hand to her cheek. 'Pah, it's just a scratch.'

'I believe I may have mentioned previously that a scratch which bleeds that perceptibly is in fact termed a "cut", my lady. And we have but thirty-five minutes left before you need to play hostess as the... ahem, lady of the manor.'

With her hands hastily scrubbed and the worst of the pine needles shaken from her hair, she was about to rejoin Clifford when her housekeeper appeared. A diminutive, soft-curved woman, her ever-ready smile and patient manner gave her the air of everyone's favourite aunt.

'Gracious, my lady, excuse my asking but what happened to your face?'

Eleanor felt for the cut, which she silently admitted was feeling rather hot and raised around the edges. 'Oh, it's just a scratch, Mrs Butters. I'm fine.'

'There's nothing fine about anything that angry looking. I can't leave you walking about like that. Whatever would your late uncle think of that, God rest his soul?'

Eleanor patted her housekeeper's arm. 'Thank you, but Clifford already insisted I douse it in something frightfully spiteful. Honestly, I ended up with much worse scrapes and bruises when I travelled the world. And none of my arms or legs fell off.'

Mrs Butters chuckled. 'I see half of your uncle and half of your mother in you, if you don't mind my saying so, my lady. Not that I saw a huge amount of your mother, as you know. But there is definitely a streak of your mother's fierce independence in you.'

Eleanor reflected that she hadn't seen a great deal of her mother either. Her parents had disappeared when she was only a young child, after which her uncle had sent her to boarding school. 'Thank you. Now, how about a compromise? Instead of dragging you away from preparing for the hordes of ravenous villagers who will soon descend upon us, I'll slap whatever you recommend on this minor scratch… er, cut. Then, together, we can finish any last-minute preparations.'

'Deal, my lady. In the medicine cabinet beside the second kitchen dresser there's a pink tin. It smells like honey and eucalyptus. Slather that on nice and generously. Then you need to find the arnica tablets and take two.'

After following her housekeeper's instructions, Eleanor checked that everything food-wise for the event was going smoothly. Mrs Trotman, her warm-hearted but no-nonsense cook, with the help of Eleanor's young maid, Polly, seemed to have everything well under control. Except, rather worryingly, Gladstone. He'd gone AWOL from his bed by the range where he'd been grounded for the stealing-baubles-from-the-Christmas-tree-and-burying-them escapade.

Out in the hallway, she frowned, trying to remember what she had been doing before a wilful bulldog had interrupted her.

'Perhaps if you would care to consult the planner I gave you, my lady?'

She jumped. 'Clifford, how many times have I told you not to do that silent materialising trick? It's most off-putting.'

'Apologies, but I am a butler. I will in future, however, endeavour to appear at your side heralded by sackbuts and cornetts.'

'It would be a help.' She spotted the ghost of a smile. Clifford had not only been her late uncle's butler, but before that his batman in the army. Despite the class difference they had become firm friends. On his deathbed, Lord Byron had asked Clifford to look after his beloved niece, a duty he carried out with unwavering loyalty, iron resolve and large doses of dry wit. She patted her cardigan down. 'But it appears my planner has... erm, misplaced itself. Again.'

'Indeed. Might I suggest then inspecting the ballroom? The luncheon tables are almost finished. The ladies have done a remarkable job, as always.'

'Of course they have. You all fulfil your duties with such dedication, you richly deserve your own treat once the villagers have retired tonight.' She smiled at him. 'Wasn't it a wonderful tradition Uncle Byron instigated, inviting most of Little Buckford to the Hall each Christmas Eve?'

'His lordship was a most benevolent gentleman, my lady.'

'And we've a few extra people from Chipstone this year. It seemed churlish not to extend the invitation as we had a few places free at the table. I've no idea who's coming, I just asked the Women's Institute ladies to arrange it. I do hope my first bash at hosting will live up to Uncle Byron's memory.' She suddenly felt lost. 'I also wish with all my heart he was here.'

Clifford cleared his throat. 'As do I, most heartfully. But perhaps he is, my lady. I believe his lordship's spirit will always live on at Henley Hall. Now, shall we finish checking all is ready? Your guests will have been looking forward to this since the twenty-fifth of December last.'

'No pressure then!'

CHAPTER 2

The lunch tables did indeed create a magnificent scene. Starched ivory cloths hung to the floor, topped with long artful sprays of white cyclamen and red roses set among the lightest green spruce. Tall silver lanterns punctuated the tables' length. At each place setting, on a square of red linen, edged in gold ribbon, sat a handmade paper Christmas cracker. Jugs of ruby-red fruit cordial stood ready and waiting beside small towers of polished glasses.

'It's beautiful, Clifford,' she breathed. 'I must find the ladies to thank them again. And Miss Moore, I think she's still here. Her floral displays are quite the centrepieces.'

As they passed back through the main hallway, Clifford paused to consult a neatly handwritten list he pulled from his morning-suit pocket. 'We have yet to check if the three games rooms are correctly set up. Then the refreshments room and the changing room for the race runners.'

Eleanor felt a slight wave of panic as she peeked past his elbow at the list. 'Oh golly, and there are still the last of the farewell gifts the guests will take home with them to finish tying the ribbons on. How on earth are we going to do all of that in' – she pulled her uncle's fob watch from her pocket – 'what is now twenty-five minutes?'

'Methodically and meticulously, my lady, of course.'

'Of course,' she muttered.

Through a window, she caught sight of a horse-drawn wagon turning in past the long row of garages. 'I've just thought of one more, most important job, Clifford. I won't be a minute.'

At the back door of the kitchen, she shivered and pulled her cardigan closer round her before stepping out into the icy air that froze her breath. Hurrying over to the wagon, she called out a greeting to the athletically built figure heaving a sack of coal onto his shoulders.

'Mr Canning, merry Christmas. And how are you?'

He turned and fixed her with piercing blue eyes, set in chiselled features. He nodded, shaking some of the coal dust from the strands of his fair hair poking out from beneath his cap. 'Right enough, m'lady.' His rough voice always reminded Eleanor of a growling beast. With a hard shrug, he jerked the sack further over his back.

'Gracious that looks rather heavy. Clifford could ask Joseph to help you with his wheelbarrow?'

Canning scowled. 'Nothin' wrong with me arms, nor anything else, if that's what you're suggesting.'

Eleanor bit her tongue wondering why on earth nature had seen fit to waste such handsome features on such a charmless man.

'No, I wasn't. I just thought it might help. Give you more time to get back home and change and still catch the coach bringing the other people from Chipstone to the Christmas lunch.'

'I'll manage right enough.'

'As you wish.' The frantic waving of a tea towel at the back door caught her attention. 'Ah, a minor emergency. Please excuse me, Mr Canning. Looking forward to seeing you later.'

Without a word, he walked away towards the coal cellar.

She shook her head, wondering if she had done the right thing inviting him to the Christmas lunch. He had been delivering coal to Henley Hall long before she'd inherited it from her uncle earlier that year. And he used to live in the village before moving to Chipstone, so it had seemed rude not to. *Besides, Ellie, mother always said to look for the good in everyone.*

Her thoughts were interrupted by her housekeeper semaphoring again from the doorway. She hastened over. 'Mrs Butters, are you alright?'

'Oh my lady, so sorry to interrupt but Father Time is fair dashing round the Hall leaving us no minutes to get all the last things done. I can't find Mr Clifford and he does like things to run to clockwork. And Trotters, I mean Mrs Trotman, is having kittens in there.'

Eleanor clapped her hands. 'Whatever it is, we can sort it out. Come on.'

Having indeed sorted out half a dozen minor emergencies, Eleanor was hastily tying the last of the ribbons on the wreath that hung on the front door. Another Henley Hall tradition, everyone contributed something to the decoration that would welcome visitors throughout the festive season. Being a part of that felt very special. As she added the crowning ribbon, Mr Canning appeared sat aboard his coal wagon.

'Thank you for delivering on Christmas Eve, I do appreciate it,' she tried one last time. 'I'll see you at the lunch later, perhaps?'

There was no reply and Eleanor turned back to her ribbon. *Even he can't find something to be unhappy about in that, Ellie. Just ignore him and finish the wreath.*

She heard him jump down from his seat. 'Lady Swift?'

'Yes?' She turned back in surprise.

He pulled off his cap. She had never seen him look nervous before. 'Just wanted to say ta like. For the invite. To the lunch,' he added as if she were a little dense.

Had there been a chair behind her, she'd have fallen into it over him uttering a 'thank you'.

'Yes. I know. My pleasure.'

He looked down at his cap and then seemed to focus his piercing blue eyes somewhere over her left shoulder. 'You know, you're not like the other toff— gentry I deliver to.'

'Ah, well perhaps not.' She sighed, wishing for the untold time that her recent inheritance of Henley Hall had also included a manual on how to be a proper lady of the manor.

'Didn't mean to be rude. No offence. Your uncle were the same.'

'None taken. I rather take that as a compliment.'

He ran his hand along his jaw, revealing the blue tattoo of a compass that ran down his neck and disappeared into his collarless shirt. 'Most fancy folk pretend I don't exist when I'm delivering.' He gestured behind her to the Hall. 'Places way less posh than this.' His face clouded over. 'Only time they acknowledge I exist is when one of them stuck-up footmen complains I've left a blooming sooty footprint somewhere.' He glanced at her face and then away. 'Excusing the language, m'lady.'

She shrugged. 'It must be almost impossible to do your job without leaving some…' Eleanor tailed off. *He obviously isn't listening, Ellie. Honestly, why did you ever think you—?*

The anger that suddenly erupted on his face stopped her thoughts. 'You know what they say? At this time of year with me breaking my back?' He jabbed a blackened finger at her. 'They say all I bring is a sack of bad luck!'

She shook her head. 'I can't see anything unlucky about having someone run a wonderfully efficient service that means I and my staff can have heat and hot water over the festive season.'

For the first time in the conversation he looked her in the face.

'You got me thinking a couple of weeks back when you invited me to lunch. Included me like I counted for something. Didn't even get your butler, old Mr Stiff, to ask me, did it yourself.'

She smiled despite herself. *Quite an appropriate name for Clifford, really. Sometimes, anyway.*

'But, Mr Canning, you used to live right here in the village before you moved to Chipstone. And you've delivered here for years, long before I came, so why wouldn't I invite you?'

He glanced over his shoulder at his wagon. Apparently satisfied his horse wasn't about to bolt, he turned back to her. His eyes bored into hers once more. 'Because. That's why. No one else in Buckford would have asked me. Or Chipstone. But I've been doing a lot of thinking. I've done what's right.' He turned on his heel and strode back to his wagon. He climbed into his seat and took up the reins. 'None of us can choose how we enter this world, m'lady, but we can damn well choose how we leave. Excusing the language again.' He urged his horse into a fast trot and was soon lost from sight round one of the many bends in the Hall's drive.

What on earth was that all about, Ellie?

Aware that Clifford had stepped noiselessly out behind her, she spun round and gave him a questioning look. 'What was he talking about?'

'Regrettably I did not overhear the exchange. There is, however, a minor catastrophe we need to address, if you are free?'

'Oh golly! Now what?'

'Master Gladstone has collected all the prizes earmarked for the treasure hunt and secreted them in his bed. He is now lying on top of them, refusing to give them up.'

'Oh dear, that won't do at all.' She tried to hide a smile as she followed Clifford inside.

Miraculously the morning's preparations were finally concluded to Clifford's satisfaction, but only two minutes before the villagers were due to arrive. Eleanor sped down the stairs, now changed into an emerald-green silk dress and matching shawl, her stomach knotting.

Having been brought up abroad by bohemian parents and having spent the last few years in South Africa, she was fine tackling dangerous animals or crash landings in the desert. Society events, however, and welcoming the entire population of Little Buckford into Henley Hall as lady of the manor were a different matter. She waited in the centre of the hallway as Clifford stood ready to open the front door.

She straightened her dress. 'Wish me luck.'

'I am sure, my lady, that you will do his lordship proud.'

How does he always know exactly what you're thinking, Ellie?

Clifford reached for the door handles. 'Shall we?'

CHAPTER 3

The villagers' excitement hadn't diminished after the stowing of winter coats and hats, and a full rundown of the afternoon's festivities. Nor had it after the complicated process of getting all fifty of them seated at the three long tables set out in the ballroom.

Eleanor had greeted them all personally and now looked to her butler for her next move. 'You've done this before with Uncle Byron, Clifford,' she whispered. 'What's the correct etiquette? Do I just say "tuck in!" when the food arrives or am I supposed to recite a limerick while standing on one leg?'

'This afternoon is the only time in the entire year when the barriers are lowered a fraction and the rules are relaxed, my lady. You may do as you wish.'

'Clifford!' She stared at him. 'I can't have heard you correctly. You said the words "rules" and "relaxed" in the same sentence.'

'And like the villagers, my lady, you will need to wait until December twenty-fourth next to hear them in the same sentence again.'

With three courses on the lunch menu, she opted to take one at each of the long tables. Over the carrot and turnip soup, she enjoyed joining in with the chatter of everyone's plans for Christmas Day. As she moved to the second table, conversation paused with a collective gasp as the main course arrived. The roast geese with chestnut and sausage-meat stuffing were accompanied by dripping pudding, crispy parsnips, creamed leeks and mashed potato with cabbage peppered with slivers of bacon.

'To Lady Swift and her wonderful staff!' a voice called from the far end of the table, setting off a raucous stamping of feet that reverberated around the room. Eleanor beamed across at Mrs Trotman and mouthed a 'Thank you, well done!'

At that moment, Clifford approached. 'You have a visitor, my lady.'

She looked around the room. 'I'd say I have about fifty, Clifford!'

'Indeed, but your extra visitor is waiting in the hall.'

Intrigued, she hastened out of the ballroom and stopped dead. A broad-shouldered man in a blue wool overcoat and with his bowler hat in his leather-gloved hand stood looking at her uncle's portrait.

'Inspector!'

DCI Seldon turned to her with a grunt. 'Lady Swift.'

What's he doing here? When she'd first come to the Hall, she'd developed a love-hate relationship with the handsome detective. They'd crossed swords on several murder investigations she'd been caught up in. Of late, however, it had been more love than hate. The fact that he had saved her life only a few months previously had helped.

For a moment there was an awkward silence. 'Inspector, please forgive me, but I wasn't expecting you. It's my first Henley Hall Christmas Eve lunch and games for the villagers. Unfortunately I'm rather… busy.' *Blast, Ellie. If only he'd called yesterday!*

'I'm sorry.' He ran his hand through his chestnut curls. 'I was passing on my way to Oxford and then London, and on impulse I thought it would be… churlish not to extend my best Christmas wishes to you. And to Master Gladstone, of course. But I shouldn't have called unannounced, especially' – he nodded towards the raucous noise coming from the ballroom – 'as you say, you are entertaining most of the surrounding population.'

Think of something, Ellie! 'Would… would you care to join us though, Inspector?'

He grunted. 'I would love to, Lady Swift, but unfortunately I have a confoundedly tricky case that will keep me occupied throughout Christmas.'

'So you'll be working all over the festive season? That's such a shame. Well, the minute you are free, do come again. Only do call ahead, I should hate to miss you.' She blushed. 'I mean, I know your time is valuable.'

He held her gaze and then looked down, turning his hat in his hands. 'Yes, I'd like that.' He glanced at the grandfather clock. 'And speaking of time, I'm afraid I must be leaving.' He placed his hat on his head and nodded. 'Goodbye, Lady Swift.'

As she watched him drive away, she shook her head and wished again that he hadn't chosen today of all days to call unannounced.

Back at the lunch and now seated at the third table, she laughed along with everyone at the silly jokes that were told as the pickled walnuts and slices of cheese were devoured. With the plates cleared, she looked up in surprise as Clifford turned off the lights. Her guests, however, seemed to have been waiting for this, as hushed whispers of excitement ran round the room.

A moment later, she saw why. Entering in a line with Clifford at the head, her four staff appeared each holding aloft two plum puddings dancing in blue flames. This brought everyone to their feet, clapping wildly. Fearing the lump in her throat would be the end of her, Eleanor tried to hide her emotion by glugging from her water glass.

Lunch over, the women among the guests cleared the tables. The men then rearranged them into two long serving stations for the Christmas drink and second pudding.

A flurry of ladies served behind the tables, having to call out to be heard over the hubbub. Their matching red-and-white-striped pinafore aprons and caps adding a seasonal holiday feel to the already festive atmosphere.

In front of each table, a line shuffled forward. On the drinks table, Mrs Trotman handed out a generous glass of her secret recipe Christmas mead, which the guests savoured as they moved forward. They then handed the empty glass to Polly, who washed it up in a bowl and placed it on a tray ready for the cook to use again.

On the other table, Mrs Butters and her helper, the local vicar's housekeeper, handed out slices of Mrs Trotman's equally secret chocolate yule log.

Eleanor beamed at her cook. 'Gracious, it's working like clockwork.'

'Right it is, my lady,' Mrs Trotman said, pouring another glass of Christmas mead.

Eleanor shook her head at the cook's quiet efficiency. 'What an amazing job you ladies are doing. Everyone seems to be enjoying themselves immensely.'

'Most folk are having a fine time, except folk like him.' She nodded to Conrad Canning standing in the queue to get his yule log. 'Old grumpy drawers over there's never got a good word to say. Only a minute ago he was arguing with another gentleman in the queue.' She leaned in and dropped her voice. 'Can't understand what women see in him. No use having eyes as blue as the sky if there's no heart to go with them.'

Eleanor looked across to Canning. He seemed his usual surly self. But then he saw her looking at him and for an instant his features changed. It was ridiculous, but he looked almost... *saintly? At peace?* She was sure he nodded almost imperceptibly, as if guessing her thoughts. A moment later he turned away from her to accept his yule log. When he turned back and left the line, his face had set itself into his habitual scowl. She remembered the odd conversation they had had earlier in the day. *What was it, he said?*

Mrs Trotman interrupted her thoughts, holding out a glass of Christmas mead. 'It'll help with the shock of getting that cut to your cheek, my lady. Shall I send Polly for some more ointment?'

At the sound of her name, the young maid spun round from the washing-up bowl, flinging an arc of water over most of the queue, Mrs Butters and Eleanor. She gasped and ran round with a soggy tea towel, which she held out with a trembling hand.

'So sorry, your ladyship.' She grabbed the top of her apron with her mouth and sucked nervously on the edge of the lace.

Eleanor smiled and gently tugged the apron free. 'No harm done, Polly.'

'Yes, my lady. Sorry, my lady.' The maid scuttled back to her station.

Eleanor took a sip of mead. 'Mrs Trotman, that is truly delicious, very warming. Just what our runners need if it starts snowing. Although I'm not sure the race should go ahead if the weather turns.'

But her cook didn't hear, being deep in conversation with the jittery maid. 'Polly, my girl, what did I tell you?' She pointed at the bowl Polly was washing the glasses in. 'Don't wait until you can't see the bottom to change the water, girl.'

Polly peered into the bowl. 'But, beg pardon, it looks quite clear, I thought.'

Mrs Trotman shook her head. 'Joseph! How full is the barrel?'

Joseph, the Hall's gardener, strode over. 'Plenty of space for lots more washing-up water still, Mrs Trotman. No point letting it go to waste when I can put it to use in the greenhouses.'

Over in the food queue, many of the fun-run entrants were staring longingly at the rapidly declining mounds of yule log. Eleanor watched Mrs Butters and her helper each place a slice on a square of newspaper. They then twisted the corners, securing the yule log, which they handed to the waiting runners.

Deciding that her next job should be to check the outdoor stage where they'd present the prizes to the race winners, she turned to go.

Before she could leave, Mrs Butters caught her eye. The house-keeper mouthed, 'Gladstone?'

Eleanor shook her head and mouthed back, 'Sorry, no idea.' Just then Clifford appeared, marching towards the kitchen with a contrite bulldog lumbering alongside him.

Good, no need to worry about Gladstone, but what about the weather, Ellie?

Polly appeared at Eleanor's elbow, her hands trembling.

'Are you alright?' she asked the girl with genuine concern.

Her maid's eyes were wide with fear. 'Must have been the whistling, my lady.'

'Whistling?'

'Yes, my lady. Red sky this morning, that means sailors' and shepherds' warning. Then someone whistled right when everything was red and changed the wind. Now the storm's coming. I don't like storms, my lady.'

Eleanor peered out through the floor-to-ceiling windows at the darkening sky and shivered. 'Neither do I, Polly.'

CHAPTER 4

'Ah, Lady Swift!' a cheery but disembodied voice hailed her as she neared the stage.

A hand then appeared clutching a shiny brass loudhailer.

'Reverend Gaskell, is that you?'

A ball of tousled grey hair and a pair of thick spectacles above a clerical collar bobbed up. 'Indeed, it is, Lady Swift. I, err… may have taken a brief tumble. I was retrieving this masterful speaking device of Mr Edison's own invention.' He hauled himself up to his full five feet five inches by leaning on what appeared to be a long-legged tripod. Beaming at Eleanor, he looked the epitome of Christmas in his red wool jacket over a purple shirt and matching jumper, his felt derby sporting a silk rose in the mauve hatband. 'However, thanks to our Good Lord, I am all in one piece. "A merry heart doeth good like a medicine," Proverbs, chapter seventeen, verse twenty-two. Gracious, but I see you may have met with a small calamity yourself. Are you alright, dear lady?'

'Perfectly fine, thank you.' Eleanor smiled and held out her hand in greeting.

Reverend Gaskell dropped the loudhailer, which hit the stage with a resounding clonk. 'Oops!' He pumped her hand exuberantly. 'Such a wonderful day. Thank you for so generously hosting this Christmas lunch and games for our most-deserving little community! I found myself still awake in the early hours this morning, full of excitement for all the fun and laughter that will ring across Henley Hall's grounds.'

Eleanor stared up at the now dark-grey sky. 'I only hope the weather holds. I don't suppose you could pull any extra strings on everyone's behalf and arrange for this snow to hold off until the Christmas fun run is over? The first and last sections are so steep I'm concerned someone will break something if the going is slippery.'

Reverend Gaskell chuckled. 'What a charming idea, but I'm not sure I have quite such influence above!' The vicar picked up the loudhailer. 'It is such an honour to be the official Christmas fun-run starter, dear lady. It is quite the highlight for me, and rather ironic as I fear "sporty" is not a term that has ever been bestowed upon me.'

'Sporty or not, you'll do a superb job, I have no doubt.'

'Well then, if you'll forgive me, I need to get into position.'

'I'll see you at the start in' – she pulled out her late uncle's pocket watch – 'gracious, only twelve minutes!'

Twelve minutes later, Eleanor was embarrassed to see everyone else had arrived at the start line before her. As she appeared, Reverend Gaskell hailed her through his brass loudhailer. 'Three cheers for Lady Swift and her generous hospitality!'

The crowd erupted, making Eleanor jump and leaving her not knowing where to look. She gave a cordial wave and looked around for her butler.

'My lady?' Clifford's voice came from behind her.

'Ah, Clifford. Tell me, how does the Christmas fun run usually get started?'

'In the customary manner, with the firing of the starter pistol as detailed in the fete programme.'

'Yes, yes, the programme. It's just that Reverend Gaskell seems to be stalling for some reason. The runners are getting restless.'

Clifford frowned. 'There seems to be some disturbance at the start line.'

Before she could reply a drop of snow landed on her nose and instantly melted. She jerked her head up. 'Oh, Clifford, we need the reverend to get this thing started, the snow's arrived.'

He nodded and walked over to the stage. Reverend Gaskell leaned down, cupping his ear as Clifford said something and held his hand out to show the first snowflakes were falling. The vicar pulled out his pocket watch and bobbed an apology. After patting Clifford's shoulder, the reverend put the loudhailer to his mouth again. 'Ladies, gentlemen, children, this is it! We are here to cheer on our most adventurous and spirited runners. Wish them God's speed, but first, please step back off the running course itself.'

This brought a hasty shuffling backwards from the spectators and a great deal of frenetic limbering up among the runners who the vicar now addressed.

'Gentlemen, I wish you every success in navigating this year's most ingenious course. Take care and be guided by Corinthians, chapter nine, verse twenty-four. "Know ye not that they which run in a race run all, but one receiveth the prize? So run, that ye may obtain."' He bowed his head momentarily, then looked up. 'I declare this Christmas fun run…' He lowered the loudspeaker and patted his blazer pockets.

Eleanor watched Clifford point at the vicar's back. With evident relief, the reverend reached behind and from the waistband of his trousers produced the starting pistol. He paused and seemed to stare intently at one of the runners, the gun pointing dangerously in their direction. Clifford gently moved the barrel to one side. The reverend shook his head and addressed the crowd through the loudhailer again. 'Good friends, my apologies. Runners! On your marks. Ready. Set. GO!'

At the sound of the shot, the runners set off like stampeding cattle, divots of grass and earth flying out behind them as they surged forward. Intense concentration was written on every face. It might be a fun run, but there was a lot of rivalry in the village. Eleanor's eye was caught by Canning. He was surrounded by a group of five men she didn't recognise – *probably from Chipstone*, she thought. She had greeted everyone at the entrance to the Hall, but there were too many faces to remember.

Clifford reappeared at Eleanor's elbow, holding an umbrella festooned with silver tinsel.

'Thank you for magicking that up from wherever you did.' She huddled under it gratefully.

'Crikey, Clifford. I thought this was supposed to be a fun run. Mr Canning for one seems to be taking it outrageously seriously.'

'Indeed, my lady. And it will probably turn combative before the finish line.'

'Well, I hope it doesn't actually get out of hand, that's all.'

'Then the crowd will be most disappointed. Shall we?' He gestured past the first obstacles that ran down the field before looping back to give the onlookers room to fan out along the length of the course. The furthest reaches were down the steep hill at the midway marker before the trail snaked back up the tortuous climb to the finish line at the Hall's main entrance.

She looked up at the snow, now falling faster, and shuffled her feet back and forth on the sodden grass. 'It is getting very slippery, you know.' An icy wind was whipping the flakes into spinning eddies, which whirled away across the ground before settling. 'We'd better get a move on, although I don't want to miss the fun of seeing the runners negotiate the first of your fiendish obstacles.' She gestured to the three lines of lorry tyres placed at intervals along the route.

Clifford pointed to a tall man in the crowd opposite with a thin moustache in a weathered trilby and overcoat belted tightly at the waist. 'The *Chipstone Gazette* reporter is enjoying the show, my lady.'

'I know, he has a pocket Kodak camera, so our little Christmas entertainment might even make the front page. Well, if he can get any photographs in this snow, that is.' By now the front runners who had escaped the tyres were tangled in the next obstacle, a large rope net they had to crawl under.

Eleanor and Clifford took a shortcut and reached their first cheering station, which was the point at which the field sloped dramatically downhill. The runners who had escaped the clutches of the rope net lurched towards them, slipping on the now mud and snow-covered grass. Once they'd passed, there was a brief gap before the next bunch of runners arrived.

One of them made Eleanor wince at the gasping sounds he was making. He looked familiar, but she couldn't quite place him. Then she remembered he was one of the group of five men surrounding Canning at the beginning of the race. As he drew level, he seemed to trip and landed hard in front of them. Clifford held out a gloved hand and helped him up, which drew a wheezing 'Cheers' before he lumbered off after the others.

Eleanor tilted her head. 'I thought I saw something in the rules about spectators not helping the runners?'

'True, my lady. Perhaps you saw the rule about runners not deliberately tripping each other up also?' He peeled off his now muddied white gloves and pulled another pair from nowhere. 'Hence, my helping him.'

She clapped and shouted encouragingly to the next straggle of runners who passed, then peered at the blackened sky. The biting wind had got up and the snow was now almost horizontal. She had to raise her voice to be heard. 'I wonder if we will be able to witness anything at all at the end. How many more are there to come through this section?'

'Approximately ten or so.'

Eleanor applauded at another small group who ran past, one of them holding the back of his leg as he hobbled to keep up.

'Oh dear.' She offered him a commiserating smile and an extra enthusiastic round of applause. As he crested the hill, he slipped and disappeared from view in a tumble of arms and legs.

'I say, man down!' Eleanor cried.

'Fear not, my lady, the noble members of the St John Ambulance Brigade are poised and waiting at the bottom.'

By the time all the runners had passed and she and Clifford had taken another shortcut to the finish line, a thick white layer had covered the course. The onlookers had their hands in their pockets and their hats pulled down against the snow and wind.

'This is actually really exciting. I wonder who will win,' she shouted against the gale. She stood on tiptoe and peered down the course. 'One man's miles in the lead!'

Clifford applauded along with the crowd's cheers as the triumphant runner, a stalwart of the Little Buckford and Chipstone running club, crossed the line. A dozen or more runners passed over the line in the next few minutes, all receiving a tumultuous welcome.

Eleanor peered down the course. 'I can't see anyone else coming.'

The crowd obviously thought the same and, chilled and soaked, made a mass charge for the warmth and dry of the Hall.

Eleanor and Clifford remained at their station. Clifford brushed a layer of snow off his coat lapels. 'This is the deciding stage of the Christmas fun run, my lady. Customarily, the last runners do not make it this far and return to the Hall in Solemn Jon's carriage.'

'Solemn Jon, the undertaker!? Seems rather close to the mark given the state they will be in.'

'Most likely. But, as you are aware, despite the name by which the entire area knows him by, Solemn Jon is a most jovial gentleman. And the cost of receiving a lift is only a pint in the local ale house.'

Eleanor laughed. 'Very crafty.' She leaned out from under the umbrella and stared down the hill. 'Well, judging by the fact that no one appears to still be running, I imagine Solemn Jon has already collected the stragglers and will be supplied with ale through to next Christmas. Oh, hang on!'

Two runners came into view. Almost on their hands and knees, they clutched at the snow-covered tussocks of grass as they hauled themselves up and over the long, steep rise. One of the runners was so thickly coated in mud his face was hard to see. He clutched his stomach as he heaved himself over the edge with his other arm, his legs wobbling, his eyes fixed vacantly on the finish line.

Eleanor watched the man, concerned by how much he was zigzagging. He panted past in the gloom of the snowstorm, followed by a giant, bearded man. As the bearded man passed Eleanor, he seemed to find a last shred of energy. Speeding up he drew level with the other runner and knocked him violently with his shoulder. He staggered past the finishing line and, without stopping, on towards the Hall.

Eleanor turned her attention back to the other runner, who now lay in the mud and snow, his head resting on a snow-covered tussock,

'Shall we go inside the Hall, my lady?'

Eleanor nodded, her eyes still on the fallen runner. 'Perhaps we should just check he's okay first.'

'As you wish.'

They approached him, their feet crunching on the freshly frozen snow.

Eleanor called out to the man, 'I say, do you need a hand up?' The thick blanket deadened her voice, making it sound hollow and lifeless.

When there was not so much as a groaned response, Eleanor darted forward and dropped to her knees. With Clifford holding the umbrella over the fallen man with one hand, he helped her turn him over by the shoulders with the other.

She gasped. 'It's Canning!' His eyes were unfocussed and he seemed in the throes of a violent internal struggle. 'We need to get Doctor Browning quickly.'

Clifford abandoned the umbrella and took the fallen man's wrist and concentrated on his pocket watch.

Eleanor's red curls stuck to her face as she looked around for help. 'Oh, Constable Fry!'

She beckoned and shouted to the policeman who was striding to the Hall's entrance, head down against what was now driving sheets of sleet. Somehow he heard or saw her and changed direction, reaching them in a few strides.

'Lady Swift, is something the matter?'

'We need Doctor Browning's assistance urgently. This man has collapsed and is in need of immediate attention.'

'Doctor Browning? Last seen in the refreshment room, your ladyship.'

'Good work, thank you. If you could fetch him then?' Eleanor turned back to the figure on the ground as Fry lumbered off. She went to remove the fun-run number pinned to the man's vest, which had twisted upwards and poked into his throat, but Clifford's cough stopped her.

'Forgive my contradictory suggestion, my lady, but I fear we should not touch the gentleman until Doctor Browning arrives.'

'Why ever not? I'm trying to clear his airway.'

'Regrettably, it is too late for that.' Clifford let the man's arm drop.

'You mean he's—'

'Dead, my lady.'

CHAPTER 5

She stared into Canning's now glassy eyes and felt a rush of guilt. 'I'm responsible for letting this man push himself too far! I should have cancelled the race at the first sign of bad weather.' She reached out again, wanting to remove the Christmas fun-run number as if doing so might somehow reverse the terrible event.

Clifford gently held her arm. 'If you will forgive the indelicacy of my observation, the gentleman has in fact ejected some of the contents of his stomach recently, my lady. That is not something associated with exhaustion.'

She snatched her hand back.

'And I do not think the inclement weather had much to do with his demise.'

'But he looked so fit, well, at least athletic. I wonder if his heart gave out.' She shivered. Too late, the wind had started to ease off and the sleet was drifting back into swirling snowflakes. She was soaked through. She knew Clifford must be too. She also knew he knew her too well by now to suggest she leave the victim.

A taut voice made her spin round. 'Constable Fry said you were calling for me, Lady Swift?'

The elderly doctor wore a tweed jacket buttoned up against the elements and a brown homburg. Like Eleanor's clothes, both were soaked through. His green patterned bow tie lay askew against his starched white collar. Fry silently brought up the rear.

'Thank goodness you're here, Doctor, although' – she glanced at Canning's now lifeless form – 'I suppose the urgency has gone.'

He tottered over, gripping his cane as his stoop caused him to rock backwards and forwards. With watery grey eyes, he peered through his round, wire-framed glasses at the fallen figure, then at Clifford. 'Mr Clifford.'

Clifford nodded back. 'Doctor Browning. Good afternoon. I rather fear Mr Canning's demise is—'

'"Demise?" I am a medical man. "Demise" is for literary writers of flowery prose. In my forty-four years of medical practice, I have never written a "demise" certificate.' He looked down at the prostrate figure. 'Conrad Canning! The fool!'

Eleanor fought the frown that leapt to her forehead. 'Are you going to examine him?'

The doctor held up a tremulous hand. 'There is no point, Lady Swift. Those eyes are staring at something in the afterlife, I can see that from here.' He turned back to Clifford. 'Have you found a pulse?'

'Not the faintest of beats, regrettably.'

'It is as I suspected. Canning understood his condition well enough to know that taking part in this Christmas fun run was beyond foolish.' Eleanor watched an expression she couldn't read cross the doctor's face fleetingly. He tottered the six steps to Canning's body, now half-covered in fresh snow, and bent stiffly from his waist. His glasses slid down his nose and landed on the dead man's chin. One lens fell out.

'Still causing trouble, even after you've passed over, you blighter,' he muttered for the deceased patient's ears only.

Eleanor's sharp hearing caught it, however, and she shot Clifford a questioning look. He raised an eyebrow in response.

Doctor Browning grabbed hold of the Christmas fun-run number and tugged it from Canning's vest. Eleanor craned her neck forward and watched as he then pulled down the vest. Having retrieved his spectacles, he pushed the lens back in and peered either side of the sternum as if watching a tennis match. He poked the dead man's throat, then pulled the mud-covered bottom lip down and grunted as a long trail of thick saliva ran down the chin. As it cleaved a path in the filth, Doctor Browning gave a knowing 'uh-hum' and straightened up stiffly, leaning on his knees to do so.

'What caused him to pass away?' Eleanor asked.

'Unofficially, I'd say his last moments bore witness to a heart attack but that is for his doctor to confirm, Lady Swift.'

'But you're here, attending the body.'

'Although this person is known to me, I was not his doctor.'

'But you said something about Mr Canning understanding his condition well enough to know he shouldn't run the Christmas fun run. What was his condition?'

The doctor gave her a withering look. 'I may have been fortunate enough not to call this man my patient, but I am an honourable physician, bound by the Hippocratic oath. Whatever I see or hear in the lives of others, I will keep secret, as considering all such things to be private. Good day.'

Eleanor stood open-mouthed as he shuffled away, his unsteady gait exacerbated by the unevenness of the ground. He soon faded into the swirling snow. Clifford stood silent. Eleanor flinched at the concern etched on his usually inscrutable expression. He shook his head and glanced up at Fry.

'I believe we have need of Solemn Jon, Constable Fry.'

'Right away, Mr Clifford.'

They waited in silence, keeping watch over the body, until the loud gasping of a heavy man running in stout boots made them both turn. Fry had returned, his chest heaving, mud streaking his uniform.

'Gracious, are you alright, Constable?' Eleanor asked, fearing another casualty.

'Quite. Alright. My. Lady,' the policeman puffed. 'That is a deceptively steep hill, if you'll pardon my giving an opinion on your property.'

Eleanor looked him over in concern. 'Have you just run all the way up the hill?'

'Almost three times, given that I slid back down to near the bottom twice. The going has become treacherous. Were this to have been a fun run involving horses and suchlike, I should have had regrettable cause to call a halt for the safety of the animals.'

Eleanor pointed at the now soaked body of Canning. 'I wish either you or I had called a halt to the Christmas fun run. Maybe then this man would still have been with us. But why run up the hill? I saw you with your bicycle earlier. Surely, taking the road would have been easier and a good deal less fraught with possible injury?'

'An astute observation, my lady. And, yes, it would have been if I hadn't had a puncture. I went down to the other end of the track to converse discreetly with Solemn Jon. I told him as you wouldn't want a huge fuss, seeing as it's the special day for everyone.' He smiled and gave a shrug. 'Jon said he would drop the runners he'd picked up at the refreshment room where they would receive an extra glass of mead.' He stared at his boots. 'I do apologise for the presumption that your ladyship would be happy to furnish the runners with an extra beverage. I would have checked first but on account of being at the bottom of the hill and Canning and yourselves being here at the top...' Constable Fry tailed off.

'A most ingenious ruse on your part, Constable. Not only am I happy to sanction it, I applaud you for your quick thinking. Ah!' She spotted the funeral wagon trundling towards them. Even without their ceremonial feather headdresses, the two black draught horses pulling the long glass and ebony-painted funeral coach brought an instant air of sombre elegance to the otherwise muddily irreverent spectacle.

'Bravo, Constable! If we can remove the deceased gentleman from the vicinity, it would be most helpful.'

'Begging your pardon, my lady, but I don't think many folks would be calling Canning here a "gentleman". There'll be precious few tears shed at the Duck and Badger tonight, I'll warrant.'

The three of them looked up as the funeral wagon drew to a stop. A short rotund man with chestnut-brown eyes, bordered by smile creases, gave a wave and raised his snow-encrusted peaked cap. The ribbed hem of a thick, blue woollen jumper hung out below his grey worsted jacket. Beside him, a whiskery Irish wolfhound sat poker straight, sporting a snow-laden matching peaked cap and hand-knitted scarf.

'Ah, Lady Swift, 'tis a pleasure.'

Eleanor nodded. 'It is good to see you too. And please accept my immense gratitude for helping out with this unfortunate situation, Mr Jon.'

The undertaker jumped down far more lithely than his rotund appearance suggested he would. 'Everyone's called me Solemn Jon for longer than ever, m'lady. It suits me just fine because it doesn't suit me at all, if you get my drift. Born happy, I was. And in this profession, you needs to see the bright side of things. Now then, shall we get this poor fellow out of the snow? He may have passed away, but that's no reason to treat him any differently to those of us still walking the earth. I've a jacket and' – he pointed to his wolfhound – 'even Patrick's got his cap on. Being left out in the snow is for rubbish and firewood that needs seasoning, not bodies.' He shook his head. 'Though I seen enough like him lying in the mud and snow in them trenches to last me a lifetime and more.'

'Will the three of you be able to manage Mr Canning? I'm very willing to help.'

Jon shook his head again. 'Goodness to heavens, m'lady! How would that look for my business if folk see me letting a titled lady sling a body over her shoulders?' He walked around to the back of the wagon. Reappearing with several lengths of wood battened together to make a ramp, he laid this against the side of the coach. Clapping his hands, he addressed Clifford and Fry. 'Gentlemen, shall we pay our respects to old Canning whilst moving him to somewhere more luxurious than the mud and snow?'

With a 'One, two, three, heave ho. Off to better pastures you go,' Jon orchestrated the awkward shuffling of the dead man across the boggy ground and up the ramp into his wagon.

'Thank you, gentlemen,' Eleanor said with relief. 'First hurdle out of the way.' She went to Jon's side as he stood ready to climb into the wagon. 'If you have any difficulty or delay in receiving payment from Mr Canning's family for any costs incurred, please send your bill straight to me.'

Jon raised his cap. 'Poor soul. There'll be no family willing to fork out for him. But it's my job to do the best by all, we're all made of the same clay in the end.' He swung himself into his seat with the nimbleness of years of practice. 'So I'll be happy to do right by him for cost of materials only, my lady. And look after Jet.' At Eleanor's confused look, he explained. 'Jet is Canning's horse. You'd have seen him pulling his wagon. He'll need a new home now, poor chap.' He stroked his wolfhound under the chin.

'That's very kind of you. But if you change your mind, let me know. Oh, just one more thing, if I might ask? Could you possibly leave Mr Canning on your fine wagon in the empty garage for a short while and continue enjoying the festivities?'

'With pleasure.'

The three of them watched him expertly turn the horses in a tight circle and head off to the long block of cream-stone garages, the wolfhound leaning his head on his master's shoulder as they set off across the grass.

Eleanor noted a troubled look pass over Clifford's face.

'My lady, I believe rather than fetch Mr Canning's doctor, it might be more appropriate to ask Oxfordshire Constabulary to send a coroner.'

She stared at him, but there was an expression in his eyes that made her keep silent. She wondered what he had deduced.

Fry's eyes turned to saucers. 'Foul play suspected? Oh dear, dear, bad show that. Telephone in the main hallway alright to use, m'lady?'

Once he was out of earshot, Eleanor tried to fight off the peculiar sorrow that washed over her. 'I suppose I should close the Christmas games now as a mark of respect?'

Clifford picked up the sodden, snow-covered umbrella and shook the worst of the weather off it. 'If I might suggest, my lady, the crowd will be deep in the throes of enjoying the delights of Mrs Trotman's parsnip perry.' He flinched. 'Possibly proceedings will even have moved on to her dandelion concoction.'

Eleanor remembered all too well the almighty headache effects that could bring on. 'I hope she isn't going to offer her chestnut liqueur.'

'I fear that may happen later this afternoon.' He gave her a rare smile. 'But if you are asking for my opinion?'

She shifted her soaking feet, then nodded.

'The Christmas lunch and games that follow are singularly the highlight of the village year. And for many of our worthy and hard-working, but lest affluent, residents, the only chance of a decent lunch and tea over the festive period. Given the less than popular regard in which Mr Canning was held by the villagers, it might seem churlish to further sour their abiding impression of him by closing the celebrations. Thus branding him as the man who cancelled Christmas.'

'Good call, Clifford, thank you.' Eleanor let out a deep sigh. 'Do you know I thought I had this Christmas event pretty well in hand, especially with all your wonderful and meticulous organisation which, again, I am grateful for.' She bit her bottom lip. 'Didn't see a dead man in my tea leaves this morning, though.'

'Most fortunate, my lady. Now, even though the snow has eased, I feel you should remove yourself from the elements and change into dryer clothing. Shall we?' He gestured towards the house.

As they walked, Eleanor broached the subject uppermost in her mind. 'You saw Doctor Browning's reaction, Clifford. Did it seem at all... what's the word?'

'Unprofessional?'

'Perhaps. But also he seemed... troubled.' She stopped and faced him. 'As troubled as you, yourself were at Canning's death. I didn't want to question you in front of Fry, but why the need for a coroner?'

By now they were standing under the imposing canopy of the main entrance to the Hall. She scanned his face.

'My apologies, my lady. I should have discussed the matter with you before Constable Fry arrived.' He busied himself brushing the ledge of snow from the shoulder of his morning suit.

She bent down into his eyeline. 'Clifford, whatever it is, you'll have to tell me sooner or later, you know.'

'Indeed.' He looked down at his gloves. 'Perhaps I should have told you the day you inherited Henley Hall.' He swallowed hard. 'Mr Canning's last moments were suspiciously similar... to those of your late uncle.'

Eleanor clasped her hands to her chest. 'Clifford?'

The same look of consternation passed over his features again. He regained his implacable demeanour with a visible effort. 'The death certificate identified the cause as an accidental overdose of digitalis from his lordship's heart pills, but I vigorously disagreed then and I do to this day. It is my regrettable belief, my lady, that his lordship was deliberately poisoned.'

Eleanor's thoughts swam. 'Poisoned? I… I can't process that at the moment.' She shook her head slowly. 'But… but that means that Canning—'

'Was also poisoned.'

CHAPTER 6

Having changed into dry clothes and half-thawed her toes and fingers by the kitchen range, Eleanor gently batted off Mrs Butters' insistence that she needed all manner of fussing over. Knowing she could rely on the discretion of her staff not to create a drama over what had happened, she slapped on her genial hostess face. Then she rejoined the noisy throng whom, Clifford had assured her, were oblivious to Mr Canning's demise.

Secretly, she wished for nothing more than to curl up on her favourite chaise longue with Gladstone while she tried to make sense of the afternoon's tragic turn of events. Not least of which was Clifford's bombshell about her uncle.

If Clifford was right, then it meant her uncle had been murdered. And that Clifford, his batman, wingman, butler and friend for thirty years or more had failed to save him. *No wonder he's so over-protective of you, Ellie!*

Doing her best to act as if nothing had happened, she willed herself to move from group to group, chatting and joining in with the festive fun and games. A wave of relief washed over her, however, when Clifford materialised two hours later and caught her eye. She hurried over to him.

'Is it the… erm.' She looked over her shoulder before she whispered, 'The person we've been waiting for?'

'Almost, my lady.' He led the way to the second drawing room in the right-hand tower that flanked the front entrance.

She stopped short. 'Inspector! I didn't expect you to be the one to answer the call. What about your other case?'

DCI Seldon spun round. 'Good afternoon, Lady Swift. I was about to leave Oxford for London when the name Henley Hall was mentioned in relation to a death. I decided my other case could wait a few hours.' His intense brown eyes held her gaze.

Despite the gravity of the situation, Eleanor felt a blush of warmth that he had taken a personal interest and come all the way back from Oxford on Christmas Eve, and in terrible weather. The sight of him now brought a wash of calm. She felt her shoulders relax for the first time since Canning had fallen in front of her.

'Merry Christmas again, by the way,' she said.

'Merry Christmas again to you, Lady Swift.' He raised one eyebrow. 'I see the death of one of your guests doesn't seem to have dampened the festivities. It sounds like the entire village is still marauding round the house.'

'Certainly, most of them.' She shrugged. 'And the festivities are still in full swing for two reasons. Most importantly because these good people are afforded very few opportunities to properly enjoy themselves but secondly, they are thankfully unaware that there has been a death.'

Seldon frowned. 'But...' He shook his head. 'I'll have words with the officer who took the original message then. I was told he had died during some sort of running race. It seems remarkable that the event went unnoticed.'

Clifford reappeared, saving Eleanor the need to elaborate for a moment. He placed a silver tray bearing two glasses of Christmas mead, a small carafe of coffee and a plate of warmed mince pies on the onyx table. A sumptuous smell of spiced cinnamon and citrus peel wafted up.

Seldon's stomach rumbled.

Eleanor waved a hand at the long Wedgwood blue settee designed to fit the exact curve of the tower. 'Why don't I tell you what happened first and then you can examine the body on a fuller stomach.' She paused midway onto the opposite settee. 'Unless that's the wrong way round? Maybe an empty stomach is better for inspecting a dead man?'

Seldon tore his eyes from the plate Clifford had placed on the side table next to him. 'I am rather afraid that after eleven years as a detective my constitution has rather accustomed itself to death.' He grunted. 'It's my thoughts that bear the struggle, however.'

Eleanor rubbed her temples. 'I feel terrible about it having happened. If I hadn't decided to hold the race, he would possibly still be with us.'

'Possibly?' Seldon reached into his jacket pocket for his leather notebook. He flipped open the cover. 'Can we start with the basics?'

She looked to Clifford for help.

He stepped forward. 'Mr Conrad Canning, previous resident of Wendover Lane, Little Buckford, latterly a resident of Chipstone, street unknown to me, regrettably. Age, I would hazard forty-five to fifty?'

Eleanor recounted the afternoon's events, ending with Doctor Browning's reserved assessment of the body.

'There you have it all, Inspector.'

He finished writing, closed his notebook and downed the last of his coffee. He looked at his watch and rose. 'Perhaps you would be so kind as to point me towards where the deceased fell so I can examine the body?'

Eleanor cleared her throat. 'Ah yes, well, he isn't exactly where he fell. We, err… might have moved him.'

Seldon pinched the bridge of his nose. 'Lady Swift, I understood that you instructed Constable Fry to call Oxford Police because you felt a doubt lay over the manner of Mr Canning's demise and yet you moved the body?'

Eleanor blushed. 'He was lying in the mud, sleet and snow. It seemed awfully wrong to leave him like that. Not much in the spirit of Christmas and all that.'

Seldon shook his head and gestured towards the door. 'Please, can we just go to wherever you have put him?'

Out in the garage where the undertaker's wagon had been parked, Seldon lifted the sheet that covered Canning's body. He checked the neck, wrists, calves and torso. Then he lifted the eyelids in turn. 'You mentioned that Doctor…' He referred to his notes. 'Browning said this man had an ongoing condition and had been advised against running in the race?'

Eleanor nodded.

Clifford appeared at her side, holding a soft, wool picnic rug retrieved from the boot of the Rolls. She gratefully draped it round her shoulders and tried to rub some warmth into her hands.

Seldon snapped his notebook shut. 'There are no evident signs of foul play, Lady Swift. I'm sorry, but I cannot justify requesting the coroner investigate his death. I'll make sure his doctor is notified. He can issue a death certificate.' He pulled the sheet back over the body.

'But, Inspector…'

He held up a hand. 'However, if Canning's doctor has no objection and the coroner has no cases to investigate, I'll ask him to take a look if he's amenable. I must warn you that even if he agrees, it will take longer than I'm sure you'd wish. The department has suffered staff and budget cuts in recent months. Politicians seem to think that they can have an efficient, motivated police force on no more than empty promises and empty purses.'

Eleanor stepped forward. 'Please, hear me out. Something definitely doesn't add up in how he died. The doctor was ruffled by what he saw… and so was Clifford.'

Seldon scanned her face, his gaze straying to her frost-pinked cheeks. He placed his bowler hat on his head. 'Unfortunately, an investigation can only be set up based on a piece of evidence, an eyewitness report or—'

'Clifford and I were eyewitnesses.'

'Indeed you were. Witnesses to a man falling down dead during an exertive race he'd been told by a doctor not to participate in. Whilst I don't know the man's medical history, I suspect he had a heart attack. Until his doctor, or the coroner, verifies anything to the contrary, there is nothing more I can do.'

Eleanor opened her mouth to argue, but stopped. She knew he was right.

Seldon glanced again at Canning's body. 'As the deceased has been placed in the undertaker's wagon, perhaps you'd be kind enough to ask if he could keep the body for the moment?'

She nodded.

'Lady Swift.' He turned on his heel. Clifford opened the door and as the inspector strode out, an icy blast pushed its way in and swirled around Eleanor.

She pulled the rug tighter around her shoulders.

CHAPTER 7

Clifford appeared at Eleanor's side by the undertaker's wagon, straightening the sheet over Canning's body at each corner to smooth out any wrinkles. Fry's bulky frame loomed in the doorway.

'Forgive my intruding, m'lady, but Detective Chief Inspector Seldon has left and Solemn Jon has said as how he'll look after the body until it is collected.'

Eleanor looked at the sodden, mud-splattered policeman. 'Constable, you have performed your duties admirably and I am very grateful. I would be delighted if you would return to the house and avail yourself of the entertainment and refreshments on offer. Perhaps a warming glass of Christmas mead or two and some hot mince pies?'

Fry's face lit up. 'If them's your wishes, my lady. Mrs Fry and the little'uns are all having such a wonderful afternoon, I could join them. Thank you kindly.'

'Just keep your eyes and ears open,' Eleanor added lightly.

'Ever watchful, my lady, that's my middle name.' With the heavy stomp of boots, he set off back towards the house.

Once the constable had left, Eleanor put her face in her hands and shook her head. 'Clifford, we can't leave this alone. The inspector's hands are tied until… no, that is, *if* the coroner even looks at the body.'

'Are you proposing we make our own enquiries into Mr Canning's demise?'

'No, I'm proposing we stick our noses into every crevice and turn over every stone and find out the truth about what happened this afternoon. A man has died, here at Henley Hall, on Christmas Eve of all days. It may end up being a heart attack but, if we're correct and Canning was murdered, whoever did it is probably still inside the house.'

'If you will forgive my offering a contrary opinion, it is more commonplace for murderers to flee the scene once their evil deed has been committed. I doubt many loiter waiting to be caught.'

'Yes, alright, but someone here might have seen something. Maybe the murderer escaping just before, or after, Canning's death?'

'Point taken, my lady.'

She shook her head. 'And I'm still reeling from what you said about Uncle Byron.' She winced at his drawn expression. 'As I know are you, even all these months later. But I do wish I had known earlier.' She held up her hand as he opened his mouth to speak. 'Please don't apologise. I merely meant that I've probably unwittingly encroached on your grief time and time again. Like dragging you into several murder investigations for starters.'

'It has been a pleasure, my lady.' He gave a quiet cough. 'In a manner of speaking, of course.'

'In the manner that someone passing away at the hand of another is never a pleasure to be embroiled in and yet here we possibly are again. But I owe it to Canning, and Uncle Byron, to discover the truth. I know Canning is one of the most disliked men in the area and Uncle Byron was one of the most respected, but Solemn Jon said it well. At the end of the day, we're all from the same clay and in my book we all deserve the same justice.'

Clifford nodded. 'I'm sure if your late uncle were listening, he'd concur, my lady.'

She looked up at the lightening sky. The snow had eased further and there was even the hint of weak sunshine behind the clouds.

'Well our murderer may be long gone but there's no sign of a mass exodus of the villagers yet. Let's go and examine where Canning fell. It might spark an idea. We can ask around afterwards.'

'Very good, my lady. Perhaps these will relieve some of the discomfort of being outdoors in this inclement weather.' He pulled two palm-sized silver cases from his pocket and held them out to her.

'What are these?' she asked, holding out her hands. 'Oh gracious, they're warm, hot even. How ingenious! An invention of Uncle Byron's?'

'An adaptation on his lordship's part. Such items were cobbled together from tobacco tins by soldiers in the war to better endure their days in the trenches in winter. Mr Canning lying in the mud and snow reminded me of them, although unfortunately he is past such comforts. These are significantly more sophisticated, however, my lady. But today they will just do an admirable job of keeping your hands from becoming too cold.'

'Thank you.' She dropped one into each pocket and shoved her hands inside on top. 'Lovely.'

He gave a discreet cough and adjusted his tie. 'You may also be heartened to know that there are still sufficient of his lordship's favourite ingredients to create an evening's worth of hot revivers once your guests have departed.'

'Hot revivers, Clifford? Why do I fear I will awake feeling as if I had spent the evening playing the drums with my head?'

'I really couldn't say, my lady. We have not yet had the pleasure of witnessing how you usually spend Christmas Eve.'

Outside, the fallen snow had all but obliterated any sign of the fun run. It had certainly hidden all signs that a man had died where they now stood.

'Oh, this is hopeless. And I'm not sure what I thought we might find now that I come to think of it.' She peered sideways at him. 'You're quietly thinking we would do better talking the scene through in minutiae with warm, dry feet, aren't you?'

'On the contrary, my lady. I was trying to determine the precise number of minutes that passed from the start of the race to Mr Canning falling in front of us.'

'And?'

'Around twenty, I believe. Perhaps a little less.'

'Well, that's a good starting point already. If you are correct and he was poisoned, timing is surely going to be hugely important. Perhaps we should also work even further back and find out his movements between the time he arrived until the beginning of the race.' She walked in a small square, staring at the ground, kicking the snow aside. 'We're absolutely sure it was just here that he fell, are we?'

'As we made our way back to the house, I counted the number of strides from where Mr Canning fell. That being exactly sixty-nine.

She pulled out one of the hand warmers and gathered her skirt up to squat down on her haunches. Patting the silver case from one hand to the other, a peculiar sense of not wanting to leave overtook her. And this despite not being able to feel her toes for the second time that day.

'You know, Clifford, it's dashedly hard when people expire out in the elements amid the wildest and woolliest of weather to really get much out of the scene. Perhaps that's why the inspector didn't bother to come out here. Oops!' Her hand warmer slipped from her grasp. She leaned over to retrieve it but as she tried to pick it up, it slid away down a frosty mound until it buried itself into the layer of fresh snow.

Clifford watched her dispassionately. 'Might that also have been because Chief Inspector Seldon suggested any investigation had been compromised by the body having been moved?'

'Maybe, but forget about that for a moment.' Eleanor jumped up. 'Look!' She held up the hand warmer and then turned it round, revealing a small metal object sticking to the back of it. 'It must be that the hand warmer rolled onto this thing and somehow it has frozen to it.' She frowned. 'But how could it have frozen to the warm case?'

Clifford took the hand warmer and examined it and nodded to himself. 'The explanation is really quite simple, my lady. His lordship included a magnetic strip in each of the silver cases for a reason that is of no consequence at this juncture. However, when used as a hand warmer, the heat significantly reduces the strength of the magnet.'

She frowned. 'But it's still roastingly warm so that should mean that the magnet was less strong and it wouldn't have been attracted to it.'

'Quite so, my lady, which leads us to only one conclusion.'

'It does?'

'Yes.' He pulled the object from the back of the case and held it up. It was a small, ornate key. 'That this key itself is magnetic.' He frowned. 'Which means it fits into a very unusual, and rare lock.'

He handed it to Eleanor. She turned it over in her hand. It looked like an ordinary key to her, if rather ornately made.

'So whatever it unlocks either contains items of great value to their owner. Or—'

'Or items that their owner did not want found.'

CHAPTER 8

Back in the house, Eleanor was delighted to see the ladies of Henley Hall enjoying themselves as much as the villagers. With all the guests full from their hearty lunch, and the excitement of the race over – *if only they knew, Ellie!* – each of the adults was now fortified with a glass of Christmas mead.

Mrs Butters had joined the happy group of women and children at the long table filled with a variety of Christmas craft materials. Painted pebbles, holly, ivy and fir cones were being turned into festive decorations they could take home with them at the end of the afternoon.

Mrs Trotman had stationed herself in the middle of the entertainment section, umpiring the hotly contested games of blind man's buff and twenty questions. Mrs Butters was too busy laughing from the craft table to referee the charades players as they tried to act out the name of a festive book, song or phrase using Clifford's meticulously prepared cards. Good-natured heckling accompanied each turn on the floor as the exuberant crowd tried to guess the answers.

Polly scampered past with a gaggle of fifteen or so excited children on a treasure hunt with Gladstone lolloping after them, festooned in tinsel. In another room, a huddle of children were being read *A Christmas Carol*. Sitting cross-legged on the rug by a giant fireplace, the youngest had already fallen asleep snuggled against the next child.

Eleanor dropped her voice and leaned towards Clifford. 'Where do you think we should start? Somehow, I hadn't considered just how many people there are. Who knows who might have seen something suspicious?'

A wave of exhaustion overtook her as she watched the fun and games still underway. The strain of playing the perfect hostess amid the tragedy of a man dying mid-festivities had drained the last of her energy. She rubbed her hands over her cheeks, trying to conjure up some extra stamina.

'Might I suggest, my lady, that Master Gladstone would greatly benefit from fifteen minutes resting on the chaise longue with you? Perhaps over a reviving pot of coffee and a slice of something sweet and sticky?'

She laughed. 'He'll get in an awful mess, won't he? But yes, I'd love that. For Gladstone's sake, of course.'

'Of course, my lady. And at the same time we could make a plan of attack?'

She nodded, and they quietly left.

With the door of the snug closed, Gladstone nuzzled into her legs, and the smell of coffee and warm gingerbread wafting around the room, Eleanor was already feeling better. She bit the arm off a gingerbread Father Christmas and let the sweetness dissolve on her tongue.

'I confess, I'm more disappointed about the inspector's insistence that there is no suggestion of foul play over Canning's death than I had realised.'

Clifford cleared his throat. 'One's opinion becomes quite the barbed thorn when it is refuted by someone whose respect we desire.'

'Perceptive, as always. It was horribly awkward with him out there in the garage. It seems he hasn't… you know.'

'Ah, the inspector is still torn between following protocol and following his heart, perhaps?'

'Well, protocol won.' She sighed. 'Oh dash it, Clifford! It's Christmas and we're tangled in another mess. I wanted you and the ladies to have such an easy time once today's lunch is over. You all work so hard all year.'

'Thank you, my lady. But I am mindful that you've had more than your fair share of death in the last twelve months.'

'As you have too. And it's no good doing the stiff upper lip thing, you thought the world of Uncle Byron. I'm sure after living and working with such an eccentric character, you believed my coming to stay at the Hall would make for a horribly routine time.'

'Were it able to respond, the routine of the Hall might not agree, my lady.'

This made her laugh. 'I really am doing my best not to mess up the order you've created here, but I'm just rather used to it being only me to account for. For a while too long, if I'm honest.' She held up her coffee cup. 'Are you aware of a superstition that says you mustn't propose a toast over coffee instead of champagne?'

'I have never encountered one, my lady.'

'Then a toast. To justice for Canning, and Uncle Byron.'

Clifford clinked his cup against hers. 'To justice. And finding the truth.' He held her gaze. 'Wherever it is hiding.'

She put her cup on the saucer and pushed Gladstone's heavy head gently off her back where it had slid down. Clifford handed her a notebook and the gold fountain pen her uncle had given him. She opened the book at a fresh page and wrote the name Conrad Canning at the top. Then she drew a key next to it. A frown crossed her face.

'We are assuming two key things here, no pun intended.'

Clifford raised an eyebrow.

She laughed. 'The first thing we are assuming is that the key we found belonged to Canning. Any of the runners could have dropped it.'

Clifford nodded. 'True, my lady. However, if it had been dropped by one of the earlier runners, it would almost certainly have been trodden into the mud and would not have stuck to your hand warmer. This suggests that the key was resting in the freshly laid snow and the snow had no chance to settle on the course until the majority of runners had passed.'

'Okay, we'll assume it belongs to Canning until proven otherwise. The second thing we're assuming is that the poison was administered before the race.'

Clifford nodded again. 'True once more, my lady. However, administering a poison during would have been very difficult. The fun run is too short for anyone to need drink or sustenance while taking part, so I doubt if Mr Canning was given poisoned drink, or food, during the race. The only other method that comes to mind is the poisoner might have used a syringe and plunged it into one of Mr Canning's veins as they ran. However, there were too many spectators and other runners along the route to imagine no one would have noticed. And it would have been fiendishly tricky to execute successfully on the go, as it were.'

Eleanor bit the head off a gingerbread man and felt a jolt of horror as she pictured Canning lying dead in the snow. *Pull yourself together, Ellie, it's just a gingerbread man!* 'Okay, we'll assume that the poison was administered sometime before the race, but not later than… than when?'

Clifford cleared his throat. 'If I am correct and Mr Canning was poisoned in the same manner as his lordship – and his symptoms were similar – then the poison used was digitalis. It could have been something else, but digitalis is easy to obtain being the main constituent in many heart pills. It has a very interesting history. In 1775 the Scottish doctor William Withering had a patient come to him with a heart condition he considered incurable. On being told this, the patient, being a somewhat strong-minded individual, told the good doctor to go to the devil. He then left, insisting if the doctor wouldn't help him he'd find a gypsy who would. Naturally, Doctor Withering believed that would be the last he'd see of this, in his view, terminally ill man. However, the patient strode back into the doctor's surgery some months later, seemingly fully cured.'

Eleanor gasped. 'That's amazing! How?'

'The gentleman had indeed gone to a local gypsy who had given him a "magical potion". So amazed was Doctor Withering, that he spent the following months himself scouring the highways and byways of his home county of Shropshire to try and hunt down this elusive gypsy.'

'And did he?'

'After much searching he did locate the woman. And after much haggling he persuaded her to part with the secret recipe, the key ingredient of which was digitalis, a substance obtained from local foxgloves.'

Eleanor laughed. 'So it seems that there is sometimes truth behind some of these old wives' tales and handed-down wisdom.'

'Absolutely, my lady. Doctor Withering treated over a hundred patients soon after his discovery, many with remarkable results.'

'So this digitalis, it comes from foxgloves? And it's safe in the correct dose, but can be fatal in larger doses?'

'Exactly. Which is why many poisoners have favoured it over the years. If the victim is already taking heart pills, as his lordship was, an overdose looks much like a heart attack and may be signed off by the victim's doctor as such.'

'Which is exactly what Canning's doctor is probably going to do, unless the inspector keeps his word and asks the coroner to do a post-mortem.'

'Indeed. However, even if a post-mortem is carried out, it merely reveals a dangerous level of digitalis present in the victim's system. This is then, as in his lordship's case, put down to the victim accidentally taking a double dose of his medicine. And if the post-mortem is not performed soon after the poisoning, as may be the case with Mr Canning, the levels of digitalis in the system will inevitably fall.'

Eleanor thought for a moment. 'So how did our poisoner get hold of the poison? Steal heart pills?'

'Possibly, but not necessarily. As I said, digitalis is actually easily obtained from the common purple foxglove. One can simply use the dried, powdered leaves, or berries, for instance, and dissolve it in any liquid with a reasonable taste of its own to disguise it.'

Eleanor digested this piece of information. Her mind flashed back again to Canning lying in the mud and snow. 'So how long would it take to kill a man?'

Clifford pursed his lips. 'It would depend on a number of factors that we do not know, such as how much was administered. At a guess, around ten to twenty minutes before any severe symptoms would start to show themselves. And, if the dose was high enough, which in the case of Mr Canning it was, maybe another ten to fifteen to prove fatal.'

Eleanor tapped the pen on her chin. 'Well, Canning was still alive – just – when we reached him… and the race was roughly how long, Clifford?'

'It started at two fifteen. As I was checking his pulse using my wristwatch when he expired, I can accurately place the time of his death at two thirty-seven.'

'Twenty-two minutes after the race started. Which suggests he must have taken the poison no more than fifteen to twenty minutes or so before the start of the race.'

'And, my lady, if you look at the day's programme, one of which is on the table there, we can find out roughly what Mr Canning may have been doing.'

Eleanor ran her finger down the items on the agenda, silently giving thanks for employing such a detail-orientated butler. 'Ah! If you wanted to compete in the race, you would have had to queue up for your number from about quarter to two. That's thirty minutes before it started. Does that sound a reasonable starting point?'

Clifford nodded slowly. 'There are a great many variables we do not know, but it is the best we have, and perhaps good enough for the moment.'

Eleanor went back to her notebook and wrote under Canning's name:

1.45 p.m. – Canning queues up to collect race number.

2.15 p.m. – Race started by the reverend.

2.37 p.m. – Canning dies.

She tapped the pen on her chin again. 'Now, if only we knew what he did next.'

Clifford coughed. 'When Mr Canning died, I observed he was not wearing the same clothes as when he arrived at the Hall.'

'Of course! He changed into more suitable racing clothes, like a lot of the runners who came in their Sunday best. So he'd have gone to the changing room we provided.'

She added:

1.55 p.m.? – Changed into race clothes.

'And after that? Ah! I can answer that one.' She wrote down:

2.05 p.m. – 2.10 p.m. – Queues to get Mrs Trotman's Christmas mead and log.

Clifford looked over her shoulder. 'So that only leaves a few minutes for Mr Canning to leave the refreshment room and walk over to the start point. We can therefore assume that he must have been poisoned sometime between the registration and the commencement of the race.'

'Top-notch deduction, Clifford! So let's retrace Canning's movements and find out who he was in contact with before the race started. Someone must have slipped the poison into… into what, Clifford? His drink? Or food?'

'Possibly either, my lady. Most likely whatever he was drinking as it would be easier to slip the powdered leaves, or berries, into a drink than into food.'

She nodded. 'Makes sense. The killer must believe he's got away with it at the moment, so we need to ask questions without arousing any suspicion. Most people don't even know Canning is dead, and we want to keep it that way so everyone can carry on enjoying themselves.'

Clifford nodded. 'Unfortunately that shouldn't be too difficult as I doubt many of the villagers will miss Mr Canning or feel the urge to seek him out.'

Eleanor nudged Gladstone off her legs and stood up. 'Sorry, old friend. Right, let's go investigate the murder of a man who isn't even officially dead yet.'

CHAPTER 9

Eleanor beckoned to Clifford as he chivvied Gladstone through the door and closed it behind him. 'We need to start by finding out who gave out the race numbers and if they saw anything.'

'I believe the ladies are over there, my lady.' Clifford pointed to elderly twins in identical frilled blouses and ankle-length pleated skirts enthusiastically whirling their partners around the phonograph table to Tchaikovsky's 'Christmas Waltz'.

Eleanor smiled. 'Ah, bad timing. They are having a wonderful time.'

As the couples whirled in their direction, the corners of Clifford's lips twitched. 'Although I believe the gentlemen would appreciate an excuse to leave the dance floor.'

Eleanor laughed. 'I see what you mean, they do look a little puffed.' She scooped up four glasses from the drinks table behind her and approached the dancers.

'Breathtakingly graceful, ladies and gentlemen.' Eleanor held out the glasses. 'You've definitely earned this. You really have put on quite the spectacle.'

Clifford nodded at the men. 'Gentlemen, perhaps when you have regained your breath, you might like to join the yule log gathering party? We're still a few volunteers short.'

The two men nodded, took their glasses and hurriedly made their escape.

Eleanor gestured to a row of unoccupied seats by the floor-to-ceiling windows. 'Ladies, have you a moment? I haven't had the chance to thank you properly for your efficient organisation in registering the runners.' She steered them towards the chairs by holding onto their drinks.

Helpfully, the twins had indeed seen something: Canning arguing with an unruly looking man with an unruly looking beard. Unhelpfully, they had no idea who the man was, and hadn't seen him in the ballroom or elsewhere since.

Unruly and bearded? *Could it be the same man who knocked Canning over just before he died, Ellie?*

Having thanked the twins for their help once again, Eleanor and Clifford were stopped as they left the ballroom by a gaggle of young girls. The group pushed the tallest one forward, who hesitated, and then spoke up. 'We've made you all a newspaper Christmas hat.'

'How delightful.' Eleanor accepted hers and turned it over in her hands. It was decorated with feathers, holly and buttons in beautiful swirls and had been enthusiastically painted. 'I appear to have a very fine creation here. A wonderfully painted scene of… a woman in… in a lovely house?'

A rosy-cheeked girl in a pinafore pulled on her dress. 'It's a princess in a castle, like you.'

'Oh golly.' Eleanor blushed.

The girls all turned and stared at Clifford, who dutifully set the one handed to him on his head.

'Lovely ribbons, Clifford.' Eleanor stifled a chuckle at the sight of her usually impossibly stiff butler regaled in a homemade paper hat liberally threaded with ribbons all tied in voluminous bows.

He bowed. 'Thank you, ladies.'

The girls skipped off, giggling excitedly.

At that moment, Eleanor caught Constable Fry's eye. It seemed he wanted a word. They met in the middle of the room.

'Is everything alright, Constable?'

'Oh goodness, yes, m'lady. It's just that the little'uns are getting scratchy, what with being so tired on account of all the fun we've had.'

His wife appeared behind him, holding three blanket-wrapped bundles with difficulty. 'Thank you so much, Lady Swift. We've all had such a wonderful time, I hope you won't think us rude if we slide away and get the boys to bed?'

'Gracious, not at all. I imagine keeping the routine is triply important.' Eleanor was genuinely in awe of Mrs Fry coping with three young wilful triplets. Sometimes she struggled to cope with one elderly wilful bulldog. A thought struck her. 'Constable, where were you when we all went out to get the race underway?'

'Hurrying up the last of the hill, m'lady. The Atwoods' pigs broke out again. Proper escape artists they are.'

'So you didn't see the reverend fire the starting pistol then?'

'Oh that I did, m'lady, but only by the skin of my teeth. Good job Mr Clifford was there. Afterwards I had words with the reverend about the appropriate way of handling such a dangerous device. He seemed quite agitated.'

'That's not like the reverend. He's always so jolly and easy.'

Fry ran his hand over his chin. 'Well, for him, he was in a right old fluster. Probably worried he might have accidentally shot one of his flock, I imagine.'

His wife bumped her hip against his. 'Well, the reverend didn't injure anyone. And it all went off on time, which was lucky seeing as a couple of the men were getting all over-competitive.' She laughed awkwardly. 'Silly boys, it was only for fun.'

'No one came to blows, I hope?' Eleanor said.

'Gracious, better not have.' Fry looked stern. 'I've no problem having stiff words with troublemakers to break up a brawl, even on Christmas Eve. Course I'd have taken them off out of sight first, m'lady.'

'So kind.' Eleanor wondered for the hundredth time how this gentle giant had ended up in the police force.

His wife shuffled one of the babies into his arms. 'Ooh, heavy now. Anyhow it wasn't anything serious, just Canning up to his usual. It was ever so thoughtful of you to invite him, Lady Swift. I'm sure most people wouldn't have.'

'Oh really, but he's been such a loyal coal merchant to the Hall for a long time.'

'It's just that he's unpredictable at times. But then I think being a loner can do that to you, don't you?'

Fry caught up. 'Canning was the one going at it, was he, luv?'

'No more than usual. Couldn't see who the other chap was, nor Canning himself mind, but you can't miss Canning's voice. Rough and raw, all those years at sea shouting over the wind, I imagine. Shame, Lady Swift, you having put on such a special do for us all, as well.'

Eleanor tried to choose her words carefully. 'Gracious, what could possibly be so important that it was worth arguing over on Christmas Eve, I wonder?'

Mrs Fry shrugged. 'No idea. All I heard was him saying something about there'd been nothing before and there was nothing now.' She rocked her babies. 'Funny how some folk can even fight about nothing, eh?' She looked around the room. 'Speaking of the devil, I haven't seen Canning since the beginning of the race.'

Eleanor caught the constable's eye. He shook his head and whispered, 'I'll tell her when we get in. Didn't want to upset her afternoon.'

Mrs Fry looked at him quizzically. 'What's that, Bob? Honestly, sometimes your face goes as long as a horse. 'Tis a party not a funeral!'

CHAPTER 10

Once the constable and his wife had left, Eleanor turned to Clifford. 'Fry has done an admirable job of keeping the news quiet, but it will be all over the village by the morning I'm sure. Now, we know Canning changed into his running clothes after he got his number, so let's head to the changing room and see what we can find.'

Disappointingly, the room itself offered nothing despite their detailed search. Eleanor pursed her lips. 'Again, Clifford, I find myself wondering what on earth I hoped to uncover. Criminals never actually leave a signed confession note or vials of poison behind, do they?'

'Only in penny dreadful novels, my lady.'

'Ah, that's probably where I got the idea from,' she confessed.

Clifford clicked his fingers, the sound muffled by his pristine white gloves. 'Was there not a lady in charge of the changing rooms?'

Eleanor's eyes lit up. 'Of course, she was manning them for us, how could I have forgotten. Come on, let's see if she saw or heard anything.'

In the ballroom, the lady was easy to spot. Her long silver tresses hung down the back of her voluminous, green cotton dress as she supervised a crowd of excited children playing musical chairs.

As Clifford hung back, Eleanor slid in next to the woman and joined in the clapping. 'I think they might all sleep well tonight, don't you?'

The woman turned to her. 'Oh, m'lady, the children are having so much fun. And the parents, too. It's a wonderful afternoon, thank you.' She pulled a lace handkerchief from her pocket. 'Oh that reminds me, I left the changing room nice and neat. Honestly, men think throwing something on the floor near the rubbish bin is being tidy. Tsk!'

'So kind. And thank you for manning the door. Did you find any items which need to be returned to their owners, by any chance?'

'Oh goodness, m'lady, has someone lost something?'

Only his life! Eleanor shook her head. 'Not that I'm aware of, I just thought that it would be easier to pair any lost items with their owners now rather than later. I'm sorry it wasn't perhaps the most glamorous of tasks, however.'

'Chivvying a bunch of men is no different to chivvying children.'

'Gracious, did you have to play the part of usher then? I thought they were all so keen.'

'Too keen! That's why the room needed a tidy and no mistake.'

Eleanor felt she had no choice but to be more direct. 'Did you happen to notice if Mr Canning came to change?'

She rolled her eyes. 'Canning? He did, and without wishing to be a negative Nancy, he was his usual grumpy self. Even Christmas isn't enough to bring out any decent bones he might have in his body. I don't know what's wrong with that man.'

'I hope he wasn't rude to you.'

'Oh, he knows better than to show me his lip, m'lady. He's not too old to get a clip round the ear.'

'He didn't have an argument with any of the other men while he was changing?'

'Not that I heard. Mind, he was one of the last to change, even though all he went on about was getting his free drink and food. Some folk will do anything to get what they think they're due for nowt.'

'Well, thank you so much and also for supervising the children.'

''Twas and is nothing, m'lady. And, honestly, it was nice to be a part of all the festivities. Oh, and thanks for sending someone to relieve me for a… a comfort break.'

Eleanor frowned. 'Sending someone?'

The woman laughed. 'Not very ladylike to admit it, but when you get to my age, sometimes you need to pop off sooner than you expect, like. She must have thought I'd deserted my station, having got there and me nowhere in sight. Then she must have got called away herself. I just hurried back round the corner, and she was going off round the other one. 'Twas like one of them farces in the theatres in London, people just missing each other all the time. Mind you, she got the short straw as only Canning was left in the changing room by then.'

'And remind me, who came to relieve you? It would be so rude of me not to thank them.'

The woman looked blank. 'No idea, m'lady. All I saw was her skirt and woollen stockings disappearing round the corner.'

'Well, if you see the lady again, do tell me so I can thank her properly.'

The woman tutted. 'Mr Clifford will know who it was, I'm sure. He knows everyone, and everything, doesn't he?'

'Very nearly. I sometimes wonder why Uncle Byron kept such an extensive library here at Henley Hall, when his butler is a veritable encyclopaedia on legs.'

The woman laughed. 'And such long legs too,' she ended, fanning her hand at the blush that ran across her cheeks.

Oh, Clifford has a secret admirer, Ellie! How fabulous.

On spotting Clifford watching them from behind the safety of one of the ballroom's marble pillars, Eleanor realised the woman's admiration had not perhaps been kept so secret. She made her excuses and joined him.

'Admiring the craftsmanship?'

He straightened his perfectly aligned tie. 'It is an exquisite example of the work of a highly skilled artisan.'

'It's okay, you're safe for now. But don't worry, I'll tell you everything she said later.'

He swallowed hard.

Eleanor laughed. 'About her time outside the changing room, of course.'

Before he could answer, Mrs Trotman walked over, trailed by a sheepish-looking Gladstone.

'Oh dear, whatever has he done?' Eleanor leant down and ruffled the bulldog's ears as he pressed himself into her leg.

'Master Trouble here has called a halt to the skittle alley by stealing every ball until there are none left. And then he's only gone and toddled off outside and buried them all somewhere.'

Eleanor couldn't help laughing. 'Well, that's his way of joining in. Poor chap, his house has been overrun by excited people, all wafting slices of your delicious cooking past his nose all day. I think he's been extremely well behaved.'

'I think Father Christmas might have other ideas, my lady. It's a piece of coal for him for sure!'

Eleanor started, remembering her and Canning's interrupted conversation that morning when she'd asked why people weren't pleased to see him at Christmas. *Folk say I bring a sack of bad luck.* She shook her head. Maybe he was right. She turned to Clifford.

'Clifford, is it good or bad luck to give someone coal at Christmas?'

He looked at her oddly for a moment, but then answered. 'In many countries, my lady, it is considered bad luck. Father Christmas, or St Nicholas if you prefer, is supposed to come down the chimney and leave presents for good children. If they have been bad, however, he is supposed to simply grab a piece of coal from the fireplace and leave that. Hence the idea that it is bad luck to receive coal at Christmas. Why do you ask?'

She shrugged. 'I just wondered.' She turned to her cook. 'I think giving poor old Master Gladstone a piece of coal for his Christmas supper might be a little harsh. Perhaps I should have told him the rules about all balls being his except for today?'

Mrs Trotman smiled. 'I suppose no one told him, my lady. I'll shuffle him off to the kitchen and read him the rules so he knows next time.'

Polly appeared, looking flushed. 'The treasure hunt is finished, your ladyship. 'Twas ever so hard, but ever so fun.'

'Marvellous. Thank you for supervising it all so well.'

'Super...?'

'I meant thank you for making sure it went without a hitch.'

Mrs Butters and her helper stopped on her way past. 'Is there anything you need, my lady? We're just off to finish the last of the clearing up in the refreshment room but it'd be no bother to get you something.'

'Gracious, you've all worked so hard. Surely it can wait until later? Or even tomorrow?'

Out of the corner of her eye, she saw Clifford give an involuntary shudder.

'Oh my stars, a mess left overnight is thrice the task in the morning. Besides' – Mrs Butters nodded to Eleanor's left – 'Mr Clifford wouldn't get a wink of sleep for the nightmares it would bring on.'

'Fair point.' Eleanor turned to Mrs Butters' helper, the reverend's housekeeper, Marie Fontaine. 'Mrs Fontaine, I'm so grateful for all your help today.'

'It was a pleasure, Lady Swift.'

As they turned to go, Eleanor cleared her throat. 'Oh, by the way, did you serve Mr Canning his mead and log?'

Mrs Fontaine shook her head. 'I was helping on the food table, but I think Mrs Butters gave him his log, non?' She spoke with a strong French accent even though Eleanor was sure the vicar had told her she'd lived in England most of her adult life. But Eleanor had noted that the longer a French man, or woman, lived abroad, the more pronounced their accent seemed to become.

Mrs Butters shrugged. 'I've served that many people, my lady, I can't rightly remember who. I know Mrs Trotman poured him his mead because the great lummock had the cheek to complain about his measure.'

Eleanor laughed. 'Oh, I'd forgotten all about that. Then that man in the other queue shouted at Mr Canning for his rudeness, you said. Did any of you manage to see who it was?'

There was a general shaking of heads.

Outside in the hallway, she sighed. 'Well, Clifford, I can't work out from what we've learned so far if Canning argued with one, two or three people!'

Clifford coughed gently. 'Actually, my lady, I believe you can. Consider the fact that none of the witnesses were able to identify the man's voice or features in the three separate incidents? In a small village like Little Buckford that eventuality is very unlikely. It suggests, therefore, that all three involved a man from outside the village.'

Eleanor clapped her hands. 'And the likelihood of Canning arguing with three separate men from another town is also very unlikely.'

'Exactly. And as we know the only people at the Christmas luncheon not from Little Buckford came from Chipstone on the coach—'

'We can deduce Mr Canning argued with one man.'

'And that man also came from Chipstone on the coach.'

'Excellent! It may have nothing to do with Canning's death, but it's the best we've got to go on at the moment.'

Clifford fetched the list of those who had come from Chipstone, and they looked down the names.

1. John Singleton
2. Jenny Johnson
3. Alvan Moore
4. Conrad Canning

5. Stephen White
6. Hubert Wraith
7. Albert Wainfleet
8. John Dickens

Eleanor sighed. 'We can cross Jenny Johnson off, as we know Canning argued with a man, but how can we narrow this down to just one?'

'It is not as hopeless as it seems, my lady. Mr Singleton and Mr White are both well-known in Little Buckford, so I'm sure someone we've spoken to would have recognised them or their voice.'

'It's a start.' She crossed off the two names.

Clifford's brow furrowed, and then his eyes lit up. 'If we are to assume that the man Mr Canning argued with three times is the same man, then that man must have also been in the race alongside him.'

'Brilliant, Clifford!'

Clifford went in search of the list of those who had entered the race, while Eleanor gave Gladstone a tummy tickle.

A moment later Clifford returned, and they compared the two lists. Of the remaining four men on the first list, one, Albert Wainfleet, had not entered the race. Eleanor crossed off his name and looked at the remaining three.

1. ~~John Singleton~~
2. Alvan Moore
3. ~~Jenny Johnson~~
4. ~~Conrad Canning~~ (victim)
5. ~~Stephen White~~
6. Hubert Wraith
7. ~~Albert Wainfleet~~
8. John Dickens

She wrote the three names in her notebook under the rough timing they'd worked out earlier for Canning's death.

'So now we find out which of these three had a reason to quarrel with Canning and maybe we'll have found our poisoner.' She glanced at Clifford and looked back at the original list. 'I know, it's not likely to be that straightforward. And, anyway, we've forgotten the mysterious woman in the changing rooms. She could have been from Little Buckford or Chipstone as no one really caught sight of her.'

She added 'Mystery Woman' to her list.

'So we have a mystery man from Chipstone and a mystery woman, also possibly from Chipstone, as our suspects. Who's your money on?'

Clifford coughed. 'Well, my lady, they do say poison is a woman's weapon.'

CHAPTER 11

The white flakes swirling round in the evening air nipped at Eleanor's face. The temperature had dropped dramatically in the last few hours and she swore she could see her breath freeze.

At least it wasn't horizontal sleet, she comforted herself.

As the remaining villagers trotted down the lantern-lit front steps of Henley Hall, they called their final farewells and thank yous and waved exuberantly.

'And thank you so much for coming. Merry Christmas!' she called back as the darkness swallowed their retreating forms, the snow muffling their footsteps and chattering voices. Then the world fell silent as nature held her breath lest it spoilt the peace left behind.

Pulling the collar of her sage woollen jacket up round her neck, Eleanor leaned her head against one pillar of the central stone arch. She felt a wash of comfort that the day had gone well, at least in part. That Solemn Jon had discreetly removed Canning's body to his undertaker's yard unnoticed had been a great relief.

As if reading her mind, Clifford said, 'A job well done, my lady. Keeping the news of Canning's demise from the villagers.'

She straightened up. 'But, Clifford, it will also hinder us. I mean, unless people know Canning is dead, it's going to be devilishly hard to investigate his death, isn't it? I think, on reflection, it will actually be a good thing when it's out in the open. We'll be able to tackle this investigation front and centre, as it were. It's all very well trying to be circumspect and ask leading questions, but as you know, I favour a more direct approach.'

As she walked off, she was sure she heard him groan.

Four hours later, warmly wrapped for Midnight Mass, Eleanor sat on one of St Winifred's hard wooden pews and wished she'd accepted Clifford's suggestion to bring a cushion. Despite the chill, however, the small church had a cosy, familiar feel. Built in the twelfth century, the deep ribbed carving on the pointed early Gothic arch threw a long shadow down the stone nave to the simple altar.

She relaxed as she looked at the flickering candles through half-closed eyes and listened to the serene voices of the young choir ascend way beyond the tiny upper balcony. As clear as glass, the innocence and purity of their harmonies were at odds with the events of the day.

She'd trusted Clifford's judgement and before the service had started, they had informed Reverend Gaskell of Canning's passing. The reverend had artfully included a reference to Canning's death in his sermon, without going into too much detail.

As they filed out at the end of the service into the moonlit churchyard, she caught whisperings about Canning and the reverend's impromptu tribute to the dead man. It had been brief and, to Eleanor's surprise, rather short on warmth. But Canning's life had been honoured, however summarily, and respects paid, although she hadn't noticed any tears being shed on his behalf.

Eleanor stepped to the side of the path to allow the rest of the congregation to shake the reverend's hand before they set off home.

'Is it terrible of me to feel something of a weight has been lifted, Clifford? I mean, now that people know Canning died at Henley Hall. If I'm honest, I think I've been dreading the news getting out. I so wanted to honour Uncle Byron's memory and keep the tradition he started. Someone dying the first time I host the event isn't a great start, is it?'

'My lady, his lordship would have been proud of the way you ran the luncheon, games and race today. And, as you yourself said, the greatest honour we can afford his lordship, and Mr Canning, is to achieve justice for their passing.'

He gestured towards the reverend who was almost at the end of the line of his parishioners leaving the church.

Eleanor joined them and took both of Reverend Gaskell's hands in hers as she greeted him. 'What a wonderful job you did, Reverend. Not just with your uplifting service but in breaking the news of Mr Canning's death and honouring his memory.'

The vicar's face clouded slightly behind his round spectacles. 'Good gracious, dear lady, it is what I am here for.'

'Well, you've lifted my spirits enormously tonight.' She tilted her head. 'Christmas means different things to different people, I've found.'

The vicar clapped his hands together. 'And yet we were all united at this special service. I suspect tomorrow, however, will be more material than spiritual based. But our local people work hard and richly deserve some unadulterated rest and recuperation.'

Something tugged at Eleanor's thoughts. 'Was Mr Canning a member of St Winifred's flock when he lived in Little Buckford?'

Reverend Gaskell let out an uncharacteristic snort. 'No, dear lady, he was not. Despite… well, that doesn't matter now. But succinctly, no, he wasn't.'

'But will you permit the funeral service to go ahead here at St Winifred's? I'm very happy to cover any costs.'

'It is not a case of cost, Lady Swift, although I appreciate your kind and thoughtful offer.'

His words baffled Eleanor. 'So, you're saying no?'

The vicar sighed, then shook his head. 'He will be buried here, I'll see to it. All men have the chance to atone for their misdeeds. Whether they choose to do so or not is between them and their Maker. I am minded of Matthew, chapter four, verse forty-five: "For he makes his sun rise on the evil and on the good, and sends rain on the just and on the unjust." If the Lord can treat men equally, so must I.'

She searched for the right words, but the vicar's unexpected response had thrown her. He was always so compassionate towards everyone. She'd never heard him utter a single cross word or uncharitable comment. Perhaps there was some history between the two men she was unaware of?

Eleanor stole a peep at Clifford, but his expression gave nothing away.

'As you think best, Reverend,' she said.

He nodded. 'I shall make the initial arrangements for the funeral in our burial ground, but I fear it will be a poorly attended affair. A man who continues to make enemies on Christmas Eve is going to leave this earth more alone than those who treat their fellow man with civility and respect.'

Eleanor flinched at his words. 'Did you overhear Mr Canning fighting with someone this afternoon then?' She thought back to the bearded stranger the twins had mentioned.

He nodded. 'Mr Canning thought fit on such a day and such an occasion to fight with another runner on the start line before I set the race underway. But let us not dwell on such things. It is Christmas Eve. Perhaps you would both care to join a few of us at the vicarage after our ten o'clock family communion tomorrow? It has become something of a custom to partake of a sherry and exchange some glad tidings on the special day itself.'

Eleanor didn't need to look at Clifford to know he would be nodding in agreement. She smiled. 'We would be delighted, thank you, Reverend. Good evening, sleep well.'

The vicar gathered up the many folds of his white surplice and turned back towards the church.

Eleanor suddenly realised how chilled she was. Peculiarly though, the snow didn't seem to have penetrated her thick boots, nor the frosty air her thick gloves. This was like a block of ice gnawing at her stomach. She placed her hand over her middle. 'What an unnerving sensation.'

Clifford arched one eyebrow and dropped his voice. 'Perhaps it is the result of having unexpected misgivings, my lady? That was not quite the conversation I believe either of us anticipated having with the reverend.'

'I know!' she whispered back, her breath frosting on the late-night air. 'So much for the season of goodwill. Even Reverend Gaskell struggled to find a good word to say about Canning.'

As they crunched back through the snow, she found herself frowning. 'Well, Clifford, do you think the man the reverend saw fighting with Canning was the same man we are after?'

Clifford pointed out a patch of ice on the path and waited until she had skirted around it to reply. 'If it involved any other man than Mr Canning, one might reasonably assume so. But, if I am not mistaken, he seems to have offended even Reverend Gaskell, a feat I had thought impossible, so it may well have been a different man.'

Eleanor shrugged. 'I suppose you're right. We'd better add him as another person we need to find out the identity of and talk to.'

As they walked on in silence, she remembered what had been tugging at her memory. She turned to Clifford. 'Everyone may not be good, but there's always something good in everyone.'

He nodded. 'Oscar Wilde.'

She shook her head. 'My mother. She used to say it every time people had nothing but bad things to say about someone.'

'I mean that is a quote, my lady. From Oscar Wilde. "Everyone may not be good, but there's always something good in everyone. Never judge anyone shortly because every saint has a past, and every sinner has a future."'

Eleanor walked on in silence, thinking it would appear from Reverend Gaskell's demeanour he considered Canning a definite sinner. But someone had robbed him of his future. Perhaps a future where he'd intended to make up for some of those sins? She remembered again his words and changed demeanour on his last trip to the Hall. She turned to Clifford. 'It would seem then that all we have to do to track down our poisoner, is to find a saint with a past.'

CHAPTER 12

Arthur Treddle had passed away in 1899, after seventy-six years that were dedicated to serving the community of Little Buckford he'd loved so dearly. Eleanor's uncle had bought Arthur's flint house and outbuildings and had them converted into a new, more spacious village hall. Among other local groups, Little Buckford's Women's Institute had proudly held their fortnightly meetings there since February 1916. And their Christmas morning gatherings were always a special occasion.

By eight o'clock, laden with two wicker baskets, Eleanor bumped open the door with her hip and jerked to a stop.

'Gracious, that is a lot of boxes!'

'Forty-three this year, Lady Swift.' Alice Campbell's untameable grey curls bounced round her beaming face as she leaned out of the nearest doorway, her green gingham dress setting off her intelligent eyes. 'And happy Christmas to you.' Her bubbly voice was as cheery as her words. She wore her perennial housekeeper's apron, despite having retired from such a job when her employer, a government official, had been murdered at the start of the year. That Eleanor had caught the murderer meant she could do no wrong in Alice's eyes.

'Happy Christmas to you too, Alice.' Eleanor wiggled an encumbered arm by way of greeting. 'Forty-three, that is wonderful. So many deserving families receiving a little something extra to help them celebrate the festive season.'

Alice beckoned her towards the doorway. 'And folks won't just be getting food this year. Look!'

Struggling past the boxes, Eleanor peeped inside the low-timbered-ceiling room. 'Oh! Linens, soaps, wool and toys!' An unexpected lump jumped into her throat as she knew that many people who had donated would have little enough of their own.

Alice was still nodding. 'And you so kindly provided the pile of children's clothes and shoes. So generous, m'lady.'

'Not at all. I just hope it's sufficient.'

Alice held out her hand for one of the baskets Eleanor still hadn't put down. 'You've only to see the faces of all the folk who will be getting their Christmas surprise in two hours to know we'll have made their day a special one. Mind, if we don't get a move on, they'll have nothing packed ready to take home at all!'

'Only two hours? Have you ladies time for a small break?' Eleanor looked down at the baskets. 'Mrs Trotman sent three Thermoses of tea to go with these almond and apricot pastries she somehow fitted into her busy cooking schedule this morning.'

'Such a treasure, she is. Bit of reviving tea and sweet treats will make us work all the faster.' Alice cupped her hands around her mouth and called out. 'Ladies! Time to feed the workers.'

It was a hasty break, filled with easy chatter about the mischievousness of nieces and nephews, the extortionate price of meat and the vagaries of Christmas weather. Struggling to join in with much of the subject matter, Eleanor was relieved, however, that Canning's death hadn't featured. Although she rather suspected that might be out of deference to herself and the Christmas spirit.

With their cups washed in the small adjoining kitchen, the eleven ladies of the Women's Institute set to ensuring they provided the best possible Christmas for the neediest local families.

Eleanor peered at the first box in her pile. She couldn't read the recipient's surname or decipher most of the suggested things to include. She looked round at the other women who were all selecting items from the piles and efficiently ticking them off their lists. Worried to ask one of them in case it was their writing she couldn't read, she stepped out into the hallway to see if she could find someone else to ask. She, however, was halted in her tracks by voices coming from the end room.

'But Canning would never be told, you know that,' said a woman.

'Too busy being the one doing the telling, that's why,' came a second female voice. 'Too much of a stubborn mule to listen to an expert. You can see him setting his jaw all hard, like he did before he got riled when poor old Doctor Browning tried to tell him, can't you?'

'But Doctor Browning weren't his doctor anymore, was he? Not after, well, you know.'

'True, but he's a good sort. He had to offer his advice, having taken that hypocritical oath.'

Eleanor had to cover her mouth to stifle a good-natured laugh.

The first woman's voice continued. 'Yes, but after all that business I wouldn't have blamed him if he'd helped Conrad put his shoes on and told him to run as fast as possible!'

'What a wicked thought!'

'Speak as I find, you know me. And, well, I'm not one to gossip, but there's rumours that Canning didn't pass away of his own doing, if you know what I mean.'

The sounds of boxes being moved stopped. A sharp gasp pierced the air. 'You mean he was… murdered?' The last word was said in a dramatic whisper.

''Tis only hearsay.'

'If it is true, he probably got himself killed 'cos of him and all his tall stories.'

'That may be, but there's talk that maybe those tales weren't as tall as we all imagined.'

'Really? Go on.'

'We'd best stack those boxes while I do then.' Sounds of scraping and stacking restarted along with the first voice. 'I heard that if you were to strip all the nonsense he spouted away, what was true was that he really did go to most of the places he boasted.'

Eleanor's ears pricked up. She knew Canning had been a sailor years back. Clifford had mentioned it to the inspector, after all, but why were the two women interested in that? With a quick peek over her shoulder, she leaned forward to hear better.

'Why would that have got him killed?' the second voice said.

''Cos they say he wasn't above joining the likes of pirates out on the high seas. Smuggled all sorts of stuff in his time. Word is he was sitting on more than a pretty packet of money.'

There was a pause. Eleanor found she was holding her breath. The second woman's voice filtered out to her.

'But that can't be right. He lived almost as poor as a church mouse. It's a wonder that tiny cottage of his is still standing. He never spent a penny on it. Besides, why would he have gone round humping coal like a labourer if he went home at night and laid his weary bones on a mattress stuffed with money? No sense in that at all.'

Eleanor clapped her hand over her mouth. *The key, Ellie! Maybe it opens some kind of treasure chest of stolen bounty?*

'I reckon he was a miser,' the first voice said. 'But why did Canning do any of the things he did? That's like asking what on earth women saw in him.'

'Oh yes, but that was ages back. I'd not seen him with a woman for years.'

'Me neither.'

Eleanor felt the hairs on the back of her neck stand up.

'Lady Swift?'

She spun round guiltily to see Mrs Fontaine standing in the doorway. Her shoulders relaxed at the sight of the vicar's housekeeper.

'Are you alright? I thought something happened? You disappeared?'

Feeling guilty for eavesdropping, Eleanor's cheeks coloured. She held up her list. 'I'm embarrassed to say I was looking for someone to ask what these items are. I couldn't read the writing.'

Mrs Fontaine laughed. 'Then let me help you. I have almost finished. Together, we make a fast job of your list too, non?'

Eleanor smiled with relief. 'Thank you. I would greatly appreciate that. I had a horrible fear that some families might receive all kinds of items they neither need nor want.'

'Ah, now this I think could not happen. Good things come to good people. Only good people, though. Shall I take your list and call out the items to be placed in each box?'

'Yes, please. You're a lifesaver. I'm supposed to be at the vicarage at ten o'clock.'

The woman laughed again. 'And I should be there at the twenty minutes to, otherwise the, how you say, ah the nibbles, they will be all muddled. The reverend is a wonderful man but I think he might need the new spectacles sometimes.'

Eleanor laughed this time. 'He's very lucky to have you, Mrs Fontaine. He appreciates you very much.'

She waved her hand. 'It is a pleasure to help him. We are perhaps a little like you and Mr Clifford, I think. The reverend and me, we have the good understanding of each other.'

Eleanor smiled. 'Maybe, but I'm pretty sure you've worked for the reverend a lot longer than Clifford has worked for me.'

Mrs Fontaine nodded. 'True. Eleven years I think. Now to work! These boxes will not fill themselves.'

'Oh gracious, no. And here we are chatting away.'

Mrs Fontaine grinned. 'Do not worry, I will not tell Mr Clifford. He is one to keep the time, I think. A man who studies the details always, non?'

A slight groan escaped Eleanor. 'Only so as you'd notice.'

CHAPTER 13

On the top step of the village hall, Eleanor pulled off one glove to catch some of the softly falling snowflakes. 'It's so beautiful,' she said with a sigh as she closed the door behind her, staring out over the postcard view. A white carpet covered the village green and surrounding trees and rooftops.

A quiet cough from the pavement broke her reverie.

'Ah, hello, Clifford.' The gossip about Canning was still ringing round her mind. She gave him a conspiratorial look. 'We really need to talk.' She looked around. 'But I say, where is the Rolls?'

'It is waiting for us at the church, my lady. Forgive my presumption, but I thought you might prefer…' He held up a pair of her stout-heeled, lace-up boots.

She clapped her hands in delight. 'A walk in the snow! Clifford, you truly are a mind reader. I've waded through waist-deep snow abroad, but I've never skipped about in the snow in England. Not even ankle deep. As a child, I always dreamed of a proper, white English Christmas.'

She bounded down the steps, catching herself as she slipped at the bottom by grabbing the thick overcoat sleeve of his outstretched arm. 'Oops! Thank you.'

She bent and swapped her Oxford lace-ups for her boots. Mrs Fontaine's comment about Clifford's meticulous timekeeping popped back into her head.

'But won't we be frightfully late for drinks at the vicarage? Surely you're not going to countenance such tardiness?'

'In the words of Oscar Wilde, my lady, "experience is the one thing you cannot get for nothing". I am sure Reverend Gaskell will understand the need to indulge in a childhood dream.'

'Excellent! There is something so magical about snow on Christmas morning, isn't there?'

'Indeed. This is only the fifth time I have experienced it in this country.'

That niggling question popped into her mind again. *Just how old is he, Ellie?* He looked almost the same to her now as he had on her few rare visits to Henley Hall when she was a child. During their recent murder investigations, despite his slightly advanced years, she'd also seen him scale fences and carry an unconscious person with the strength and agility of a much younger man. But, then again, he and her uncle had been in the army for much of their lives.

He took the pair of Oxfords she held and brushed the snow off with his gloved finger before placing them in a soft cloth bag. He held the gate open. 'Shall we, my lady?'

Placing her feet deliberately, Eleanor listened to the crunch of each footstep. She couldn't resist kicking the snow up as they started off towards the centre of Little Buckford, where the vicarage sat nestled behind a thick yew hedge, next to the church. She ran her hand along the tops of the lower bushes and garden gates, scooping the snow into balls and throwing them in front of her.

'Gracious, Clifford, this is such a pretty part of England, isn't it? Always so picturesque, but now covered in a veil of white, it's perfectly magical. Murder can't really happen somewhere so... tranquil, can it?' She smiled ruefully. 'Despite what everyone thinks, I'm not sure if it isn't safer out in the wild and woolly places I cycled abroad than in a small English village!'

'His lordship was always greatly heartened by your resourceful-ness in the precarious situations you found yourself in. He—'

'Oh no you don't!' She waggled a finger at him. 'Not unless you intend to tell me exactly how much, and indeed how, Uncle Byron was aware of those times.'

He cleared his throat. 'Perhaps another day, my lady.'

Her intrepid travels had generated a reasonable amount of newspaper coverage at the time, but he'd alluded to her uncle knowing a lot about her adventures abroad. A lot more than it would have been possible to learn from the confines of an armchair at Henley Hall, that was certain. She guessed that as her guardian, and only remaining relative, her uncle had had her followed on occasions. Or at least had paid for information on her whereabouts from time to time.

Clifford coughed. 'I was saying, there is the rather more pressing matter of Mr Canning's demise. I am confident the majority of the reverend's guests will also have been at the Henley Hall luncheon yesterday.'

'Absolutely and just wait until you hear the rumours that are flying about!'

He arched one brow.

'It seems a fair proportion of the villagers think Canning had some sort of smuggling racket going on when he was at sea. And that something in his past life as a smuggler led to his being murdered. There is also a strong consensus that he was not the man of meagre means he seemed.'

'Interesting, my lady. The intimation thereby being that he had a fortune hidden away?' He stared at her. 'Then perhaps the key…'

'My thoughts exactly, Clifford! But what I can't fathom is why would he have come back to sleepy Little Buckford? And, even more so, why would he live so sparsely and spend his days selling coal to make a living if he had a secret fortune lurking somewhere?'

'Both excellent questions. Perhaps we should take one at a time.' He paused as they reached the Rolls parked outside the church.

'What would induce a man who not only survived but was successful on the dangerous high seas to settle back into a village? Unless…' He seemed to run over a scenario in his mind. 'Forgive what might be an indelicate observation, my lady, but men who have been at sea for an extended period sometimes—'

'Have a girl in every port, they say.'

'Indeed. But only one who is special enough to return home permanently for.'

'Good theory, Clifford! But if accurate, who was she, I wonder?' She pondered for a moment. 'Hmm, more to the point though, whatever happened to her?' A frown knitted her brow. 'But why am I assuming she's gone, or passed away? Although I've just heard two women gossiping about the lack of a woman in Canning's life for years. Gracious, Clifford, perhaps our murderer is a woman, a woman scorned in love by Canning?'

He nodded. 'Indeed, the flames of fury do not necessarily diminish with time. Rather, time tends to feed them. Brooding over old injuries all too often leads to one result.'

'Revenge,' Eleanor breathed. She watched as two turtle doves fluttered overhead in the snow-laden sky and landed on the ledge of the church bell tower, the smaller of the two nestling into the other.

Clifford followed her gaze. 'Rather off course, my lady. They should have left for Africa in September at the latest. I suspect her mate has stayed to help her through a hard winter.'

'Unlike Canning did, perhaps.' A hollow feeling washed over her. 'Maybe it's because it's Christmas Day but I don't wish to dwell on… on broken hearts right now.' She thought of her own, once turbulent but now rather stagnant, love life.

Clifford straightened the seams of his leather gloves. He pointed at the snow-capped yew hedge separating the church from the vicarage. 'If I might suggest, my lady, we could start with a more matter-of-fact issue, namely pursuing the hearsay regarding Mr Canning's potential hidden fortune?'

She smiled. 'Tsk, tsk, Clifford. I never realised you were such a gossipmonger. Quite scandalous!'

CHAPTER 14

'Lady Swift, Mr Clifford, welcome, welcome!' Reverend Gaskell sang out from the arched porch before they had even reached the open front door of the vicarage. Pleased to see he was back to his usual jovial self after their uncomfortable conversation, Eleanor hurried across the gravel driveway to the attractive yellow-stone building and its decorative chimneys.

She beamed back at him. 'Happy Christmas, Reverend! Thank you for inviting us. What a treat to share such a special day among friends and neighbours.'

'Ah, so true, dear lady. Come in both and join our little throng, do.'

As she followed him down the hallway towards the sound of chattering, she couldn't help marvelling at the sunny ochre-coloured walls and patterned runner beneath her feet. The ambience suited the reverend's bright and chirpy personality perfectly.

But she was surprised to discover his previously unmentioned hobby. An avid amateur artist, his sketches and paintings covered the walls, all signed 'Gideon Gaskell' in soft brush strokes. A mixture of religious- and nature-themed works of varying sizes showed a marked improvement in skill the further they walked into the main part of the vicarage. The top half of the end wall was dominated by a simple but polished wood frame displaying a painting of two odd-looking leafless trees. The trees tapered up to a wide crown of bare branches fanning out over a basic wooden building.

She stepped back to make sense of the perspective. 'How captivating, Reverend. I didn't realise you were such an artist.'

'Oh goodness, hardly, dear lady. But I have tried over the years. This one was my little evening project during last winter. I intended to capture my time with the missions in Madagascar. This building was our modest HQ as it were. And these' – he pointed at the odd-looking trees – 'are supposed to be the baobab trees, they are an important symbol out there. But goodness how quickly the precision of memory fades, although it has been ten years.'

Mrs Fontaine appeared with a tray of delicious-looking savoury nibbles. 'Hello again, Lady Swift, Mr Clifford.' Clifford nodded and took the tray. 'Ah, *merci*.'

Reverend Gaskell waved down the hallway. 'Why don't you come through to the drawing room and join the festivities.

Eleanor followed him to find Clifford already offering nibbles to two couples, both turned out in their Sunday best. Four ladies sat in a circle on honey-coloured button-backed chairs chatting. By the piano, three men in suits were deep in discussion about something that appeared frightfully important. Recognising all but two of the guests, she gave a general wave and a 'Merry Christmas everyone!'

Eleanor sniffed the air, trying to identify the delicious aroma. Mrs Fontaine came over to her and whispered, 'It is cinnamon and orange peel, sprinkled on the logs.' She held her finger to her lips. 'A trick from France to make guests feel extra bienvenue.'

'It's wonderfully effective.'

Whilst listening to Mrs Fontaine, she failed to tear her eyes away from the view through the tall arched windows. The vicarage garden was filled to bursting with bushy plants of all descriptions, bowing under their increasingly heavy snowcaps and capes. A now white higgledy-piggledy path weaved through the beds like a lazy river, with inviting-looking tributaries sneaking off to secret corners. Beyond a perfectly cut box hedge the church of St Winifred's sat serenely, its spire disappearing into the sky.

Eleanor took the glass held out to her and stepped to the window. 'What an exquisite view, Reverend.'

'Why thank you, dear lady, although I confess I'm not one for the more traditional form of gardening, forever pruning and weeding. To my mind, everything the Lord makes is beautiful and has its place. And what better place for weeds and troublesome trees who shed leaves or drop sap everywhere to find shelter than in a vicarage garden? Even the poisonous yew is welcome.'

'Absolutely.' Eleanor pondered how she might persuade her own wonderful gardener, Joseph, to create such a delightfully wild area left to nature's own devices.

The vicar pointed to the still roaring fire. 'Best keep her topped up, given the weather. I'll just pop outside and get a few more logs.'

Left alone, she looked around. She needed to use the opportunity to find out more information from the reverend's other guests about Canning and his past. She plumped to start with the four ladies who were discreetly peering over at her. Two of them she knew as farmers' wives from just outside the village, whose eggs and milk she had enjoyed since her arrival at the Hall. The other two were Mable Green, West Radington's postmistress, and her elderly mother, who was prone to bouts of eccentric behaviour at the most inconvenient of times. At the moment, however, she was lying back in her chair snoring contentedly.

'May I join you?' Eleanor whispered, not wishing to wake the sleeping woman. Twenty minutes and two more glasses of sherry later, she had learned much about the tastiest plum sauce recipes and the best affordable milliner in Chipstone. About Canning, however, she'd gleaned little. The ladies clearly wanted to quiz her for details over his death, but etiquette prevented such things. Sensing she was getting nowhere, she politely made her escape and turned to one of the couples she'd noticed on arriving.

'Lady Swift, such a pleasure,' the moustached man held out his hand. 'James Trumball. And this is my wife, Esther.'

'Delighted.' Eleanor shook his hand. 'Forgive me, I don't believe we've met before?'

'No, no,' Esther said, 'but that has been our loss until today. We knew your uncle, of course. Such a wonderful man. Our heartfelt, if late, condolences.'

Eleanor smiled at her words. 'Thank you. So do you live locally? I don't recall seeing you in Little Buckford or Chipstone.'

James patted his chest, which had instantly swelled. 'Before, yes. But we had to move away on account of my business growing substantially in the last seven years. Yes, had to go north, nearer the port and the larger labour market. Outgrew Little Buckford and Chipstone, I'm afraid.' He smiled smugly, which made Eleanor think he wasn't too homesick for the area he had apparently outgrown.

'Congratulations. A lot of hard work, I'm sure.'

His wife nodded and patted her husband's shoulder. She leaned forward. 'We were so sorry to hear about what happened at the Henley Hall lunch for the village though. Such a shame.'

Her husband rolled his eyes.

'James, please,' his wife said softly with an embarrassed shrug to Eleanor.

He grunted. 'For the sake of Christmas, alright. But without wishing to be uncharitable, any man who can fall out with Gideon, and for so long, is not one I feel the world will grieve too hard for.'

Eleanor blinked. 'Gideon... as in Reverend Gideon Gaskell, our host?'

Esther nodded. 'It bothered him for so many years. A small blessing, I suppose, that he is free of that now.'

James snorted. 'We've no idea what the rascal did to anger him, save that despite every effort Gideon made, that man itched under his skin like a poisonous bee sting.'

Esther's lips twitched. 'I don't think bee stings are usually poisonous, James dear.'

'Maybe not, but I'll tell you one thing, I was told Gideon hardly managed to restrain himself from aiming for Canning's chest when he set off the firing pistol at the start of that race! Now, I'm famished.'

He strode over to the food table where he helped himself to two of most things. His wife smiled apologetically and joined him. Eleanor stayed put, her mind whirling. She remembered some kind of hold up at the beginning of the race and the reverend telling her it involved Canning and another man. At the start line, the reverend had certainly appeared, what? Angry? Furious? He certainly waved that gun around. *But Canning wasn't shot, Ellie, so that hardly incriminates the reverend.*

Throughout her musings, the vicar had been picking out Christmas carols on the piano. She watched as Clifford threaded his way through the other guests and whispered in the reverend's ear. 'How delightful, Mr Clifford. What a wonderful offer, and a reprieve for the assembled company. I fear I am, perhaps, rather over-rusty at tickling the keys.' Eleanor was surprised to see them both looking in her direction. The vicar clapped Clifford's shoulders. 'Delighted to, simply delighted.'

A minute later, Eleanor and the vicar were standing on the stone terrace in the garden.

'You should have said, dear lady, I would be delighted to give you a tour.'

Ah, so that's how Clifford engineered us being out here, Ellie. The clever bean!

'Thank you, Reverend, but I feel I shouldn't steal you away from your other guests.'

'Not at all. Mr Clifford is clearly a far more accomplished pianist than I.'

Eleanor stared through the window at her inscrutable butler playing the piano whilst simultaneously conversing with the other guests apparently with no effort at all. She wondered if later he would carry on playing while serving everyone drinks!

The vicar offered his arm before setting off on his tour. 'Do watch your step, dear lady. How fortuitous that you came prepared in stout boots.'

'Oh, what? Oh, yes.' As they started off, Eleanor wondered if her artful butler had brought her boots along for this very purpose.

With the first half of the tour complete, they arrived at a set of steps that allowed her to peep over the hedge at the church. After Mr Trumball and his wife had confirmed what she and Clifford had guessed, Eleanor felt she had no choice but to broach the topic. 'Thank you again for your tribute to Mr Canning last evening. It must be a blessing that the long quarrel is finally over.'

'What!?' Reverend Gaskell started and stepped away from her. His cheeks paled. 'Quarrel? What quarrel?'

Oh, Ellie, couldn't you have thought of a subtler way to start the conversation?

'Gracious, forgive me. I meant Mr Canning's quarrel with… the world is over. He seemed such an unhappy man. I always found him a rather tragic figure, believing there was a sad tale behind his gruff exterior. I have tried to keep looking on him compassionately, but it is becoming harder not having heard a single positive word about him from any of the villagers.'

The vicar pointed back towards the house. 'We… we should be getting in. Risk of a chill, you know.'

She touched his arm. 'I am sorry, Reverend, I fear I have upset you.'

'Upset me? No, no, dear lady.' He hesitated, looking at the ground. Then, as if decided, he looked up at her. 'I feel I owe you an explanation for my less than Christian response to Mr Canning's death. After all, he died almost in your arms, and that must have been most distressing. Your determination to find some good in him as well, makes me ashamed of the way I have behaved.'

As she went to speak he held up a hand. 'It is true that Mr Canning and myself had a long-standing quarrel. Sometime in the past he behaved despicably towards… a… parishioner of mine. She came to me for help because of the situation Mr Canning left her in and I was able to assist her through the church. I appealed to him to behave in a Christian manner and to acknowledge his responsibilities, but he would have none of it. He showed no shred of remorse for his actions from then up to his dying day. Now, if you will excuse me, Lady Swift, I really should be getting back to my other guests.'

As the reverend stomped the snow off his boots in the hall and re-greeted his guests, Eleanor thought back again to Canning's last visit to the Hall. 'Perhaps he did regret his past, Reverend,' she whispered to the icy wind.

CHAPTER 15

Back in the vicarage, Eleanor was relieved to see the vicar was once more at the piano. Without being able to jot down the snippets she had overheard, she knew there was a chance with so much going on that one or two might slip her memory. She beckoned to Clifford to join her at the nibbles table.

'My lady?'

'Well engineered, the walk in the garden with the reverend. Please remember a few things for me. Dispute. Parishioner. Never regretted.'

'Very good.'

'Dash it! I think there's something else?' She shook her head. 'Never mind, it'll come back to me by this afternoon.'

'While you are at the Fenwick-Langhams' Christmas luncheon, perhaps?'

'Oh bother, thanks for reminding me. Do you know, I had no idea Christmas Day could be so exhausting.' She laughed. 'It might take me until New Year's to recover at this rate. And I thought being a Lady of the Manor was all about languishing on chaise longues and chiding the tradesmen!'

'It might be if Mrs Butters were not so efficient with callers at the back door and Master Gladstone not so fond of commandeering the chaise longue all for himself.'

'And if you and I weren't yet again caught up in…' She peeped over at the other guests. 'Another nasty business.'

'Indeed.'

They paused as Mrs Fontaine appeared beside Clifford holding two plates of sugar-dusted tartlets, the irresistible waft of spiced fruit and citrus peel spiralling up through the lattice pastry. He made room for them on the table.

'Merci, Mr Clifford.'

Eleanor's mouth watered. 'They look amazing! As good as the finest patissier in France would create.'

Mrs Fontaine smiled. 'Or pâtissière. I studied briefly under a wonderful lady master chef many years ago. In France, it is not as unusual as here for a woman to, how you say, wear the trousers.'

As the vicar's housekeeper disappeared back towards the kitchen, Eleanor let out a lengthy breath. 'We're probably done here on investigating, I say. Perhaps we can just enjoy the Christmas celebration now, and definitely those sublime-looking pastry creations, and let our brains chew over what we've learned so far?'

He gave a deferential nod but cleared his throat at the same time.

She moaned quietly. 'I see. What wonderful scheme are you proposing we get up to instead?'

'I believe Miss Green is itching to pin you in a corner.'

'And pump me for information about Canning's death, I'll bet. But I don't want to tell her anything. It will be all round the village before the post office even reopens.'

'Undoubtedly, my lady. However, Miss Green has stood behind that counter since the day she left school at fourteen and has been establishing herself as the fount of knowledge for all things local ever since. Yesterday, she herself was at an event where a man died and yet she has nothing from the horse's mouth to share with her customers. That cannot be an easy disappointment to swallow.'

Eleanor folded her arms. 'But if she didn't see anything that she can tattle with others about, she won't have anything to tell me that's of use!'

'Might I suggest that it is not what she might have seen but what she might have heard.'

Eleanor glanced over in Miss Green's direction to find the woman was nonchalantly sidling towards her. 'Oh help!'

'My lady, if anyone knows more than we have managed to glean so far, I would bet Christmas on it being our dear postmistress.' He gave his customary half bow and turned to the drinks table. Pouring Eleanor a fresh glass of sherry, he called across, 'Miss Green, perhaps I can furnish you with a refreshment?'

'Traitor!' Eleanor whispered from the corner of her mouth.

Sitting beside Miss Green, Eleanor couldn't help but notice a prettiness in the woman she'd never spotted before. Maybe it was the soft, blue cotton dress that hugged her feminine hips and the extra effort she had made with her usually lank auburn hair. Or perhaps it was the blush of excitement at being released from the post office counter a second time in less than twenty-four hours.

Despite this, Mable was at least twenty years older than her, Eleanor thought. She did the maths. It meant Miss Green had been trapped in that tiny shop selling stamps and sending the odd telegram for longer than Eleanor had been alive.

Biting her lip, she thought back over the many adventures she'd had, to say nothing of the freedoms she was still experiencing, especially with her recent inheritance of Henley Hall. Her musings were cut short by the lady herself accepting her drink from Clifford and raising her glass.

'A happy Christmas to you, Mr Clifford. And you, Lady Swift.'

She responded in kind and leaned towards Mable. 'It's been a strange start to Christmas though, Miss Green, I have to say.'

Miss Green's eyes shone with interest. 'I dare say, m'lady. It is your first one at Henley Hall, after all. You must have been so busy with all the preparations to entertain the entire village.'

'Yes I suppose, but Clifford is meticulously organised about, well everything, actually. And so many people who came along helped as well.'

Eleanor was confused. Even though she was trying hard not to show it, Miss Green was obviously put out. *Ah!* Ironically, she felt Eleanor had snubbed her by not asking her to help out at the Christmas lunch.

'I was, of course, Miss Green, desperate to ask for your well-known efficiency in helping out but didn't wish to intrude on your free time. You have such a busy schedule already, with the post office and caring for your mother.'

Mable smiled graciously. 'Very thoughtful, m'lady, thank you. Mother can be a trial, bless her, and it truly was a treat to be free for an afternoon. It's just such a shame for you that things went awry with the race, unless' – she lowered her voice conspiratorially – 'I heard wrong, of course?'

Artfully does it, Ellie. Clifford will be watching from somewhere.

Eleanor lowered her voice as well. 'Regrettably, you heard correctly. Poor Mr Canning fell on the second half of the course but had passed away by the time Doctor Browning reached him. Such a tragedy.'

Mable's eyebrows rose. 'Doctor Browning attended to him, did he? Well, well, that is surprising.'

'How so?'

Mable glanced around her, a knowing look on her face. 'Not that I'm one to gossip, but you were not here when Canning's mother passed away, I believe?'

'Ah, I didn't realise his mother had been alive when he returned from the sea.'

'She was, although barely to Canning's mind. She was, in fact, at death's door. He took it upon himself to investigate as her health was such a contrast to what he expected. He said he'd found' – she looked over her shoulder – 'evidence that Doctor Browning had acted irresponsibly in prescribing certain… medications. Canning went to the police over the doctor having, shall we say, hastened his mother's passing.'

Eleanor was genuinely shocked. 'Gracious! So Mr Canning believed Doctor Browning was responsible for his mother's death? And what happened?'

'Well, m'lady, it turned out the evidence was inconclusive. The charge of malpractice was thrown out of court.'

Eleanor's mind raced. *Canning tried to get Doctor Browning struck off as a doctor!* That means the doctor had a strong motive to kill Canning: revenge. But was it all in Canning's mind? Or was Canning right, but Doctor Browning was too wily to be caught out?

She picked her words carefully. 'So I suppose Mr Canning moved from Little Buckford to Chipstone to avoid bumping into the doctor almost daily. After all, that would only have reminded him of his poor mother.'

There was that knowing look again. 'Ye-s, but Mr Canning moving to Chipstone meant he kept bumping into someone else, who, shall we say, was as keen to avoid him as he was Doctor Browning.'

Eleanor was now puzzled. 'But who? And why?'

Miss Green's hand went to her throat. 'M'lady, I would hate to be indiscreet.'

'Goodness yes, yes. Forgive me, it's just that I do wish to send my condolences to all the people I should. Especially' – she leaned in closer – 'as Mr Canning died at my event.'

'Naturally, but Miss Moore wouldn't thank you for sending condolences.'

'Miss Moore? As in Miss Lucetta Moore, with the delightful florist shop?'

'Oh dear, did I say her name out loud?' Miss Green said innocently. 'Well, I'm not saying there was anything between her and Canning but there was talk years back. To my knowledge they've not so much as passed the time of day since, even though they regularly "bumped" into each other once Canning moved to Chipstone. But that's what made it seem odd. That she risked being thought so unseemly as to seek Canning out in…' She raised her hand to speak behind it. 'In the changing room you had arranged.'

Eleanor struggled to keep her face neutral. 'Perhaps Miss Moore was carrying a floral arrangement when you saw her going in or coming out? I did engage her to do the flower displays for the Christmas Eve lunch, you see.'

'Well, I'm sure that's what it was, m'lady. I didn't actually see her myself, you understand. My friend told me she was passing the changing room and heard a woman's voice. Then a door slammed and Miss Moore came rushing out.' Miss Green glanced around and lowered her voice even further. 'Followed by Canning looking furious.'

'I see.' Eleanor realised Mable was waiting for more titbits of information. Aware that all she'd passed on in exchange so far was that Doctor Browning had been the one to attend to Canning, Eleanor racked her brain. If she gave away too much, there was every chance the murderer might be forewarned.

'Ah,' she blurted out, making Mable jump hard enough to spill her sherry. 'Oh dear, sorry. I just realised I probably ought to be getting along. I'm waiting for a phone call regarding Mr Canning's body.'

'For the date of the funeral, do you mean?'

Eleanor shook her head. 'Between you and me, Doctor Browning wasn't able to provide poor Mr Canning's death certificate, not being his doctor, as we mentioned. And as Canning's doctor was not at the scene, well, the certificate has yet to be issued.' *Well, it's only a minor lie in a good cause, Ellie. You don't know if it has been or not.*

Miss Green licked her lips and looked across at the other women she had been seated with for most of the sherry party. 'Well, please don't let me detain you, m'lady.' She rose and practically skipped back to the other side of the room.

A short while later, with their goodbyes made, and the reverend thanked again, Clifford held open the door of the Rolls outside the church.

Eleanor slid onto the passenger's seat. 'Enlightening morning, eh, Clifford?'

'Regrettably not on my side, my lady. I can see you fared considerably better, however.'

'Absolutely. Although now my head is swimming with information. The trouble is it's also swimming in sherry.'

He pulled out his pocket watch. 'Fortuitously you have almost fifty minutes before the Christmas luncheon party at Langham Manor begins and the champagne flows. Then, naturally, there will be wine to accompany each course, followed by dessert cocktails and, lastly, spirits for after luncheon toasts.'

This made her groan. 'But I'm so full, I could curl up with Gladstone and a good book and wake up tomorrow with the pages open in my face without having read a single word.'

Clifford gently eased the Rolls out onto the snow-covered lane. 'Enjoying oneself can be quite the trial, my lady.'

She laughed at his less than subtle comment. 'I know, what a terrible brat I am. Fancy complaining about such luxurious indulgences.' She lay back in the seat. 'Although I'm sure my poor battered head and stomach will have plenty to say about it in the morning.'

'Boxing Day at Henley Hall traditionally starts at seven, my lady. The ladies look forward to it most particularly.'

'Oh don't worry. I shall be up and presentable, if only in spirit. Oh, but you need to add some more reminders to the list I gave you previously. What were they again?'

'Dispute. Parishioner. Not regretted. Plus?'

'Malpractice. Doctor Browning. Miss Moore. Changing room.'

'All pique my interest, but changing room?'

'It would appear, Clifford, that the changing room might have been the scene of something pertinent to Canning's murder.'

He thought about this for a moment. 'If Mr Canning was poisoned in the changing rooms, then how and when he died might have been intentional.'

'You mean the poisoner might have planned it so Canning died very unpleasantly?'

'And very publicly. Although we have rather left the realm of facts for that of conjecture.'

Eleanor shrugged. 'I doubt if many murders have been solved without a certain amount of conjecturing. I rather think it's my forte. So, to continue to conjecture and play devil's advocate, if our poisoner wanted Canning to die in such an unpleasant, public manner, then there's really only one motive I can think of that would make someone act so inhumanely.'

Clifford nodded. 'Revenge.'

CHAPTER 16

'Oh, botheration!' Eleanor muttered. After a hurried stop-off at Henley Hall, she was now back in the Rolls, en route to the Christmas lunch. There was a knot in her stomach and she reflected, not for the first time, that she found it less nerve-wracking to face charging rhinos than formal society events.

It wasn't being sociable that was the issue, more that she hadn't been brought up to deal with the rigid social etiquette of 1920s England. Polite small talk came to her as naturally as rain to a desert. Her bohemian upbringing, followed by a fiercely independent life abroad, had made her more at home in the bush than at a society function. She fiddled with her beaded shawl and stared down at the jade-green silk dress she had hastily changed into. Running her hand over her embroidered organza overskirt, she sighed.

'Clifford?'

At the wheel, he stared straight ahead. 'You might wish to look in the velvet bag behind your seat, my lady.'

She turned and picked up an exquisitely made, ruched wrist purse. 'Gosh, that is beautiful and, wait though, it matches my dress!'

'A handmade gift from Mrs Butters.'

She pulled on the silk ribbon drawstrings and smiled. 'Gracious, what a treasure she is. Look, my kohl, lipstick, compact mirror and two handkerchiefs.'

'Does that answer your question, my lady?'

She nodded, still stroking the velvet purse. 'Mostly. I'm still not very comfortable at this formal socialising stuff.'

'Although you will be among good friends today.' He paused. 'And no one you have not already met.'

Her head jerked up. 'You asked Sandford for the guest list?'

'It may have come up in conversation, my lady.'

'What, when you rang him to ask for it?' She laughed. 'So you could warn me against putting my foot in it with anyone? Thank you, Clifford. That was very thoughtful. I can totally see why Uncle Byron valued your company and your friendship for all those years.'

They sat in amiable silence until the Rolls passed under the golden arch of Langham Manor's imposing gates, the stone lions still wearing manes of pristine white.

Feeling altogether less apprehensive about the afternoon, she looked in wonder at the decorations. Ornate wrought-iron stakes bearing giant holly-and-ivy wreaths decorated with red ribbons and gold baubles lined the length of the Manor's drive.

Eleanor's mouth fell open. 'Gracious! They are so beautiful. And for the first time, I'm only fractionally late arriving at one of Lady Langham's dos. And between you and Mrs Butters, I might actually survive this luncheon without getting into any trouble at all.'

'Ah.' Clifford cleared his throat. 'My lady, perhaps I should have mentioned that the Dowager Countess Goldsworthy is amongst those on the list.'

'Double botheration!'

'Merry Christmas, Sandford!' She waved to the Langhams' butler as he held the door open for her at the base of the grand entrance steps. With a shiver at the coldness of the outside air, she hugged her shoulders and looked up at the Manor. Even though the sun was yet to set, lights shone out of every window onto garlands of fir branches embellished with gold bows. A welcoming committee of tall, silver lanterns stood ready either side of the wide stone steps, each sporting a perfect posy of white Christmas roses.

'The house looks magnificent,' she said.

Sandford bowed. 'Thank you, Lady Swift, and merry Christmas to you too. Would you care to join the other guests inside, where it is markedly warmer?'

'Absolutely. And as a special treat for Lady Langham, I'm not really late, am I?'

Sandford cast his eyes down. 'I couldn't say, my lady.'

Eleanor's face fell. 'Oh dear! And I tried hard this time. Let's hope she might learn to find it an endearing part of my character.'

Sandford's silence answered her question.

'Okay, perhaps not. But listen, I do hope after we're all stuffed to the gills and dozing by the fire, you might find time to join Clifford for a quiet drink? I've given him a little something special for you to share and a basket of treats for the rest of the staff.'

Sandford gave a Clifford-worthy half bow. 'You are most kind, my lady.' He nodded to his old friend who had stepped out of the car. 'Mr Clifford is always a most welcome presence in the staff quarters.'

In the grand entrance hall, Eleanor found her feet wouldn't let her move on until she had taken in the full breathtaking splendour of the interior decorations. Garlands, candles, giant baubles and hundreds of velvet bows in red, gold and green festooned the space.

She turned in a slow circle, eyes wide. But it was the Christmas tree rising two full storeys to the galleried second-floor landing which made her tingle. The delicious scent of fresh pine needles tickled her nose as she stepped forward to stare up its full height. Wooden decorations hung from each branch, tiny painted rocking horses swinging below nutcracker dolls in smart uniforms interspersed with Lilliputian silver-cased lanterns, each bearing a flickering candle. As she stood gazing in wonder, a model train chugged slowly out from the base of the tree, its trucks filled with mini gifts, and then disappeared again.

'Eleanor, old girl, there you are.' Lord Langham's booming voice careened down the stately carved staircase, followed by his two exuberant chocolate spaniels.

'Morning, Humphrey, morning, Monty.' She ruffled the dogs' ears as they jumped up on their back legs, tails vibrating with excitement. 'Nice Christmas bow ties you're wearing, boys.' She laughed, feeling the knot in her stomach loosen. Despite knowing Lord Langham and his wife for less than a year, there was something very comforting about being in their company. Especially Lord Langham, with his affable manner and lack of interest in social stuffiness.

'Harold, how are you?' She patted the arm of his favourite plum cardigan, worn under a seasonally red velvet waistcoat.

He poked his empty champagne flute into his breast pocket and scooped up her hands in his. 'Totally spiffing thanks, old thing. It's Christmas Day. Hurrah!' His face below his monstrous walrus moustache split into an enormous grin. 'Have to confess I snuck off from the sherry and small talk. Quite deathly.'

Eleanor laughed. A man after her own heart. 'Well, the house looks absolutely beautiful. It's like standing in the most incredible fairy tale.'

'Ah, now tell that to my darling wife and she might relax a little and enjoy herself. Daft old partridge thinks it will ruin everyone's special day if things aren't perfect. Never understood the fuss about guests myself. Fill them up with good drink and plates of delectables and let them snooze it off, I say. Job done. But apparently that's not the ticket at all. So, lay it on thick about how splendid it all is, and hang on to my arm so we can survive the full roasting for being late together, what?'

Eleanor couldn't help but chuckle at this soft old bear whose only interest in life was making sure that the wife he adored was happy. But just before they reached the reception room, Eleanor

felt a hand grasp her free arm from behind and slide her gently
out of Harold's grip.

'I'll take her from here, Pater.'

She spun round. 'Lancelot!' Eleanor cursed the blush that set
her face on fire.

'Merry Christmas, Sherlock.'

Harold chortled. 'The boy's been on tenterhooks waiting for
you to arrive, old girl.'

Dash it, Ellie! You're supposed to be mad at him, remember. 'Hello,
Lancelot,' she said matter-of-factly.

Lancelot pulled a face, ever the joker rather than the sophisticated
young lord his mother, Lady Fenwick-Langham, implored him
to be. 'Are you going to be horribly formal? What happened to
Goggles? I really liked my pet name, Sherlock.'

Eleanor had nicknamed him 'Goggles' as he was a pilot and he
had nicknamed her 'Sherlock' after she had solved a murder within
weeks of arriving in the area.

'I did too, for a while.' She tried hard to remind herself again
that she was still annoyed with him for refusing to take anything
she did seriously.

He chuckled. 'Oh, you're not still doing the sulky girl routine,
surely? Darling fruit, it doesn't suit you at all.' He leaned in, his jaw
brushing her cheek, sending a tingle up her spine. 'But fret not,
being the good sort I am, I'll let you in to a little secret.'

She melted a little. 'What?'

'I don't think anyone else has noticed yet, but when you pout,
you look like a trout. One that's been hoicked out of the water
when he was right in the middle of nosing about in something
dashedly interesting.' He stuck his bottom lip out and rounded
his shoulders with a theatrical huff.

Eleanor struggled to stop herself smiling. 'I'm not sulking
actually.'

'Sherlock, you used to think I was the cat's pyjamas, what's happened?'

'Look. Lancelot, you still are the cat's pyjamas, but you made me look a fool when I stood for election as Chipstone's first female Member of Parliament a while ago, remember?'

'Ouch, Sherlock, bit of a kick to a chap's feelings. That wasn't my intention at all. I don't know how you could think that.'

'Perhaps it was the way you paraded about with your bright young thing friends reducing the entire thing to a farce?'

He took her shoulders and pulled her in close. 'I'm sorry, Sherlock. Sometimes I just act without thinking. These last few weeks with you being all huffy with me have been hideous. I've missed having fun with you.'

Eleanor felt her whole body sway.

Suddenly he slapped his forehead and jerked backwards, making her jump. 'Hey! I've got it. Your next mystery to solve! And I can be your sleuthing partner this time round. This one should be a cinch, seeing as you are, in fact, peculiarly whizzo at solving the rummiest of the things.'

'What mystery?'

'It's a bally awful case of a missing person.'

She stared at him. 'Who's missing? Is it someone I know?'

Lancelot nodded. 'Yes. She was such a bright, jolly sort, always so full of fun and life.'

'Oh my goodness. Do you know what's happened to her?'

'Absolutely. She's been kidnapped and a dull, earnest type left in her place.'

Eleanor pursed her lips. 'And this tragic girl's name?'

'Lady Eleanor Swift. Although, just between you and me, she was too peculiar and captivating to be a proper lady.'

She pushed him away, half playfully. 'Well, I've heard that Lady Eleanor Swift might have grown up and realised that the world is more than just the playground her fatuous friend keeps insisting it is. Now, merry Christmas, Lancelot. I've got to go and do my duty as a guest.'

Lord Langham, who had been discreetly admiring a painting while they talked, now joined them again. 'Better get in there, old thing, or the memsahib will relegate us to the doghouse for the rest of Christmas!'

He threw open the double doors.

'There you are, Harold!' Lady Langham's voice carried out to them, a hint of vex to her tone. 'Our guests were wondering where on earth you'd got to.'

'No they weren't, light of my life.' Harold waved an arm at the six people dotted around the room, absent-mindedly stepping aside and releasing the full whirlwind of the two spaniels. 'They were wondering who gnawed a hole in their stomachs. All that empty tum rumbling is like bally thunder, you can hear it out in the corridor.'

Most of the guests laughed. 'Harold, please,' his wife pleaded. 'And do sort the dogs, there's a dear.'

'Ay, Augusta, he's not wrong,' called an elderly female Scottish voice from beside the roaring fire. 'If we'll not be having Christmas luncheon soon, it'll be more a case of Boxing Day tea.'

Hearing this, Eleanor hurried in.

'Augusta.' Eleanor grasped Lady Langham's arm. 'I am so sorry I'm a little late. Frightfully poor guest behaviour.'

'Frightfully!' Lancelot said. 'Shall I get Sandford to throw her out with the spaniels, Mater?'

Eleanor shot him a look and turned to the assembled room. 'A merry Christmas to you all!'

Everyone in the room chorused various Christmas greetings back.

Lady Langham drew her into a warm hug. 'Eleanor, my dear, welcome and merry Christmas.' Since saving Lancelot, her only surviving child, from a murder charge, Eleanor could do no wrong in Lady Langham's eyes.

Over Eleanor's shoulder, she said, 'Lancelot, perhaps you might like to attend to some of our other guests?' She nodded towards the fireplace where the purple-tartan-clad form of the elderly Dowager Countess Goldsworthy sat. Eleanor wondered if her niece who sat opposite her, the round-faced Cora Wynne, would develop a squint from batting her lashes so wildly at Lancelot.

'Don't strain yourself, Lancelot,' the countess called over. 'I know you're not used to exerting yourself, especially at this hour.'

Her niece tutted and stared down at her hands.

'Daffers.' Harold strode over and whipped the empty whisky glass from the countess' hand. 'It's Christmas. Would be a frightful shame if you've left behind your festive cheer on the train on the way down from Scotland, wouldn't you say?'

She narrowed her eyes, but the corners of her mouth betrayed the true feelings she held for him as the husband of one of her best friends. 'Less of the old, if you please. And more of the dram. It's not a bad one.'

'Faint praise for your favourite malt, shipped down specially for you, you rascal.'

'Ay, and you wasted your money paying the carriage. I could have saved you the cost and brought it myself.'

Lady Langham tightened her grip on Eleanor's arm. 'Remind me what it is about Christmas that makes people bicker, my dear?' she whispered.

'I'm sure it's my fault,' Eleanor said. 'A delayed lunch start is enough to make anyone tetchy. I feel terrible.'

Her hostess shook her head. 'My dear, I am the one to apologise. You are not late.'

Eleanor stared at the gold ormolu and porcelain clock on the marble mantelpiece. 'But surely…'

'Actually, I might have asked Clifford to tell the smallest of fibs. He was instructed to let you know luncheon would begin promptly at one o'clock when he knew it was really planned for half past.'

Eleanor's jaw dropped, then her face broke into a smile. 'I say, Augusta, what a clever ruse!'

'I knew you wouldn't mind. And ignore Daphne, she's always rather vocal about waiting for anything Chef produces. His cuisine is quite the highlight for her.'

'And for us all.' Eleanor clasped her stomach as it rumbled loudly at the thought.

'See!' Lord Langham pointed at her. 'Thunderously hungry!'

Lady Langham stood up. 'Yes, dear. Tell Sandford we are ready, would you?'

Lord Langham quaffed the remains of his champagne flute and bellowed, 'Sandford? Troughs ahoy, old chap!'

'Oh help!' Lady Langham muttered.

CHAPTER 17

Aware that she hadn't had the chance to speak to any of the other guests, Eleanor hurried over to the stern-faced, white-haired lady in an austerely cut tartan dress by the fire. 'Countess, happy Christmas! So lovely to see you again. I do hope you are keeping well?'

'Well enough, thank you, Lady Swift. And a happy Christmas to you, even though it's terribly damp down this end of the world.' Her thick Scottish burr seemed to accentuate her displeasure. 'Better back in Scotland, and no mistake. Cold and crisp. Good for the constitution.'

'And miserably foggy all year round,' her niece mumbled, catching Eleanor's eye. Years of living with her indomitable aunt hadn't quite buried all of her spirit.

'And Cora, happy Christmas to you!' Eleanor gave the long-suffering girl a genuine smile. 'You look simply radiant, the lilac of your gown lights up your whole face.'

Her aunt grunted, instantly dashing Cora's delight at the compliment. 'Not that it'll do any good, and a ridiculous pretty penny wasted on it too. He'll not look at you now, lassie, not now Lady Swift has arrived.'

Cora threw her aunt a horrified look and then mouthed Eleanor an apology. Cora was an orphan, and the countess had always hoped that Lancelot would marry her and take her off her hands. Unfortunately, despite Cora being besotted with him, he had no intention of making her his wife and had made this clear to the countess.

'Do excuse me just a moment, please.' Eleanor escaped to the other side of the room. On a striped Regency settee sat a middle-aged man in an impeccable grey suit offset by a seasonal red cravat which brought out the strawberry tones of his fair hair. The woman next to him appeared to have lost a fight with an entire roll of tightly pleated yellow silk, which highlighted her carefully crafted chestnut waves.

'Viscount and Viscountess Littleton, happy Christmas to you both!'

Having risen as she approached, the viscount shook her hand warmly. 'Lady Swift, happy Christmas. We are indeed in top form although Delia is finding the snow something of a vast disappointment compared to her native Boston.'

'Uh, huh!' His wife slapped the seat he had vacated. 'I so did not use the word "disappointed". I merely told you that it was a feeble show compared to back home on the East Coast. We'd be skiing up in the mountains today, that's for sure.'

Her husband rolled his eyes. 'You mean you and that mad crowd of yours.'

The viscountess glared at her husband. 'And a happy Christmas to you, Lady Swift.' Eleanor caught Lady Langham's slight shudder out of the corner of her eye, which she made every time the viscountess pronounced 'you' as 'yuh'.

'Well I hope you still enjoy how pretty it looks,' Eleanor said. She turned to the pair snuggled together on the opposite settee. 'And Baron Ashley, Lady Wilhelmina, happy Christmas!'

The man's tall and lithe frame seemed to scoop his dainty wife up with him as he jumped to his feet, standing head and shoulders above her. 'Happy Christmas to you, Lady Swift!'

'And how is newly married life treating you?' she asked with genuine affection. Like the Langhams, she had a soft spot for this sweet English rose and her charming older husband. They had both defied convention and married for love, the near fifteen-year age gap, and even wider social gap, immaterial to them.

'Wonderfully, thank you, Lady Swift. And a wonderful, happy and joyous Christmas to you!' Lady Wilhelmina said. Her natural, honey-blonde curls bobbed gently, allowing a lock to free itself from her satin clip and bounce against her cheek. She smoothed down the skirt of her cornflower-blue crossover dress, which brought out her beautiful eyes.

'Blissfully,' he agreed.

At that moment, Sandford sounded the lunch gong.

'Hurrah!' Harold said, making Cora jump. 'Lunchypoos at last, everyone. Ladies, lead on.'

Just as she always did, Eleanor caught her breath as she stepped into the exquisite dining room. There was something in her that wished she could be left alone here, just for an hour, to trace her fingers over each of the delicate, gold-relief birds and roses in the cream silk damask wallpaper, and to turn in slow circles, drinking in the hand-painted ceiling with its luminescent trompe l'oeil of a glass dome spanning the full length of the sixty-foot room. Even the thick, crimson velvet curtains called to her to wrap herself in them.

Eleanor was pleased to find that she was not seated next to the contrarian countess. Instead, she had Baron Ashley to her right and Lady Langham to her left; much more agreeable lunch companions. Lancelot grinned at her from his seat diagonally opposite, where he sat beside Lady Wilhelmina. Lord Langham seemed to have drawn the short straw, presiding over the end with the countess, Cora, and the still somewhat fractious Littletons. Oblivious, he waited until the ladies had taken their seats, and then dinged his wine glass with a fish knife with enough enthusiasm that it shattered over the starched white linen.

Lancelot applauded vigorously. 'Great show, Pater!'

'Actually, Harold,' his wife called. 'Perhaps we should forgo any speechmaking? What do you say, dear?'

'I was only going to wish our good friends a spiffing Christmas nosh up.'

Eleanor tried to hide her laughter behind a hastily retrieved handkerchief from her new wrist purse.

'How delightful,' Lady Langham said drily.

Several courses later and Eleanor was in heaven. The garlic oysters to start had been divinely silky and creamy. This had been followed by the sumptuous fish soup, garnished with a carved bread boat, replete with an asparagus mast and king-prawn skipper, and the accompanying glass of madeira wine had warmed her stomach and heated her cheeks. The third course, a ring of honey-baked figs dressed with sharp white cheese and served with a glass of sweet almond liqueur made her salivate before she'd even tasted it. Out of the corner of her eye she saw Lancelot indiscreetly waving the correct fork at her.

Ten minutes later, as the footman took her plate, she patted her stomach, which was pleasantly full. But according to the number of fingers Lancelot was wiggling at her with glee, there were still another five courses to be served!

Grateful for the twenty-minute pause, she quickly realised this was to be filled with a round of sumptuous Bordeaux wines and the pulling of crackers. Much to Cora's obvious chagrin, Lancelot insisted they pulled them with the person diagonally opposite. A hubbub of chatter arose with the swapping of the neatly printed mottos and tiny silver trinkets that exploded out onto the tablecloth. A few minutes later and they all sat sporting gold paper crowns except Viscountess Littleton, who refused to wear hers as she maintained it would ruin her hair.

Then the pièce de résistance arrived. Borne with impressive ceremony on the shoulders of four of the footmen on a covered silver platter as long as three place settings, the chatter along the table hushed except for Viscountess Littleton who was heard to mutter, 'It can be a thin line between pageantry and pantomime, don't you find?' But Lancelot silenced her by leading a drum roll with two spoons.

Sandford appeared to be waiting for a signal from Lady Langham but Lord Langham called out, 'Come on, Sandford, we're all drooling to see what Chef has conjured up.' At the butler's clap, the four footmen set the platter down on a long, wheeled serving table. With a nod from Sandford, each footman then lifted one of the four tops.

Everyone craned forward.

In the centre of the platter lay an enormous turkey, roasted to golden, herb-crusted perfection. It was flanked by a dressed goose at either end and an outer semi-circle of partridges. Mounds of roast parsnips, potatoes, Brussel sprouts, calvados-glazed carrots and finger sausages wrapped in succulent bacon strips surrounded the meat. Four serving girls appeared, each holding a giant jug of delicious-smelling gravy.

As Harold took up the carving knife from the silver salver Sandford held out to him, Lancelot leaned across the table to Eleanor. 'Sorry, Sherlock, I should have asked if you're alright after the race debacle at your spiffing Christmas Eve lunch for the localites.'

'Fine,' she replied, hoping he would take the hint.

He didn't.

'Must have been quite the damper, old fruit, what? All that prep ruined by some chap choosing to go toes up just before the finish line. Tsk tsk, rather ungrateful of him, I say.'

Lady Langham looked shocked. 'Eleanor, dear girl, what is this?'

'Oh really, it's nothing worth discussing at Christmas lunch.' She glared at Lancelot, wishing he was seated nearer so she could reach his shins and give him a sharp kick. *Oh, he's irresistible in so many ways, Ellie, but why can't he ever take a hint and stop playing the clown?*

Oblivious to her thoughts, he grinned at her. 'Sherlock, it's no good pulling out the done-it-all-before card, although you do seem to attract dead bodies like some women attract cats.'

Lady Wilhelmina and their hostess both gasped. Lancelot looked around. 'Well really, she does. Little Buckford would have won Dullsville Village of the year every year until Lady Swift moved in and started a spate of—'

'Lancelot!' Lady Langham glared at him. 'If someone did pass away at the poor girl's event, I'm sure it is the last thing she wants to discuss on Christmas Day.' She put her hand on Eleanor's shoulder. 'I am so sorry, my dear, I hadn't heard at all. It's the preparations for today you see, they tend to totally occupy me to the exclusion of all else.'

'I can vouch for that,' Lord Langham called over. 'Haven't been able to exchange a word with my darling wife for days.'

Eleanor waved a hand, hoping the topic would be dropped. 'Gracious, the turkey looks divine.'

Lancelot shook his head. 'Oh no you don't. Everyone's dying to know what happened.'

'Perhaps not the best choice of words, old man?' Baron Ashley said.

'What's this about a man dying?' the countess called up the table. 'It's natural to lose more in the winter months, mind.'

Eleanor gave her hostess an apologetic look. Lady Langham glanced around at the expectant faces and sighed.

'Do tell, Eleanor dear. It seems to be quite the topic of interest.'

Resignedly, Eleanor outlined the events of the previous day.

'But you haven't told us who he was,' Viscountess Littleton said. 'Did we know him?'

Eleanor shook her head. 'I doubt it. A Mr Canning. From Chipstone. Poor fellow, such a tragedy.'

'Canning?' Harold helped himself to a selection from the salver of vegetables and wrapped sausages one of the footmen held for him. 'Not a name I know, I don't think. Augusta, my love, is he one of ours?'

His wife busied herself with her napkin. 'I don't believe we were acquainted with the gentleman, dear, no.'

'Sandford?' Harold bellowed, holding up his glass.

'Right here, my lord.' Sandford disguised his wince well.

'Ah, now as you do the rounds with the next bottle, spill all you might know on this fellow.'

Sandford nodded. 'Mr Canning was a local coal merchant for Chipstone and the surrounding villages for a great many years, my lord.'

Viscountess Littleton sniffed. 'Oh, he was a tradesman.'

Sandford nodded again. 'Yes, my lady. He became a coalman after retiring from the merchant navy, I believe. He had his own barge for a number of years.'

Lord Langham snorted loudly. 'What the devil was the man doing with a barge?'

Sandford coughed. 'To run the, err, that is, he, err, sold his… goods along the Thames as well as in the villages and towns.'

Interesting, Ellie.

The Dowager Countess banged her glass down on the table. 'Sandford, I may be from the Highlands, but nowhere in the British Isles is coal ever described as "goods".'

'No, perhaps not, Countess Goldsworthy. Mr Canning did for a time have something of a reputation for dealing in other items, I understand. That was, however, several years ago.'

Luckily for Eleanor, like the viscountess, the guests had lost interest in the discussion at finding out the dead man 'wasn't one of them', as Lady Langham had put it. The conversation drifted off to the recently created Irish Free State and the countess' outrage at the Scottish county of Haddingtonshire being renamed East Lothian.

While the other guests were occupied with these topics, Lady Langham whispered to Eleanor. 'My dear, I saw your expression when Sandford spoke just then. Tell me, you and Clifford haven't been caught up in another investigation?'

'I wish I could,' she whispered back. 'But in truth, we have.'

'Tally ho, Sherlock rides again!' Lancelot cheered, joining the conversation. 'Watch out, murderers, miscreants and maladroits, Lady Swift is coming for you!'

CHAPTER 18

The pale pink glow of the sunrise was already illuminating the frozen sky when Eleanor awoke on Boxing Day morning. As it spread across the horizon like a shimmering watercolour it picked out the silhouettes of leafless trees smothered in a frosty mist.

She threw her thick full-length woollen robe over her grey silk house pyjamas and stuck her head outside her bedroom door. Whispering and giggling floated up the stairs, followed by the sound of scurrying footsteps. She tiptoed out and peeked over the bannisters. A silent presence at her elbow made her jump.

'Agh! Clifford!' She clutched her chest.

'Indeed, my lady.' He shuffled his slippered feet.

She tried not to smile at the sight of him wearing his dark-brown dressing gown over his routine starched white shirt and suit trousers, minus his coat tails. Having innocently mentioned what fun it would be to have Boxing Day breakfast with everyone in pyjamas as she'd done with her parents as a child, it seemed he had engineered just that.

He cleared his throat. 'Perhaps you might require a small restorative before commencing?' He held out a silver tray bearing a hideous-looking green-and-yellow concoction. As a good guest, she had eaten and drunk everything put in front of her at Langham Manor the previous day and her stomach and head were paying the price.

Despite its foul appearance, having been revived on several occasions by his magical ministrations, she took the glass. 'Wish me luck.' Pinching her nose, she downed the thick liquid in as few gulps as she could manage. 'Ooh,' she smacked her lips, 'that didn't taste too bad, actually.'

'Raw herring is a breakfast delicacy in some parts of the world, my lady.'

She blanched, but then shrugged. 'Whatever it takes, Clifford. I'm not going to waste a single minute of the day. I had a wonderful time yesterday at Langham Manor, but today I fancy sharing Boxing Day breakfast with you all. And then, once you've all departed, taking the day as it comes.'

'Indeed. However, you will have to brave Polly and Master Gladstone first. Both have been spinning like tops since before five o'clock.'

Eleanor grinned. 'Let's hope there is always a bit of the child left in all of us. Especially at Christmas.'

Less than halfway across the kitchen, however, Eleanor was bowled backwards into a chair Clifford slid behind her just in time. A wild-eyed Gladstone panted in her face, his front paws poking out from his red Christmas jumper, his stumpy tail whirling in a lopsided circle.

'I see what you mean. Has he eaten an entire tray of Mrs Trotman's custard tarts or something?'

Mrs Butters appeared from the pantry, the bottom of her cotton nightdress brushing her worn slippers below a thick, calf-length, hand-knitted cardigan. 'Oh my stars, my lady. Master Gladstone's got to you now, I see. Apologies, none of us know what to do with him.'

Eleanor turned back to the dog's wide-eyed stare. 'Golly, do you think he might be sickening for something?'

Mrs Butters chuckled and walked over to ruffle the dog's ears. 'No, my lady, I think he's hankering for the presents that are waiting for him under the tree.'

'Ah, of course.' Eleanor slapped her forehead. 'I forgot how good his nose is for sniffing out treats. He must have smelt them last night when I hid them there.'

Clifford eased Gladstone off Eleanor. 'Indeed.' He pointed to the dog's quilted bed, usually laid to one side of the range, but now trailed across the floor.

Mrs Butters tutted. 'I've tidied that must be ten times this morning, he keeps pulling it out again, the toad!'

Eleanor cupped Gladstone's face. 'Sorry, old friend, I'll bring your presents downstairs with me next year.' She fanned her own face. 'Isn't it rather warm in here for him to be wearing his jumper?'

This brought more tutting from the housekeeper. 'Oho, you can have a go at wrenching it off him, my lady. I've tried, Mr Clifford gave up and Trotters too. Polly ended up on her... well, lying on the floor trying, but Mr Wilful here seems to have decided he's going to keep it on until twelfth night!'

'But, you silly boy, you'll be a boiled bulldog soon.' Eleanor tugged on the shoulders of the jumper but, with a deep grumble, Gladstone made himself as stiff as a board.

'Ah! Perhaps we should poke him out the back door for a moment to cool off instead? Are Silas and Joseph joining us this morning?'

Clifford gave a quiet cough. 'Silas has regrettably sent his apologies, my lady.'

Eleanor shook her head but smiled. She had been at Henley Hall for nearly a year and had still to meet the man. Clifford called him 'the gamekeeper', but she had come to realise he was actually the Hall's elusive security guard.

Mrs Butters beamed. 'But Joseph'll be along in a moment. Not in his nightwear, mind. A rare enough thing to get him further than the kitchen step, but he promised.'

At that moment, the back door opened and Joseph came in backwards, shaking the snow off his clothes. He used the doorsill to pull his boots off then jerked to a stop on seeing Eleanor, his weathered face frozen in horror.

'Apologies, m'lady, didn't realise you were in here, specially in your erm...' He stared at his thick wool socks. Without looking up, he snatched his cap from his head, leaving his thinning hair sticking up. Gladstone shot over to greet him, climbing up his leg.

'Morning, Master Gladstone.' Joseph ran a calloused hand along the bulldog's back.

Eleanor smiled. 'Joseph, good morning and merry Christmas. I do apologise for the slightly unusual state of attire you find us all in. I rather dreamed of reliving a precious childhood memory, you see.'

'Ah, merry Christmas, m'lady. Memories are important. Worth breaking the normal rules for and no mistake.'

Mrs Trotman's voice cut through the door from out in the hallway. 'It's alright, my girl, it was the mistress' idea. You were excited 'bout it before. 'Tis just a bit of fun. Like proper family would do.' The cook appeared, pushing the young maid before her. Polly appeared somewhat star-struck by the audience staring at her long nightdress.

After only minimal coaxing from Eleanor, the staff were all settled round the table with steaming cups of tea. Despite the mounds of toast, sausages and eggs, they were all determined to save enough room to end with a plate of the jammy buns finishing in the range. Gladstone retired happily to his bed with a knucklebone, which he spent the first ten minutes pouncing on from different angles and nosing across the floor. Easy chatter filled the warm air as the staff discussed their plans for their highly prized day off.

'The coach will call at nine, my lady.' Mrs Butters topped up Eleanor's tea. 'Your late uncle arranged it that way for years, I do hope that still suits?'

'Gracious, yes.' Eleanor winked at Clifford as a thank you for organising it. 'I want you all to do exactly as you wish and to return not one minute before you are all done and in whatever state you see fit.'

This was met with laughter from the ladies and a shared look of horror between Clifford and Joseph.

'Them's dangerous words, m'lady, if you'll forgive me saying,' said Joseph. There was fear in his eyes. 'You haven't seen this lot when the parsnip perry's been cracked open.'

Eleanor laughed. 'Actually, I have. And the last time I think we managed to demolish not only the perry but also half the dandelion wine.'

'And the chestnut liqueur.' Clifford shuddered at the memory.

'Ay, I remember now too,' Joseph said, shaking his head.

With the jammy buns finished and the consensus divided on whether the damson, quince or gooseberry and ginger were best, the table was cleared and the washing-up dispatched.

Eleanor clapped her hands. 'I want to thank you. For a great many things, actually, but firstly this morning for indulging me in sharing Boxing Day breakfast in pyjamas.'

Polly giggled and then clapped her hands over her mouth. Eleanor gave her a reassuring smile. 'But I don't actually know how to thank you all enough for just how hard you work all year. I know Uncle Byron liked to keep things simple, but how you manage this enormous house with so few of you is a genuine miracle. And I am hugely grateful.'

'Oh, 'tis our pleasure, my lady!' said Mrs Butters.

'Work's not hard when you love what you do and greatly appreciate who you're doing it for,' Mrs Trotman added.

'Me and the gardens have an understanding alright,' Joseph said. 'I know every inch better than the back of me hands, I reckon. And you've been so kind in complimenting the way I do things, m'lady.'

'Well,' Eleanor started and then paused. She glanced around at the staff she'd inherited from her uncle and swallowed hard. 'Oh dash it. In truth you, and Gladstone, are the only reason I didn't run straight back to South Africa a week after I arrived at the Hall.' She took a deep breath, not daring to look any of them in the eye.

'And we are collectively delighted that you stayed, my lady,' Clifford said.

'Present time!' Eleanor said rather more loudly than intended. 'I mean to say, this is your day and here I am stealing your minutes.'

Mrs Butters rose and patted both of Eleanor's shoulders. 'You can't steal what is willingly given. Polly, come on, girl, we'll bring the presents in together.'

Twenty minutes later, Mrs Trotman, Mrs Butters and Polly were all still twirling in front of the range in their new, soft velvet dressing gowns and matching slippers.

Polly pulled on the soft wool hat, scarf and gloves they had also each been given, which made everyone chuckle.

'I shall pretend I'm still wearing my princess dressing gown even when I'm outside in my woollies,' Polly breathed, hugging her velvety arms.

Gladstone trotted excitedly past with more leather slippers than he could manage in his jaw. Eleanor laughed. 'A few extra for your collection, boy. And a basket of balls too.'

'My lady, you are too kind,' the housekeeper repeated for the fifth time.

'Not at all. I suddenly realised how cold it must be when you get up so early to make it toasty for when I clamber out of bed and appear ready to devour Mrs Trotman's legendary breakfasts. I hope you can warm yourselves up first now.'

Joseph waved his smart new waxed jacket and thick mittens. 'Very much obliged, m'lady.'

Eleanor nodded. 'I didn't want to buy you something for you to work in, really though, Joseph.'

'If I'm awake, I'm gardening, m'lady. 'Tis the only thing I enjoy, save for a quiet cuppa with a mischievous bulldog in the tool shed of a lunchtime.'

'Ah, now that brings me onto your second present. Please think of it as a joint present to share with Gladstone. I hope you don't mind but I asked Clifford to arrange for a wood-burning stove to be fitted in the shed, so you can stay warm in this freezing weather.'

His face lit up. 'Right kind, m'lady. Shan't know myself.' He frowned. 'Best hope I don't start going soft though.'

Eleanor wasn't sure if he was serious or not.

Clifford was unusually quiet. He seemed to struggle to maintain his composure. His present, which he'd unwrapped and then neatly re-wrapped, lay in front of him.

'Right,' Eleanor said, clapping her hands again. 'Off you all go, enjoy time with your family and your friends. There is also an envelope for each of you on the settle in the hallway. Please scoop it up on your way out, once you've dressed of course.' She winked at the ladies. 'And remember, as late and as loud as you wish for your return.'

'Don't be tempting Trotters, my lady.' Mrs Butters chuckled. 'She's a terror for mischief when she's let out.'

Eleanor laughed. 'Don't worry, I shall cycle down with the bail money if necessary.'

CHAPTER 19

Still waving and calling out their thank yous, the ladies and Joseph climbed into the hired coach. This would ferry them to various points around the area, collect them later and return them to the Hall late in the evening.

As Clifford closed the front door, he gave that cough that Eleanor knew meant he had something difficult to say.

'Yes, Clifford?'

'I am sorry, my lady. It was unforgiveable of me to lose my composure, especially in front of the rest of the staff, but…' He pulled her gift out from under his arm and unwrapped it again. 'Your choice of inscription caught me by surprise, hearteningly so, I might add.'

Eleanor bit her lip. 'You're very tricky to buy for, you know.'

'I do.' He swallowed hard as he held up the silver fountain pen she'd had engraved with the inscription. 'For caring for me as Uncle Byron would, thank you.' He turned it in his hand, then patted the leather-bound diary and matching notebook.

She smiled. 'I've also snuck a Voltaire trilogy into the snug. I noticed you were missing three from your collection. I promise I haven't broken into your quarters again though, not since I thought—'

'I was trying to kill you?'

She laughed. 'Seems impossible now, that I could have ever doubted you. Now, please go and do whatever you have planned. I don't wish to detain you any longer. And I'd best change before taking Gladstone for a walk round the grounds in the snow.'

'I have arranged to meet Mr Sandford for luncheon in the Dog and Badger, my lady. I shall not be leaving for a while if you require anything.'

'Nothing, really.' She shook her head in frustration. 'Dash it, though, why is it Boxing Day? I'm itching to go and ask so many questions. The reverend is definitely hiding something from us. However, I want you to have the day to yourself, so I shall get myself to the vicarage this afternoon.'

He pulled out the pen and turned the inscription towards her. 'My lady. I shall enjoy my lunch with Mr Sandford and return to accompany you in the Rolls.'

She went to argue, but saw the look in his eye. 'I always thought I was the most stubborn person I knew, Clifford, but I think I've met my match in you. Okay, I'll wait for you. But only if you promise not to rush.'

'Scout's honour.'

'You couldn't possibly have been a scout.'

'Indeed not, my lady.'

Ten minutes later, Eleanor thought she might just about have sufficient layers on to treat Gladstone to a snowy walk when the telephone rang. Unwrapping a long woollen scarf from her ears, she hurried down the stairs and swept up the receiver.

'Hello?'

'Lady Swift? Is that you?' A familiar, deep male voice came down the line.

'Inspector Seldon, good morning. And happy Boxing Day to you.'

'And to you, Lady Swift. I see you've added answering the telephone to your list of flouting the rules of propriety.'

'Most unseemly, I'm sure, although none of the staff are here to witness my disgraceful behaviour.'

There was a momentary silence at the other end. 'Do you mean there's just you there?'

'Of course, the staff always have Boxing Day off. It is a tradition in many country houses.'

'Then it is common knowledge you are likely to be home alone. I hardly think that is safe.'

'Why, Inspector, whatever do you imagine will happen? I'm really very self-sufficient after all my years travelling. Besides, Gladstone is here.'

'And if an intruder thinks to bring sausages in his pockets!'

Eleanor laughed, although she realised he hadn't meant it as a joke. He was clearly concerned about her. This thought brought a strange butterfly feeling to her stomach. 'I greatly appreciate your solicitude, but really, I am fine. Now, tell me, you didn't ring to check that I was safe from sausage-wielding miscreants, what can I do for you?'

There was the sound of papers being shuffled at the other end. 'I promised I would keep you informed of any news from the coroner's office.'

'Forgive me, but you said it would take ages.'

'Perhaps I did.' He cleared his throat. 'However, the report has just come in.'

'Yes?' She held her breath.

'Firstly, I need to say that the medical examiner is new, and less experienced than we would normally like, but with the cuts there was no one else available. In fact, he is our only man for the foreseeable future.'

'I see. Well, I do appreciate him, and you, making this more of a priority than it might seem to merit. What did he find?'

'The report notes that rigor mortis was fully established in all the muscle groups.'

'Hardly surprising.' Eleanor failed to stop herself interrupting. 'He didn't receive the body for a while, did he?'

The inspector left her question hanging in the telephone wires and continued. 'Signs of visible injury, none. Fingernails, undamaged. Bruising, none obviously detectable, however a multitude of tattoos on torso, arms and legs make this difficult to confirm definitively. Lungs, normally inflated.'

'Inspector, I appreciate the doctor's thorough approach but what does he believe killed Mr Canning?'

'Stomach contents, evidence of recent vomiting.'

'We knew that,' she muttered.

'Blood sample contained unusually high levels of—'

'Digitalis?'

There was silence on the other end of the line.

Eleanor was careful that her words didn't sound confrontational. 'Inspector, I take your silence as a yes. Clifford said that is exactly what you would find.'

'Quite. You also reported to me that the doctor who attended Mr Canning after he collapsed had himself warned Mr Canning against running in the race.'

'Yes, but—'

'And I am sure you are aware that most common heart medication contains digitalis. Mr Canning was probably taking such pills daily.' He paused. 'I am sorry, this entire episode is too close to home for you. Both in the location of where he died, but more so, with the similarity to your late uncle's demise.' He paused again. 'Lady Swift, running yourself into the ground to prove Mr Canning was murdered when there is no evidence to that effect cannot bring your uncle back.'

Hot tears pricked the back of her eyes. She ran her hand through her red curls. 'I appreciate your call, genuinely I do. But I have learned to trust both my intuition and Clifford, and they are both in agreement.'

'Would it make you feel differently to know that the death certificate has been issued and—'

'Not a bit. Inspector, I am not questioning your judgement, not with Mr Canning, nor… nor with Uncle Byron's death, but—'

'Lady Swift, if there was any evidence pointing to the excess of digitalis having been deliberately introduced, I would open this as a case instantly.'

'Thank you. So, you've signed the whole thing off then?'

'Actually, no, I have not, although I probably should. I've learned after our previous encounters, Lady Swift, to listen when you speak, even if I am then often limited in what I can do. Constable Fry has been tasked with ascertaining from Mr Canning's doctor if the patient was on heart tablets. And to send any samples he can of what Mr Canning might have drunk or eaten on the day of his death to be analysed. That of course means Constable Fry needs to come to Henley Hall.'

'He's very welcome to. Although he will be disappointed, the ladies are meticulous at clearing up and it was two days ago now.'

'Perhaps you are not the only one who can be dogged, Lady Swift. I also believe in leaving no stone unturned. If I were able to attend, I would come myself, but I am stuck on this dratted case in London.'

'Well, I hope you find a moment or two to enjoy some of the festive season. Thank you for calling.'

She hung up. He really was a good man. And a dashingly handsome one. Those chestnut curls, broad shoulders and endlessly long legs… the thought caught her by surprise. She slapped the telephone table.

Ellie, you're supposed to be in love with Lancelot!

CHAPTER 20

Half an hour later she had returned from her walk with Gladstone and was drying his feet on a towel, one reserved for muddy or snowy dogs she hoped. On her first day at Henley Hall she and Gladstone had been caught out in a storm. She'd dried the mud-streaked bulldog with a mound of what turned out to be towels for human, not canine, use. Not that Mrs Butters had complained, but Eleanor had felt rather bad about it afterwards.

In truth, her walk with Gladstone was over far too quickly, but she was worried that he would catch a chill, even in his snug-fitting Christmas jumper. 'We need to fit you out with stout boots to stop you getting snow between your pads, don't we, old friend?'

He clambered into his bed and completed several circuits of the quilted cover before choosing two slippers to push his nose into and falling into a deep snooze.

She pulled out a chair and sat at the table, drumming her fingers. If anyone had been there to ask, she might have confessed the house felt horribly empty. Thus it was that when Clifford returned at half past two, she jumped up and hailed him rather over enthusiastically.

He arched one eyebrow. 'Are you alright, my lady? Have you perhaps made yourself some particularly strong coffee and drunk the entire pot?'

'No, thank you for asking.' She waved her notebook. 'I tried to work on the case but without you to bounce ideas off, I didn't get very far and… oh, nothing.'

'The Hall does tend to echo and creak considerably in the colder months, my lady. It is only when one is alone that there is sufficient quiet to really hear them, I find. It can be disquieting if you are not used to it.'

'I'm okay with the noise a desert makes at night as the wind whistles across the sands. Or the myriad noises of night-time in the jungle, but it was a little odd being here on my own. I used to be on my own all the time, but I seem to have fallen out of practice.'

'I should have thought ahead and made arrangements.'

'No, you should not! And neither should you have returned so early. It's Boxing Day.'

Clifford ran the grey wool scarf from his neck and folded it into four perfectly equal lengths.

She nodded as he took up the kettle from the range. 'Yes, please, a pot of that coffee you mentioned would be lovely.' She sighed. 'Oh, the inspector telephoned to inform me that the coroner found nothing suspicious when he examined Canning's body.'

Clifford paused, kettle midway under the tap. 'Nothing suspicious, my lady?'

She shook her head. 'Apparently, there is nothing suspicious about having one's bloodstream overloaded with… digitalis.'

She watched his reaction. His silence worried her.

'Clifford? Are you alright?'

'Of course, my lady. I had hoped for once that I might have been wrong.'

'Me too.' She rose and pulled out another chair. 'Now, to heck with the rules. Sit, please. And, besides, these are the rules. It's Boxing Day and all the staff have the day off, that was Uncle Byron's rule and it's mine. So if you're going to be here, I'll serve you.' She waited until he'd reluctantly taken a seat before continuing. 'I shall do the coffee, you leaf through my notebook and see if you can fathom anything I've miss—'

Clifford looked at her inquiringly.

She set the kettle down, her eyes on a bag hanging in the corner of the kitchen. 'Of course, there is something useful we could do before visiting the reverend this afternoon…'

The overgrown hedge on either side of Canning's small and otherwise empty back garden afforded them helpful cover as they nipped through the rusty iron gate and paused under the porch, which leaned at an alarming angle.

Clifford reached into Canning's bag. 'Thankfully, Mr Canning was helpful enough to leave his house keys in his bag which we recovered from the changing room.'

Had she'd been asked, Eleanor might have confessed she was desperately curious to see inside Canning's forlorn-looking cottage. In her heart, she still clung to the belief that there had been more to him than just the belligerent man who seemed set on alienating everyone he came into contact with.

In a trice, Clifford had unlocked the back door. Hurrying inside, they took stock of their surroundings.

'Not the materialistic type,' Eleanor whispered, looking at the scrubbed wooden kitchen table and its lone chair, the upholstery neatly patched. Next to the sink stood a large metal pail, filled almost to the brim, suggesting the only water coming into the house had to be hauled in by hand.

'Nor the sociable type.' Clifford pointed at the single tin plate, mug, bowl and pint glass that stood in a line on one of the three shelves of the top half of a wooden dresser screwed to the wall. Quietly opening the two frosted glass doors of the wooden cupboard below the rectangular porcelain sink revealed only two scrubbed copper pans.

The adjoining sitting room was considerably brighter as the weak December sun penetrated the worn but clean cotton sailcloth curtains, which were thankfully drawn closed. Next to the single armchair stood a small table with a tin ashtray and a burned-down candle set in an empty rum bottle. Two more candles in matching bottles were the only addition to the mantelpiece above the fireplace.

Eleanor peered into a tin mug on the hearth. It was half filled with a collection of candle wax drippings, ready to be resculpted into another evening's worth of dim illumination.

'Gracious, he really does seem to have lived as frugally as the two women at the Women's Institute suggested.'

Clifford nodded. 'Mr Canning's abode is certainly not suggestive of a fortune stashed away somewhere.'

'And I never imagined he would have been so… neat. It's like sneaking a peek into the home of your double, Clifford. In rather straightened circumstances,' she added with a sideways glance at him.

'Perhaps not so surprising, if we remember he spent many years at sea in a cramped, shared cabin, I shouldn't wonder.'

She looked around the room again. 'There's nowhere here to hide anything the key we found when he fell at the race might fit, though. However, strangely, there's no sign that he was actually ever at sea either.'

'Save for a predilection for rum as a favoured tipple perhaps.'

She joined him in the doorway of the only other room on the ground floor. The entire space was set up as a sewing room. Squares, scraps and patches of leather, sail cloth and cotton sat in neat piles on a long bench beside the treadle-foot sewing machine.

Clifford gestured inside. 'Only a single man who was an ex-sailor would have a make do and mend room.'

She sighed in exasperation. 'But unless there's a secret panel in the wall, there is nothing in here that the key could fit either.'

He gave an uncomfortable cough. 'Perhaps I should inspect the gentleman's bedroom alone?'

'Good idea.'

She watched him clear the short staircase in three long strides. Turning left at the top, he reappeared on the handkerchief-sized landing in seconds. 'A bed, a chair and a small desk, without drawers. Minimal clothes, a stack of dated newspapers and a notepad, pen and half-empty pot of ink on the desk.'

She frowned, then as she peered up the stairs at him, she noticed a small square hatch above his head. 'The attic!' she hissed.

Nodding, he reached up and nudged the cover up and to one side. He pulled a torch from his pocket, switched it on and held it in his teeth. With a lithe jump, he grabbed the wooden support sides of the recess and poked his head up inside. Eleanor held back a laugh at the sight of her impossibly measured butler's legs wiggling as he spun side to side to swing the torch round.

She joined him on the landing and held her hands out as he grunted for her to catch the torch. Then dropping nimbly back down, he jiggled the cover into place and carefully brushed the shoulders of his coat. 'Empty, except for a rather startled pair of glis glis.'

'Glis what?'

'Glis glis, my lady. Edible dormice. Introduced in 1902 by the keen zoologist, Lord Walter Rothschild. They quickly proliferated from his estate in Hertfordshire into Buckinghamshire and the surrounding area.'

'Edible?' She grimaced. 'Breeding rodents in your attic for supper is surely taking frugality a bit too far?'

They stole down the stairs. Turning back through the sitting room into the kitchen, she blew out a long breath of frustration through her cheeks. 'My great idea feels like a complete waste of time now.'

'Uncharacteristically dispirited of you, if you will forgive my observation, my lady. If a cottage has an attic, what else is it likely to have?'

'Bats?'

He pointed to the blue rug below the coal scuttle. 'A cellar.'

He pulled back the rug, revealing a small trap door, neatly recessed in the floor.

'Locked,' he grunted after pulling on the inset brass ring, worn smooth with use. Reaching into his jacket, he pulled a set of skeleton keys from his inside pocket.

'Does one of them always fit?' Eleanor said.

'Not always, but then we can use these.' From another pocket, he produced a slim kid leather pouch and flipped the top to reveal a set of picklocks.

'Do you know, there's a large part of me that doesn't want to hear the truth about what you and my uncle got up to for so many years. Fanciful stories of the imagination can be so much more interesting.'

'And yet, sometimes still fall short of the truth!'

In the event, the picks were not needed as one of the skeleton keys soon had the trapdoor unlocked. Eleanor peered past her butler's crouched form at the steps that led down into inky blackness.

Having descended into the cellar, the torch beam revealed a dirt floor with nothing more than three empty tea chests and a pickaxe handle resting against the furthest wall.

'Dash it!' Eleanor muttered. 'Do you think he hid whatever it is at his coal yard?'

'I doubt it, my lady. Something precious, or indeed dangerous, if it were to fall into the wrong hands, would be more secure in one's home than a patch of ground at the end of a track. Unless he buried it, I suppose.'

After a brief circuit of the cellar, they had to admit there was nothing they were looking for. As they turned to remount the stairs, she noticed something glimmer as the torchlight swept the walls.

'What's that?'

He shone the torch in the direction she pointed.

Partly hidden from view, in a recess in the stone wall, the end of an iron-studded box glinted back at them.

In the kitchen, Clifford set it down on the kitchen table. Out of the gloom of the cellar, Eleanor could see it was a small, ornate chest with an arched lid and a series of iron bands running up and over the top of the smooth dark wood.

'Care to?' Clifford offered her the key.

'Do I ever!' She took it and tried to insert it into the lock only to frown at the feel of something pushing it back towards her. 'What? It's like it's alive.'

'It is the magnetic polarity. May I?' Forcing the key into the lock, Clifford frowned as it refused to turn.

'I wonder.' He turned the trunk over and ran the key along the first iron band until it snapped onto it at one point. He pulled the band back with surprising ease to reveal a second lock.

'Ingenious, Clifford!' He handed the box back to Eleanor, who turned it over in her hands. 'Whatever is in here, Canning really wanted it to remain hidden.'

He frowned. 'And yet we found the case with relative ease.' He shook his head. 'Something doesn't quite add up.'

'Well, maybe the contents will explain.' She started to slip the key into the lock, but this time, rather than repelling it, it pulled it in. She looked up at Clifford and then back at the box as she turned the key. There was a faint 'click'.

She put her hands either side of the lid. 'Ready?' Lifting it a few inches, she froze at the sound of a voice from outside.

'Thieving from a dead man afore he's even in the ground, are you?'

Clifford silently, but quickly, closed the chest lid, slid the key into his pocket, and shot back down the steps into the cellar with it. Eleanor scooped up Canning's bag and called out, 'Gracious no, quite the opposite!'

Clifford reappeared and covered up the cellar door with the rug. The coal scuttle back in place, he stepped to the back door and opened it.

'Oh, Alice, it's you,' Eleanor said with barely disguised relief at the sight of her Women's Institute colleague.

'Lady Swift, Mr Clifford, whatever are you doing in Canning's house?' Her grey curls shook like aspen leaves, her sharp eyes flicking between them.

Eleanor tried to laugh off her previous panic. 'Goodness, you made me jump.'

Clifford held the door open. 'Mrs Campbell, do come in. It is markedly less cool inside than out.'

Still looking slightly askance, Alice joined them. 'I was visiting old Mr Woolney next door with a little extra pot of supper and heard a peculiar scraping noise while I was in his pantry. Mr Woolney said it must be Canning come back from beyond the grave seeing as he heard that very noise every night. He said he'd always thought it was the water pail being dragged across to the sink.' She looked from one to the other of them and then over at the water pail.

'Mr Woolney must be a most perceptive gentleman in regard to the noise,' Clifford replied seamlessly. 'Having dropped in to leave Mr Canning's bag, which he regrettably did not have the opportunity to return home with after the Henley Hall luncheon, we noted that a pail of water left indefinitely would soon give off a most stale and unpleasant odour that might penetrate through to next door.'

'To say nothing of creating damp,' Eleanor added. 'Poor Mr Canning, without family to deal with his house and possessions, we thought it was the least we could do.'

'Although the pail proved heavier than either of us expected,' Clifford added, placing a hand on his back.

Eleanor patted the bag she clutched. 'I confess, I wanted to return this in the hope that it might relieve some of my remorse that Mr Canning passed away at my event.' She shrugged. 'I still wish I had cancelled the race, you see.'

'Oh, m'lady!' Alice said. 'You are such the virtuous and upstanding member of our community. And to think I rushed round here suspecting whoever was in the house of creeping about seeing if they could pilfer something valuable and make off with it.'

'Oh.' Eleanor swallowed hard. 'How funny!'

CHAPTER 21

The jangle of the telephone out in the hallway interrupted her. 'Sit!' She gave Clifford a stern look. 'It's still Boxing Day and you've spent half of it in a dead man's cellar. I'll make that coffee I promised you in a moment.'

They'd been forced to abandon their quest at Canning's house and had just returned to the Hall. She strode out to answer the call.

'Ah, Constable, so good of you to telephone.' She listened for a moment. 'Yes, all the staff… I know, but it's only one day a year… You spoke to Canning's doctor? Jolly efficient of you… oh… yes… yes, I do see, Constable… and yes, Clifford is now home… oh, Inspector Seldon asked you to let him know that, I see. Good day, Constable. Best Boxing Day wishes to Mrs Fry and the little ones.'

She hung up and stared thoughtfully at the telephone. Clifford appeared at her elbow. She looked into the mirror, speaking to his reflection. 'Apparently Canning's doctor warned Canning not to run in the race due to his heart trouble. He also confirmed to Fry that Canning was on daily medication.' She spun round. 'But he had been for years.' Her voice dropped. 'Just like Uncle Byron. It seems highly unlikely that they would both have made the same error, wouldn't you say?'

'I would in fact use the word "inconceivable", my lady. I think it much more likely that they both took the correct dosage and were then fed another dose, disguised most likely in a drink.'

She nodded. 'So, who would have had access to heart tablets? Obviously Doctor Browning.'

'And Alvan Moore.'

'Alvan Moore? Wasn't he on the list of Chipstone guests on Christmas Eve?'

'Correct, my lady. He is also Miss Lucetta Moore's son and a delivery driver. In these rural parts it is customary for shops, including chemists, to come to an arrangement that their goods are all delivered by the same driver to their most outlying customers.'

Eleanor frowned. 'I can see that would be more efficient and save the shops money, but we don't know that Alvan Moore delivers medications specifically. I suppose it might be easy to find out, however.'

Clifford gave a discreet cough. She gestured that he had the floor. 'Forgive my contradiction, my lady, but I have myself been at Langham Manor when Mr Moore has delivered such an item. It was when Lord Fenwick-Langham's gout had flared up most vociferously.'

'So there's a good chance Alvan Moore might regularly deliver heart pills as well?'

'Indeed. And then, of course, as we've already noted, digitalis is readily obtainable from foxgloves.'

Eleanor clicked her fingers. 'And you know who would understand just how poisonous they are? A florist!' She groaned. 'Why did I ask her to do the floral arrangements for the Henley Hall Christmas Eve lunch! I might have given her the perfect opportunity.'

'You are referring to Miss Moore? Then, forgive another correction, but she is far more than just a trained flower arranger. She used to be a botanist, working at Kew Gardens before her son, Alvan, was born.'

Eleanor whistled softly. 'Yes, I remember her mentioning it. In which case, I'd wager she knows a fair amount about native poisonous plants. So Doctor Browning, Miss Moore and Alvan all had the means.'

'However, Doctor Browning attended Mr Canning's body and seemed surprised, not at Mr Canning dying, but at the manner of his death. I believe he recognised the signs were not necessarily that of a heart attack, which is why he insisted on us calling Canning's doctor.'

'Which puts him way down on our suspect list then. Because if he'd killed Canning, he could easily have pronounced it a heart attack himself without arousing anyone's suspicion.' A puzzled look passed over her face. 'He certainly made no bones about showing his lack of sorrow at Canning having passed though. That seems odd.'

'A double bluff?'

'Maybe, but let's not forget our fourth suspect, the reverend.' She shook her head. 'Although I still can't believe he might do something like that.' She tapped her chin. 'Where would he have found out about foxgloves being poisonous?'

'Country folk are very aware of such things, my lady. I think you will find it is fairly common knowledge. However, it would be exceptional to also be aware of the similarities to poisoning by heart medication.'

'And the reverend would have had to go sneaking about in the woods to collect the plants. He could hardly say they were for a floral display, his flock know him too well for that. Setting off with a sack and a fork round the village hoping not to be noticed isn't very subtle for a murderer.'

Clifford held up a finger. 'Or he could have simply walked through the graveyard gate to the burial ground on the other side of the church wall, where there are a great many foxgloves in spring. Mr Rogers, the warden, only clears them in the churchyard itself.'

'The burial ground?' Something tugged at Eleanor's memory. 'Why is that ringing a bell… oh no! That's where the reverend said he would bury Canning.'

'Among the very foxgloves—'

'—that killed him.' She shook her head. 'It does seem rather off that our chief suspects include a man charged with saving lives and a man charged with saving souls!' She rapped the table. 'You know we should really have had this discussion in the kitchen with my notebook and that pot of coffee I never made us. How about instead though, I finally telephone the reverend and cheekily invite us both to tea? I need to hear from him why he had such a long-standing dispute with Canning, and I've the perfect pretext.' She picked up the handset and then slapped her forehead. 'Oh, Clifford, how selfish of me. Here I am including you in my schemes yet again and it is still your Boxing Day time off. Please ignore what I said, I shall invite myself and cycle over there.'

Clifford tilted his head. 'That might be rather a waste of effort. Not to mention the ruined clothes for Mrs Butters to return to after you have retrieved your bicycle from several ditches after slipping in the snow. Especially when I would be following directly behind you in the Rolls.'

Her face broke into a grin. 'Sure?'

'Unshakably so, my lady. Boxing Day afternoon alone in Henley Hall would be a terribly dull affair.'

'Fibber. You and Voltaire would enjoy a wonderful time together. But thank you.'

On leaving her bedroom, she heard the phone ringing and by the time she'd descended the stairs, Clifford was holding out the receiver for her.

And when he entered the drawing room with a sherry a few minutes later, she was pacing the room. He set the sherry down and arched an eyebrow in enquiry.

She stopped pacing and took the sherry. 'That was Canning's solicitor as you know, Clifford.' There was only one solicitor in the small market town of Chipstone, and Eleanor had helped him over a lean patch by recommending him to her rich acquaintances. 'It seems that someone' – she looked pointedly at Clifford – 'put the idea into his head that I very much wanted to know who the benefactors of Canning's will are.'

Clifford coughed. 'Indeed, my lady. I may have mentioned it to the gentleman.'

Eleanor smiled. 'Well, he revealed, on condition that it goes no further, that Canning never had a will.'

Clifford nodded. 'Many people of less affluent means do not.'

'I can understand that. However, Canning did then make a will a few weeks ago leaving everything to… Miss Moore and Alvan!'

Both Clifford's eyebrows shot up, showing an unusual degree of surprise. 'Indeed, my lady.'

Eleanor resumed her pacing. 'Oh, how I wish we could speak to Miss Moore and Alvan this minute!'

'Or the reverend, my lady.'

'Reverend Gaskell? How does the news of Canning's will incriminate him?'

'I was not necessarily proposing that exactly, although I do agree that line of thought might have merit. I was thinking more that we probably now know the reason the reverend had such a long-standing dispute with Mr Canning.'

'Clifford! You think that Canning was Alvan's father!'

'I believe it a distinct possibility. Why else would he have included him in the will?'

'But Miss Moore has brought Alvan up alone all his life. I know because she said something along those lines when I visited her shop once. She has a photograph of him as a young boy on her wall. Canning had lived in the area without exception since he returned from the merchant navy, hadn't he?'

'As confirmed by many we have spoken to about Mr Canning. But how much harder would it have been to bear the pain of a father spurning his own son when he lived but a stone's throw away, in the next village?'

Eleanor tapped her chin. 'Gracious, now I know what Canning was talking about on Christmas Eve. He said everyone believed he'd never done a good deed in his life, but that he'd show them they were wrong.'

'A troubled conscience greatly eased by a decent act, however late it was made.'

She stopped pacing. 'Drat! The chest.'

Clifford nodded. 'I was having much the same thought myself, my lady. It is one thing to enter and search Mr Canning's house, as he is deceased—'

'But quite another to now break in and search Miss Moore and Alvan's house, as it now is.' She sighed. 'Drat, again! And until we have eliminated her as a suspect in Canning's murder, we can't hand over the key.' She shook her head. 'Anyway, I was about to telephone the reverend, so there's still plenty of avenues to explore.'

The telephone call successfully made, Eleanor paused in the kitchen doorway and then tiptoed to the table. 'Has Gladstone ever been more cosy?' she whispered, pointing at the bulldog stretched out on his back, still snoring, his two front paws crossed on his chest.

Clifford shook his head. 'I am sure Master Gladstone will be quite content here until our return. How long do we have until we are expected at the vicarage?'

She pulled out her uncle's pocket watch. 'I spoke to Mrs Fontaine and she confirmed the reverend was due back in an hour and then has a few tasks to do. But she was kind enough to say she knew the reverend would always be happy to see us, so say, about two hours?'

'Perfect timing for us to commit our thoughts about the case to your notebook, my lady.'

*

A few minutes later, they both stared at the results. Eleanor had added their chief suspects and anything she could think of that might help:

Main suspects

Dr Browning. Motive: Canning tried to get him struck off medical register believing he killed his mother.

Reverend Gaskell. Motive: Canning enraged him with his treatment of Miss Moore, one of his parishioners.

Miss Moore. Motive: revenge for abandoning her and their son, Alvan. Also, if she knew she was a beneficiary of Canning's will then she had two motives.

Alvan Moore. Motive: revenge for his father abandoning him and his mother. Also, if he knew he was a beneficiary of Canning's will then he had two motives.

Man Canning argued with at Hall – identity unknown. Likely to be one of the men from Chipstone. Motive: unknown.

She shook her head. 'What do you make of it all, Clifford?'

'At the moment, nothing jumps out at me, my lady. I wonder if you might like to continue whilst indulging in your late uncle's Boxing Day afternoon tradition?'

'Absolutely! What is it?'

Clifford disappeared into the pantry, returning a moment later with a glass decanter of ruby liquid and a round metal tin.

'Port and cheese?' asked Eleanor.

'Sloe gin, and walnut and plum cake, both made by Mrs Trotman's fair hands.'

'You see, that's why I love cake so much. It's not that I'm greedy, it's hereditary. And before you say anything, if you don't join me, I shan't honour the tradition.'

Clifford poured them both a measure.

She raised her glass. 'To a wonderful man, Uncle Byron.'

'To his lordship.'

Two hours later, Clifford eased the Rolls to a stop outside the vicarage. Eleanor stepped out and looked up at the building. In the early evening darkness it seemed gloomy compared to the sunny impression it had made on Christmas morning.

As Clifford rapped the heavy brass door knocker in the shape of a cross, the door swung open a crack.

A frown crossed Eleanor's face. 'Gracious, it's far too cold to have an open house today. I hope Mrs Fontaine has got all the fires burning.'

Clifford knocked a second time. And then a third.

Eleanor tried to keep a feeling of creeping dread at bay. 'Oh this is silly. If the reverend had been called away, he would have telephoned, or at least left a note.'

Clifford frowned and said nothing. Eleanor returned to the gravel drive and went to the nearest window. She tapped loudly and waited. Leaning over the snow-capped flower bed, she pressed her face against the glass, her hand over her eyes. She blinked, then spun round.

'Clifford! Get inside! Quick!'

CHAPTER 22

Clifford shouldered the front door aside, Eleanor hard on his heels. She jerked to a stop in the doorway.

'Is he—?'

'Alive?' Clifford knelt next to where the vicar had collapsed on the floor, his ear to the man's chest. He pulled off his leather driving gloves and held the collapsed man's wrist. 'Just. But his pulse is very weak and irregular.' He pulled back one of the vicar's eyelids, receiving a quiet moan in response. 'Significantly dilated pupils,' he noted as he lifted the other eyelid. 'Reverend?' There was no reply.

He loosened the vicar's dog collar and looked up at Eleanor, the same look on his face she'd seen too many times already in the last few days.

'Do you think he's been p—' She caught her breath. 'Wait! Where's Mrs Fontaine?'

She leapt up and ran down the hallway, throwing open every door and calling out the woman's name. *Please, please don't let it be her too!*

In the kitchen she found the housekeeper slumped on the floor, a tray of broken china around her.

'Clifford!' Watching the woman's chest rise and fall unevenly, she felt for a pulse. As Clifford rushed in, his coattails swinging round his legs, she glanced up at him. 'She's the same as the reverend but slightly more conscious.' She patted the woman's hand. 'Can you hear me?'

'Help the reverend. Urgent!' Mrs Fontaine managed with a wheeze. 'Doctor.'

Eleanor and Clifford shared an anxious look before he darted forward. 'I've dialled for the operator to put an emergency call through to Constable Fry. In the meantime, we need to get them to Chipstone Hospital urgently.'

Eleanor shook her head. 'Surely we should get them to Doctor Browning? His surgery is much closer…' She shook her head again. 'Of course, he's on our suspect list. If this is poisoning and related to Canning's death—'

'Then the doctor may already have "attended" to the reverend and Mrs Fontaine,' Clifford said grimly. He dropped to his haunches and shuffled the woman into a half-seated position. 'Excuse me, madam.' He slid her top half over his shoulder and stood up with the nimbleness of a much younger man. 'Please keep her head up, my lady. And if you would be so kind as to retrieve my hat from the puddle of tea.'

'Thank goodness we drove here!' Eleanor panted as they hurried down the hallway. As they did so she dabbed her handkerchief over Mrs Fontaine's clammy brow and held the woman's chin up with her other hand.

Having carried the housekeeper out to the Rolls, they returned for the vicar. With his, thankfully slender, frame also manhandled into the car, Clifford pulled away, the wheels of the Rolls spinning on the icy road.

Eleanor had never seen Clifford drive at any speed other than 'stately', except the one time he had smashed through a burning barn to save her. But in the back seat, with one arm around each of the patients, she concentrated on supporting them while ignoring the effect the lurching was having on her stomach.

'Wretched snow!' Clifford muttered as the heavy car made it round one particularly sharp corner sideways.

The main road was relatively free of snow and ice and the Rolls picked up some speed. It still seemed an eternity to Eleanor before the gates of Chipstone's cottage hospital appeared. Clifford sped to the entrance of the low grey-stone building and slid to a stop. A single lamp burned above the entrance, with only two of the windows dimly lit.

Eleanor leapt nimbly over the vicar's lap and shot out of the car. Running up the ramp, she burst through the door, into an empty reception area.

'Help, please! We need a doctor urgently!'

Silence. Then a flurry of footsteps running from two different directions. The first to arrive was a middle-aged doctor, clutching a sheaf of papers, his white coat flying out behind him. 'What's happened? Is it a birth?'

'No. Suspected poisoning. Two patients. Critical condition,' she called over her shoulder, dashing back out to the car. She was relieved to see Constable Fry leaping down from a delivery van. He thundered over in his heavy boots and pulled off his helmet, running a hand over his dark side parting. His heavy breath frosted on the air as he spoke.

'I got your message, Lady Swift, Mr Clifford.' He peered through to the back seat. 'Oh my stars, it's the Reverend Gaskell and Mrs Fontaine.' He straightened up and stared at Eleanor. 'Most fortuitous for them that you happened along to the vicarage in time. And very public-spirited of you to rush them here.'

They moved aside as the doctor and a nurse hurried past and knelt in the back of the car. The doctor took one look at the two now unconscious patients and muttered something Eleanor couldn't catch to the nurse.

Clifford stepped back to allow the other two nurses who had appeared to lift the vicar and his housekeeper onto wheeled stretchers. They both lay helplessly, arms hanging limply from under the thin grey blankets hurriedly lain over them. Eleanor shuddered. It reminded her too much of her time with the Women's Auxiliary Army Service during the war.

With the patients wheeled inside, a suffocating silence enveloped the three of them. Eleanor bit her lip and looked at Clifford.

'We have done our best, my lady. We can only hope the good deed will win out on the bad intention that did this.'

Fry stiffened. 'You don't think—'

'Yes. We do.' Eleanore marched up the ramp and back into the hospital.

Fry and Clifford followed her into the whitewashed antiseptic-smelling waiting room. Fry turned his police helmet in his hands. 'I telephoned through to the chief inspector to let him know of the situation. Just as a matter of routine, you understand, m'lady.'

'Yes, of course. I also understand entirely that the good inspector most likely asked you to reiterate that there is currently no case for investigation?' She gave him a weak smile as he nodded hesitantly.

He pulled his notebook from his breast pocket. 'But he asked that I take down all the details, just in case.'

A young nurse appeared bearing a tray with three tin mugs of steaming tea. Clifford rose and took it from her with a nod. 'Most kind. Has the doctor been able to ascertain what—?'

'Not yet, sir.' She smiled reassuringly. 'But I'm sure he will be along as soon as he can. You needn't worry unduly.' She turned and left.

Eleanor caught Fry's enquiring look. 'Shall we tell you everything while we enjoy our tea, Constable?'

This proved to take the entire duration of the three mugs and beyond as Fry made meticulous notes in large, spidery writing.

'So to conclude, you witnessed no sign of a break-in at the vicarage?'

'None, although the front door was not latched.'

'Not too uncommon for Reverend Gaskell, m'lady. He does like his flock or anyone in need to be able to rouse him if necessary.'

'Even in the depths of winter?'

'Ah, yes, well you may have a point there. He isn't one to waste church resources like firewood.'

The sound of approaching footsteps halted the conversation. A doctor appeared in the doorway, his face pale, eyes heavy as if sleep had been a long time coming and Christmas had passed him by altogether. He looked round the three of them, his gaze resting on the enormous policeman. In his hand, he held two sheets of paper.

Eleanor jumped up. 'Doctor, what can you tell us, please?'

'Are you relatives?' he asked sharply.

'No, but right here and now we are probably the closest either of them have.'

Clifford stepped forward. 'This is Lady Swift, Doctor.'

'Ah.' This seemed to tick the required box. 'Lady Swift of Henley Hall. And Mr Clifford, of course. Forgive me, we need to be careful in cases such as these.'

'Cases such as what? Were they poisoned?'

The doctor motioned for them all to sit. He closed the door and also sat. 'Constable, you are here because?'

'Because I was called to attend by Mr Clifford. This lady and gentleman felt something suspicious had occurred and did the right thing in alerting myself to come and take the details.'

This also seemed to satisfy him. 'Lady Swift, why did you think something suspicious had happened?'

'Because we arrived at the vicarage to find both the reverend and Mrs Fontaine sprawled on the floor, at different ends of the house. Both were barely conscious with failing pulses and wildly dilated pupils. Symptoms distressingly similar to those of Mr Canning, just before he died in front of Clifford and myself.'

The doctor ran his hand over his face. 'Let us keep our discussion to our current patients, please.'

'Of course.' She chided herself for not having bitten her tongue as she'd planned.

He consulted his notes. 'I will be frank with all of you. The two patients are both in a bad way. Had you not got them here when you did, we might have been having a very different conversation.'

Eleanor gasped. 'But they were still conscious. Just.'

He nodded. 'It is not uncommon for symptoms to significantly worsen with little warning when the heart is affected. If we are lucky neither will experience further kidney dysfunction although that is a possible prognosis.' He watched Eleanor's face fall. 'I am sorry I cannot give you more optimistic news but it is my duty not to build false hopes. A slight consolation is that the lady…' He peered at one of the papers. 'Of course, we haven't had time to take the details yet. Mrs Fontaine, is it?'

All three of the others nodded.

'Mrs Fontaine's condition is more stable than the reverend's. It may simply be that her system has a higher tolerance of the toxin. Or maybe she ingested less. She appears to be ten or so years younger, that is often enough to save a person.'

'So it was poison!'

'My diagnosis at this stage is that both patients ingested something toxic. Something sufficiently toxic, in fact, to significantly impact function of the major organs. Poison could be an appropriate term. However' – he held up a finger as Eleanor opened her mouth – 'my job is to ascertain only the nature of the substance, not how or why it was ingested.'

This time he smiled warmly at Eleanor. 'Lady Swift, your reputation for solving several recent murders has not escaped the local medical profession. It is worth noting, however, that there are cases of accidental poisoning seen in rural hospitals every year. People collect what they believe are a particular berry or herb from the hedgerows and fields only to find they were sorely mistaken.'

'But not usually at this time of year, I imagine?'

'Throughout the year, actually. Toxic plants innocently made into preserves, chutneys or home brews can sit innocuously in pantries like a time bomb.'

'I see.'

He shook his head. 'I am sorry, but I really do not have any further information for you at the moment.' He rose wearily. 'I am afraid I must return to the patients. Constant surveillance is required for the next twenty-four hours if we are to save them. Fortunately, nine of our twelve beds were empty when you arrived so they will have the best medical attention we can give them.'

'Thank you, Doctor.' Eleanor shook his hand. 'We greatly appreciate your dedication and expertise.'

'Not at all. If perhaps you would take a moment to leave the patients' full names and any other available details with the nurse on reception?'

'Of course.'

'And you are welcome to send for an update on your friends,' he called as he nodded to Clifford. 'As I said, the next twenty-four hours will decide. One way or another.'

CHAPTER 23

The Rolls' headlights cut two broad beams through the late evening darkness, illuminating the now steeply falling snow. Theirs were the only tyre tracks on the road. Having dropped Constable Fry home, Clifford eased the car to a stop at the T-junction that met the street turning right from Henley Hall and left towards the centre of the village.

'Have you sufficient stamina, my lady?'

'To revisit the scene of the crime?' Eleanor nodded. 'Always. But we could go first thing in the morning, and you could still make your date with a Boxing Day brandy and Voltaire.'

'As the gentleman himself noted, the opportunity for doing mischief is found a hundred times a day, and of doing good but once a year.'

'In that case' – she tapped the dashboard – 'en avant!'

With all the time spent waiting at the hospital, it was well past nine o'clock in the evening when Clifford parked up outside the vicarage again. A small wall of snow had already settled against the front door. Eleanor pushed, but the door failed to budge.

'No! How can it be locked? Now what? It's hardly appropriate to break in through a window.'

Clifford gave a discreet cough and pressed a large brass key into her gloved hand. 'What?' She stared down at it. 'You mean amongst all the panic, you locked the door behind us.'

'It would appear so, my lady.'

The inside of the vicarage felt eerily quiet. Few of the rooms had lights on but those that did threw long shadows out into the hallway. The upstairs was inky black.

Clifford closed the door behind them and turned on the hall light. The vicarage was one of the few houses in the village to have electric light throughout. They both stared at the spot where they had found the vicar sprawled on the floor.

Eleanor squatted down. 'Why do you suppose he was lying here?'

Clifford pointed to the telephone. 'I found the handset hanging by its cord when I went to ring the message through to Constable Fry. I believe the reverend or Mrs Fontaine was trying to ring for help.'

'Shame we didn't learn more from the doctor. I thought he was dashedly reserved in what he would tell us, didn't you?'

'It is to be expected, my lady. As Constable Fry noted when Doctor Browning attended Mr Canning's body, medical men have little choice but to be cautious.' He looked around. 'Shall we retire to the kitchen? There is nothing here in the hallway I can see that could be associated with the incident.'

'Of course, the tea!' Eleanor stood in the kitchen doorway, pointing at the smashed crockery and the pool of brown liquid on the floor. 'I bet whoever poisoned them, put the foxglove leaves or berries in the tea.'

'Perhaps because we were due to join them for tea?'

Eleanor started. 'You think we may have been the target?' She tilted her head. 'Good point, but no one except the reverend and Mrs Fontaine knew we were coming. And why were they drinking tea just before we arrived? Gracious! Is that why the door wasn't closed? They could have had another visitor who left before we appeared. And if so, it was almost certainly the killer.'

'Artfully deduced, my lady. Regrettably, with the weather and it being Boxing Day, we are unlikely to find many eyewitnesses, which means we need to wait until either the reverend or Mrs Fontaine are sufficiently recovered to ask them directly.'

She was grateful he hadn't said 'if they recover', but she knew the thought was there.

'Hmm, and you and I will have obscured any footprints in the snow in the driveway and on the step. Might be worth checking the path to the church though?'

'Another excellent suggestion.' He tightened his leather driving gloves against his fingers and moved to the wooden dresser that filled an alcove created by one side of the wide chimney breast. Whipping out an impeccably pressed handkerchief from his pocket, he used it to pick up the first of the tall biscuit tins. 'The tea.' He tipped it forward for her to smell. She sniffed it but shook her head.

'Nothing easily detectable. We should drop that off with Fry and insist he sends it off to be sampled.' She rolled her eyes. 'If Inspector Seldon's superiors will authorise the expense and the paperwork, of course.'

Clifford appeared to be deep in thought, staring into the tin of tea leaves. 'On second thoughts, I have a doubt, my lady. If the poison had been administered to the tea in the caddy, how could the murderer be certain it would only kill the intended victim, who we are assuming was the reverend. Or possibly yourself?'

Eleanor shuddered. 'Maybe the murderer is the kind of monster who doesn't care how many other people are dispatched along the way? Or he was trying to kill the reverend and Mrs Fontaine, though I've no idea why.' She let out a deep sigh. 'This must be connected with Canning's death somehow, but I don't feel we've discovered much in that regard except for the reverend's long-standing dispute with him. Which, of course, we came this afternoon to ask him about.'

'I believe the reverend understood we were coming so that you could discuss how you might support the orphan's fund, my lady?'

'Thank you for reminding me that I've now deceived him three times and he is lying at death's door in the hospital, so I can't even apologise.'

'Perhaps the best apology would be to find out who poisoned him and Mrs Fontaine?'

She took a deep breath. 'Agreed.' She shook her head at the odd mix of emotions in her chest. The largest part of her was horrified at the dark turn events had taken, but a small part of her was not… glad, no, no, that was the wrong word… relieved, that was it.

She looked up at Clifford. 'At least we know he can't have been the one who poisoned Canning. And that is a tremendous relief. It has been bothering me enormously to think it might have been him.'

'If it eases your conscience, he is probably totally unaware of the scandalous suspicion we briefly held.' He paused. 'It seems plausible that he, or Mrs Fontaine, might have seen whoever murdered Mr Canning and that person decided drastic action was needed?'

'But then why didn't one of them say anything?' She shook her head in frustration.

Clifford disappeared into the pantry and reappeared with an empty jar. Picking up a spoon from the draining board, he carefully scooped several inches of tea from the puddle on the floor into it and screwed the lid on tightly. Eleanor took a home-sewn shopping bag from its hook by the back door and held it open. Clifford carefully placed all three of the biscuit tins, the jar with the tea sample and the pieces of the broken teapot inside. Taking the bag, he adjusted his perfectly aligned cufflinks and cleared his throat gently.

'What is it, Clifford? You can say whatever you need to.'

He held her gaze. 'I fear, my lady, that we have both been delaying fully discussing the potential connection of all this with his lordship's death.'

Eleanor ran her hand through her curls. 'I was afraid I might open up too painful an old wound for you.'

'Thank you, and likewise.'

She smiled. 'Then let's agree to be brave first thing tomorrow and lift the lid an inch or two and see what we unearth, shall we? Maybe it will provide the link between Canning's poisoning and the reverend's and Mrs Fontaine's. Right now, I'd like to go back to the Hall and see if the ladies have returned so they can tell us how much fun they've had. It is Boxing Day after all.'

He nodded. 'I have no doubt they will be highly delighted to regale you with the minutiae of every minute since they left this morning.'

'And let's not tell the ladies about all this until tomorrow. I'd hate to spoil their one day of real freedom and joy.'

Clifford nodded. 'Agreed.'

She sighed. 'You know it's possible you're right and neither the reverend nor Mrs Fontaine saw anything. Perhaps the tea was intended for you or me and the poisoner's plan went wrong? Maybe whoever it is thought we were getting too close to the truth?'

Clifford locked the door and dropped the key in his pocket. 'Maybe, my lady, we are.'

CHAPTER 24

'Really, I had no idea the sloe gin was quite so formidable, Clifford.' Eleanor pulled her cheek down and peered at her bleary eyes in the hallway mirror. It was the morning after Boxing Day and she had stayed up till the early hours to make sure her staff's day of freedom wasn't curtailed by the lady of the house retiring early and putting a damper on their festivities. 'We might have to plan to do very little today.'

'Except catch a killer, my lady?'

'Except that. And on that note, I have it on my mind to telephone the hospital. That was a nasty shock. Imagine if we hadn't gone to the vicarage? They would have lain there until...' She shuddered and rubbed her temples. 'But it won't help to dwell on such things. Tell me, how are the ladies this morning? It did turn into quite a late night again, didn't it?'

'Perhaps instigating a sixth round of the card game Hearts was where prudence left.'

'Just as well she did. She's no fun at all.' She smiled at Clifford's groan. 'It was a wonderful evening. I missed out on all those typically English Christmassy things growing up abroad and the ladies loved it. I could see they didn't want their Boxing Day to end. Mind you, Mrs Trotman was fiendish! Good job we were playing for matchsticks and not pennies. But onto more important matters. How do I look?' She pulled a feeble face. 'If I'm going to ask him to book me in for a medical check, I can hardly bounce in there the picture of health, can I?'

Clifford studied her face. 'I am confident, my lady, you need not concern yourself on that score this morning.'

Doctor Browning's surgery was an unsympathetic, rectangular, red-brick addition to his rather austere, grey-stone house at the head of Cowgate Lane.

'How fortunate that I haven't needed to see the doctor here before.' Eleanor nodded at the hand-painted sign that greeted them as the garden gate creaked open. 'Keep off the lawn!'

Clifford gave his contradictory cough. 'Aside from the most regrettable episode when you were knocked unconscious in the Rolls, my lady, and I brought you here.'

'Ah, so you did. Can't remember much of that, really. Anyway, best keep to the path. From what I saw when he attended Canning's body, I shouldn't like to end up on the wrong side of the good doctor. Especially if our suspicions are correct.'

Eleanor had to duck under the low door into the surgery. Inside, the only furnishings were two hard wooden chairs, a small well-worn but polished table and a bucket. A list of the doctor's charges hung in a glassless frame on the wall. Underneath was a poster stating:

Do you or anyone in your family need to see a doctor? Are you having difficulty in affording the doctor's fee? If so Lady Swift of Henley Hall will cover the seven shillings charge for each and every appointment. If you are also struggling to pay for the medicines prescribed, Lady Swift will cover the cost of these until the treatment has run its course. Please call in person at Henley Hall or telephone Little Buckford 342.

Eleanor smiled. While standing as Chipstone's first woman MP she'd become aware that many people couldn't afford doctors' fees. And that, even if they could, they couldn't then afford the medicine prescribed. She hadn't realised, however, that any doctors in the area were displaying her poster, and hadn't especially expected Doctor Browning to be.

Next to the poster was the doctor's framed medical certificate, these being the only things to break up the otherwise white-painted walls. Another low door led off to what Eleanor imagined was the consulting room.

As Clifford closed the door behind them, a bell dinged. She pulled her coat tighter around her shoulders.

'Not very warm in here, is it?'

'Warmth breeds germs, Lady Swift,' Doctor Browning's taut voice came from the doorway.

'Quite right.' She turned with a smile. 'And how noble of you to work in such cool conditions for the benefit of your patients.'

He snorted, which made him rock backwards on his walking cane. 'January will see the start of my forty-fifth year in practice. Do you think I notice the temperature any more?'

She racked her brain for a way to get the conversation onto a more genial footing. 'Actually, I was rather hoping I might book an appointment with you for a health check?'

The doctor shuffled out into the waiting room. He adjusted his round glasses and scanned her face with his watery grey eyes. 'Lady Swift, you are a perfectly fit young woman. What possible reason could you have for wasting your money and my time to find out what you already know?'

'Well, it might be something to do with recent events, I suppose. Learning that Uncle Byron had fatal heart trouble and seeing Mr Canning collapse and pass away in front of Clifford and myself, both came as a tremendous shock.'

'Comparing yourself to people of the opposite gender who were double, or almost double, your age is hardly relevant, is it?'

'But that's just it. It's my birthday in March and I will enter my fourth decade! I think it is prudent to take care of one's health.' She ignored Clifford's quiet clearing of his throat at this. 'Look at Mr Canning, he thought he was fit enough to run in the Henley Hall race, didn't he? How does one know for sure?'

'One doesn't. That's why people should listen to their doctor. And I am telling you a consultation would reveal nothing other than that you have the constitution many of my patients would fight tooth and nail for. And Mr Canning might have, if he was still with us.'

Eleanor nodded. 'You see, that's just what I said to Clifford. I think Mr Canning pushed himself to run in the race to prove that he wouldn't follow in his mother's footsteps. I understand the poor lady suffered a great many years of ill health. That can't be easy for a loving son to watch.'

She jumped at the doctor's raucous, wheezy laughter. 'Loving son! Lady Swift, Conrad Canning ran away to sea when he was a nipper to be among other blackguards as calculating as himself. And when he returned, he gave his mother nothing but heartache over his continued nefarious activities.'

'Really? How strange. I heard he cared deeply for his mother and was distraught when she passed away. In fact, I heard that he refused to believe that she was even that ill, and—'

'No, Lady Swift. What I imagine you heard was that Canning tried to have me prosecuted and banned from medical practice for hastening his mother's death. It is common knowledge, however, that the court ruled entirely in my favour as I did... Nothing. Wrong. At. All!' With each word he banged his cane on the floor. 'Nothing, do you hear? But Canning came swanning back and thought he could assuage the shred of conscience he found goodness only knows where, by announcing to the world that I'd killed her. Preposterous!'

He poked himself in the chest. 'I saved that poor lady a great deal of pain by meticulously regulating her medication. She was fully compos mentis and agreed to the prescriptions.' His chin shook. 'That was the thanks I got for doing my best by another lady he had abandoned.' He slumped down into a chair, taking the clean handkerchief Clifford offered and wiping his brow.

Eleanor took the seat next to him. 'Doctor Browning, I am sorry. I didn't mean to upset you. That must have been a difficult experience for you.'

He nodded, leaning his chin on his cane. 'I've given my life to medicine. I may not have gone up to London and become a fancy gentlemen's doctor, but I have cared for the people in this community from the day I obtained my licence. Over forty years of delivering generation after generation into the world, treating their every ailment, and signing my name to the passing of many of them.' He stared at her. 'No, Lady Swift, it was not a pleasant experience by any means. And I've been the one advising against excessive drinking, but that sent me to the bottle for a short while, I won't lie.'

Eleanor nodded. 'I've found on a few occasions that being in someone else's shoes has left me with much sharper understanding and vastly more compassion.'

He shook his head. 'Not where Canning was concerned. Think what you will but I have no good words for that man. He treated his mother shabbily, and… and other women. And his own flesh and blood! He appalled me at how he treated them.'

Eleanor decided she needed to take a risk. 'Like poor Miss Lucetta Moore?'

Doctor Browning jerked as upright as his stoop would allow him to. 'What is this now? What do you know of Miss Moore and Canning?'

'Possibly nothing more than unfounded gossip. You know what the village drums can be like. Of course, because Mr Canning passed away at Henley Hall, people have been very keen to talk to me about him.'

He frowned at her. 'Which you haven't encouraged, naturally!'

She let this go. 'Of course, the rumours are totally implausible. But I don't wish to upset you any further. Shall we look at a date for my consultation?' She stood up and pulled out her diary.

'Sit.' Doctor Browning struck the leg of the chair with his cane.

She did as he asked, holding his gaze. 'Yes?'

'You are infernally nosy, but you were there when I saw the signs that Canning might not have passed naturally. It was inevitable that you would arrive, asking questions, especially when I heard the police elected not to open an investigation. However.' He held up a shaky hand. 'I will not have mine or Miss Moore's name dragged through the mud over this. She has suffered enough and risen from it all by pure resilience. Let me state here and now that whatever you have heard about her and me years back is utter fiction. I befriended her in her hour of need, nothing more.'

Eleanor nodded, feeling the intensity of his gaze.

With one hand hard against the wall, he rose with a grunt. 'There is no point my asking you to let sleeping dogs lie. And I am too long in the tooth to fight your determination to poke about in Canning's sordid past. So, I shall bid you farewell with two suggestions.'

She waited.

'Firstly, if you insist on dragging Miss Moore into this, ask the man who was far more involved than I, despite all the rumours.' His jaw clenched. 'A man of the cloth who should have known better. And ask him what he was doing with Canning's bag not half an hour before the man died!'

She froze. 'You mean… Reverend Gaskell?' *Either he hasn't heard about the vicarage poisoning or he knows all about it, Ellie!*

The doctor gave a single, terse nod. 'And secondly, Lady Swift.' He shuffled to the doorway of his consulting room. 'I suggest you do not induce the early onset of ageing by sullying your countenance with wrinkles and grey hairs brought on by worrying about your health. As you have just demonstrated, it would take a rhino to penetrate your vitality and stamina. Good morning.'

The door slammed shut.

Clifford raised an eyebrow. 'How fortuitous that you did not tread on his grass, as well as his painful recollections, my lady.'

CHAPTER 25

The next step in their investigation took Eleanor and Clifford to the furthest end of Chipstone High Street. The sombre tones of the town hall clock struck midday. Here the pavements stopped as if to highlight that the best of the shops were now behind you. Even the festive window decorations looked as if they had seen their best many Christmases ago. Clifford parked the Rolls outside a tiny flower shop. Like all the buildings in the street, it was dilapidated and forlorn, but the window was spotless and expertly arranged with a mixture of colourful blooms against two artistically hung lengths of cream cotton. Through the gap in the middle of them, Eleanor could make out Miss Moore staring at a small bouquet of red roses. She rubbed her hands over her cheeks. *Let's hope this conversation is easier than I fear it's going to be, Ellie.*

Stepping inside the tiny shop, all the spring-fresh greenery and floral perfume tingled Eleanor's senses. She took a deep breath, relishing the scent of the flowers, bunched in mismatched, often chipped, glass vases laid out on a series of thin wooden shelves.

'Lady Swift, I wasn't expecting to see you here.' Miss Moore stepped out from behind her workbench, retying the strings of her calico apron. Lit by a single large lamp, her long, fair curls loosely held in a delicate ring of rowan berries gave her the look of Botticelli's favourite muse. 'Mr Clifford.' She nodded to him where he stood, the shoulders of his smart black overcoat and bowler hat filling the narrow doorway.

'Miss Moore, merry Christmas.' Eleanor smiled, trying to get her words together. 'I wanted to stop by to thank you for the floral displays you made for me. Henley Hall has never been so exquisitely decorated, I'm sure. Except for when you did the same for my late uncle's events, of course.'

'Oh, there's no need to thank me. It was my pleasure. I spend my days making bouquets, nosegays and pomanders but I rarely get to see how much joy they bring anyone. Once the flowers leave here, they're gone.' She smiled wistfully. 'I'm too sentimental for this job, really.' She picked up a single stem red rose from amongst the discarded pile of tall green euphorbia. 'Every flower is so perfect and unique, I find it hard to let them go. Leaves me feeling sad every time a bouquet is bought. It's very silly.'

Eleanor shook her head. 'I don't think it is, not at all. You just have a passion for flowers, and it shows in every arrangement you make.' She took the rose and sniffed its beautiful scent. 'We all have something we get misty-eyed over.'

'Even you, m'lady?'

This took Eleanor by surprise. 'Erm, yes. Even me. I'm not that different, really.'

Miss Moore reached her hand out, but then pulled back. 'Oh forgive me, I didn't mean to be rude. It's just that when you arrived, no one could talk of anything but your amazing travels and incredible adventures.' She fiddled with her thumbnail. 'For some reason, I thought that would make you rather…'

'Harsh? Unfeeling?'

'No, no, nothing like that. Just, well, not at all sentimental. Oh, my silly runaway mouth, I am so sorry.'

Eleanor leaned forward. 'I'll let you into a little secret I never realised until I went travelling. It was very lonely on my own sometimes and I found myself reaching out to all kinds of strangers. People are so kind, everywhere, you know. And the greatest lesson I learned is that I'm actually just a hopeless romantic. Who knew?'

'I had no idea you might feel that way. Lonely, I mean.' Miss Moore bit her lip. 'It's such a horrible place to be.'

Without needing to turn around, Eleanor knew Clifford would melt discreetly from the doorway at this turn in the conversation.

'Lucky you though. You have Alvan. He seems an intelligent and pleasant chap.'

'Oh, he's wonderful. Something of a tearaway a few years back. Not surprising really, he had plenty of reasons to be.'

'Growing up in Chipstone probably had a hand in that. Rural town life is surely enough to incite mischievousness, I imagine. Tons of energy and not many outlets for it.'

Miss Moore looked down at her empty wedding-ring finger. 'And no father to be an example for him.'

'That can't have been easy for him. Nor for you. I'm sorry. Life doesn't always turn out the way we plan, does it?' Eleanor's voice was gentle.

Miss Moore sighed and shoved her hands in the big front pocket of her apron. 'I can't blame life. How could it have gone to plan when I never made one? Any crooked turns were all my own doing. Anyway, that's all over now. He's gone. For good.' She ended forcefully. Then she let out a single dry sob, her chin quivering.

'Oh dear.' Eleanor wished she could do that wonderful thing Clifford always did of producing a pristine handkerchief at moments like this. Instead she stared helplessly, trying to read the emotions flashing in the woman's eyes.

Miss Moore fanned her face and swallowed hard. She picked up the euphorbia and ran it over her forehead, round her cheek and over her nose. 'Plants calm me down. I am so sorry, really. This is most unlike me. What must you think?'

Knowing this was her one chance, Eleanor bit the bullet. 'I think… what happened at the Henley Hall Christmas lunch was tragic.' Miss Moore stiffened. Eleanor hurried on. 'I also think that Mr Canning's passing has brought that loneliness back to you.'

Miss Moore sniffed. 'Gossip can be very hurtful, m'lady.'

'As can being abandoned,' Eleanor said softly.

Miss Moore closed her eyes. When she spoke, it was through her fingers, palms clasped tightly together. 'Who told you?'

'Honestly, no one, exactly. I saw Doctor Browning this morning, and he said—'

'That nothing happened between us? Same as he did all those years back then. But I can't blame him either, I suppose. He did help me when I badly needed someone. Conrad didn't want anything to do with me the minute he realised I was pregnant. Lord, what a fool I was! And what a bigger fool, staying in the same town and trying to bring my illegitimate son up myself. You say people are kind everywhere, but they can also be judgemental and cruel if you break the rules.'

'And you broke the rules?'

Miss Moore laughed bitterly. 'I was supposed to give the baby away and pretend I was never pregnant. Instead I kept him and refused to feel shame or guilt. They hate that, the judgers and stone-throwers. But I was a fool to think I could keep who his father was a secret.'

'We hopeless romantics always are. Fools who love, that is.'

Miss Moore nodded, her eyes welling up. 'I'm sure like everyone else you probably thought Conrad was a miserable, selfish man. And he was. But he wasn't like that in the beginning.'

'I didn't, actually. Honestly, I thought he seemed troubled, and that's what made him, well, perhaps rather gruff on occasions.'

'You're too polite, m'lady. He fought with everyone, all the time. Then Alvan came along, such a darling little bundle, and I thought everything would magically change. But he, and me, we meant nothing to Conrad. Or so he made me think back then. All those years I scrimped and scraped to bring up his son while he contributed absolutely nothing!' This brought an angry scowl to Miss Moore's face.

'Did Alvan know that Conrad Canning was his father?'

'Not for a long time. But then he worked it out himself. Physically they were very similar, after all. And he must have heard the rumours about me from years back, I guess. Oh, I should have moved away when Conrad came back from the sea and then moved to Chipstone. When I think how hard I studied to be a botanist! But I gave up my dream to bring Alvan up.' She closed her eyes for a moment. 'All I had was a flower stall in the street across the road over there. Until my aunt passed and left me enough to scrape this cupboard of a shop together, we were lucky to have two meals a day. Conrad never gave us anything, not a penny, not ever.' A line of tears spilled out over each eyelid.

'I hope Alvan hasn't taken the news about Mr Canning too badly.'

'Very badly, actually. I've never seen him like this. He went quiet and then he started raging that he never got to say his piece to his father about what he thought of him. I can't help him when he gets like that. It was inevitable he would end up with some of his father's temper, I guess. But maybe the news might bring back the Alvan I know and love when it's had time to sink in.' She sighed and wiped a tear from the corner of her eye. 'I... I told him some news this morning and he flew into a temper. He's going to come flying out of the Nest soon in a fearful mood, I shouldn't wonder, and then I've no idea where he'll go or when I'll see him next.'

Hmm, he's leaving home, Ellie. Interesting! 'News? A solicitor, perhaps?' Immediately the words were out of her mouth, she regretted them.

Miss Moore looked panic-stricken. 'How could you possibly know that?'

Think, Ellie. 'Oh, I didn't. Lucky guess. Did he have good news for you?' She hoped her tone wouldn't give away that she already knew the answer.

'I'm sure it will be all over Chipstone soon enough and then more rumours will start to fly.' She paused. 'Conrad left us everything he had.'

'Really?' Eleanor tried to feign surprise. 'That must have been… quite a shock.'

'What?' Miss Moore faltered. 'A shock? After refusing to help us all those years?' She shook her head. 'I'm not travelled like you, m'lady, or I'd have another word for it. As it is, all the words I have for it I couldn't repeat in front of a lady.' Anger welled in her eyes. 'At first… at first I thought it was some kind of sick, last joke on Conrad's part. I mean, I knew of the rumours.' She glanced quickly at Eleanor and then away. 'I'm sure by now you've heard them, you and Mr Clifford seem determined to… find out everything.'

Before Eleanor could reply, Miss Moore continued. 'People said Conrad had a small fortune hidden away somewhere, but that's all I ever thought they were. Rumours. When the solicitor told me Conrad had left us everything, I imagined a pile of debts and his tumbledown house, if you can call it a house. But then, then he told me how much.' Her eyes widened as if picturing it. Then she seemed to snap to, and they dulled again. 'I… I mean it's always helpful to receive some money, but if only I could turn the clock back I'd have done things so differently. Honestly, I'd swap every penny for him not to have died. It shouldn't have been like that.'

'Is there ever a way it should happen?' Eleanor wished Clifford was there by her side. Miss Moore was hiding how she really felt about inheriting the money and Canning's death, that Eleanor was sure of. But whether she meant it about swapping the small fortune she'd just inherited for Conrad still being alive, she doubted it. *The man deserted her and her son years ago, Ellie. Surely no woman could still love a man who behaved that way?*

Miss Moore was wiping her eyes, but Eleanor sensed she was watching her at the same time. Eleanor ploughed on. 'Perhaps you hadn't spoken to Mr Canning for a while although you were both at the Henley Hall lunch.'

'I tried,' Miss Moore burst out. 'I tried to warn him, but it was too late.' Her face paled, and she ripped off her apron. 'I have to go, please excuse me.'

Outside, Clifford fell into step with Eleanor as Miss Moore locked the door of the shop behind them and hurried off. Eleanor pointed randomly across the road as if she was discussing something in the dress shop's window. 'Did you hear all of that?' she asked quietly.

'Certainly the vast majority of the conversation, my lady, by shameful eavesdropping whilst pretending to attend to the engine of the Rolls.'

'Tsk, tsk. And on our last investigation, you were here gossiping like a publican's wife. Quite scandalous. However, do keep it up.'

'Very good, my lady.'

She sighed. 'However, I'm sorry you had to overhear such a sad story.'

He nodded. 'One can only admire Miss Moore's determination to bring up her son herself.'

'Absolutely. I tell you what isn't so good, though.' She stamped her feet as she walked to numb the insidious cold creeping through her toes. 'We need to talk to Alvan immediately, but Miss Moore said he was flying the nest today, and she had no idea where or when she'd see him again. So, unless we're quick we may never get a chance.'

Clifford pulled out his pocket watch, then nodded. 'I believe, my lady, all may not be lost.'

CHAPTER 26

Trusting Clifford's judgement, Eleanor followed him, figuring she would find out where they were going soon enough. Her mind jumped back and forth between her talk with Miss Moore and the delightful Christmas displays in each shop's bow-fronted window, which she couldn't help but pause at. Ingenuity, creativity and a great deal of foraging for red-berried holly and shiny, green laurel had transformed this more affluent stretch of Chipstone's quaint but practical high street into a Christmas wonderland.

Amongst the multitude of greenery and berries, cut-out paper snowflakes hung among homemade red fabric bows, both hanging above whatever else had been to hand, it seemed. Swathes of fir cones dusted in icing sugar nestled against short stacks of boxes wrapped in anything vaguely seasonal. Many of the boxes were decorated with the addition of a miniature knitted figure sporting a winter hat and mittens. Centrally placed in every window was a beeswax candle, secured in a jam jar. Surrounded by tinsel, the candle jars made it seem as if a radiant fairy had flitted from shop to shop with a lit wand, bringing the town together into a shimmering, flickering theatre set.

Eleanor turned to Clifford. 'I keep expecting Charles Dickens himself to pop out of one of these shops scribbling out his scene of Scrooge with the Ghost of Christmas Past.'

'The town does indeed have such an air, my lady.' He scanned her face. 'It is, however, a shame that Yuletide has been marred by such an unfortunate event.'

'Do you know, if you learn to read my mind any better, I shall have to wear some sort of densely formed iron hat.'

He gave a quiet cough. 'Forgive my observation, but I rather think it might need to be a mask. A large and all-encompassing affair.'

This made her chuckle. 'Alright, I'm not too adept at stopping my face from being a barometer for my feelings.' She stopped as he seemed to turn to mount the steps of the Eagle, Chipstone's oldest, and grandest, coaching inn.

'The Eagle? I love the idea of lunch, but for once I must insist we put our stomachs second. We need to find Alvan first, before he disappears for good.'

A smart waiter opened the door. 'Good afternoon, Lady Swift. Mr Clifford. A table in the dining room?'

'No, thank you.' Clifford pointed a leather-gloved finger towards the tall archway through to the sixteenth-century, black-timbered stables and outbuildings. 'We are going around the back.'

The waiter looked pointedly at Eleanor. 'Sir…? I mean, are you sure? With the lady you might prefer…' He tailed off at Clifford's impassive stare. 'Enjoy your drink.' The waiter hurriedly closed the door.

'Okay, now I'm really intrigued.'

She followed Clifford under the arch and across the higgledy-piggledy cobbles worn smooth by the stagecoaches over the centuries. The yard was empty save for two horse-drawn carts and a very dented delivery van. He paused in front of a low, black-painted door. 'Most regrettably, it is inappropriate for me to have brought you here, my lady, for which I sincerely apologise. I fear, however, that it is imperative we make progress in our investigation before our poisoner walks free.'

'Or strikes again?' She tried to peer through the tiny, diamond-shaped glass in the door but its bottle-bottom thickness made it impossible to distinguish anything clearly. 'I'll be on guard for anyone with an eyepatch and a hook for a hand, shall I?'

'Thankfully, that will not be necessary. Welcome to...' He clicked the stable latch handle and eased the door open a crack. '... the Nest, that being the local name for the tradesmen's bar of the Eagle Hotel.'

Eleanor slapped her forehead. 'So that's what Miss Moore meant. Alvan isn't leaving "the nest" as in home today. She thinks he's here, getting drunk.' She went to step forward but then leaned back. 'Crikey, let's hope the roof holds. I've never seen anything lean so precariously.'

She wasn't at all surprised that the hum of chatter stopped as she ducked under the door frame and entered the dark, timber-ceilinged bar. Neither was she thrown. In her years of travelling she had ventured into far more dubious, and dangerous, drinking dens out of necessity for a hot meal or a bed for the night. This one was cleaner than many she'd been into and happily devoid of patrons with eyepatches or hooks. The furniture was scuffed and worn, but overall the place exuded an air of modest respectability.

She looked round the huddles of curious faces staring at her, but there was no sign of Alvan. Clifford appeared at her elbow and gestured to the only man who had not turned at her entrance. Elbows propped on the bar, a hunched-over figure, fair-haired and athletically built, was deep in conversation with the barmaid. She was flicking her thick brown curls over her shoulder and running her hand down his arm. Three empty jug-handled pint glasses sat in front of him.

'Bad timing,' Eleanor whispered. 'It seems Mr Moore is in thrall to a charming lady.'

'I feel she may turn out to be less than charming,' Clifford said uncharacteristically and strode up to the bar.

Eleanor hung back, pretending to examine the multitude of horse brasses hanging on the rough-plastered walls. She'd seen first-hand how much smoother conversations went when a male suspect wasn't first met by a woman, especially one with a title.

'A gin and a dark porter, please,' she heard him order. 'Ah, Mr Moore.' Clifford turned to the man they had come to question. 'Good afternoon. Perhaps I can get you another pint?'

'Kind enough, thank you, Mr Clifford.' Alvan slid his empty glass across the bar. 'Haven't seen you in here since…' He tailed off as Eleanor joined them.

'Good morning and merry Christmas, Mr Moore, if it isn't too late for seasonal greetings of course.'

Alvan stared at her, his jaw slack. Coming to, he jumped off his stool and ran his hand through his hair. 'Merry Christmas to you, Lady Swift. Excuse me being surprised like, to see a, um… lady like yourself in… here.' This drew a loud huff from the barmaid who was watching the exchange rather than the stream of peat-brown ale pouring from the hand pump she was pulling.

'Indeed, it's a little on the unusual side, but it's almost 1921 and times are changing. We're allowed out of the kitchen now, you know.' She frowned. 'Although, to make things rather complicated, titled ladies, like myself, were never actually allowed in the kitchen in the first place.' She smiled at his confused look. 'Still, I insisted that Clifford give me the full tour of the town today. Do you know, I've been here almost a year, and I hadn't even heard of the Nest?' She settled herself on the bar stool Clifford had pulled out for her.

'That so, m'lady?' Alvan said.

'But how lucky that we've bumped into you. I wanted to find out how you enjoyed the lunch at Henley Hall on Christmas Eve.'

A muscle twitched in his cheek. 'It was great. Kind of you to lay it on and everything. I've never had anything as tasty as that afore, delicious it was.'

The barmaid slapped the drinks down and shot Eleanor a black look.

Eleanor ignored her. 'Well, thank you, but don't be over polite. I genuinely want to see if I can improve anything next year. That's why I'm asking people now, while the day is fresh in the mind, as it were.'

'I couldn't complain about nothing, m'lady. It was all fine until… just fine, it was all fine.'

Eleanor took the glass Clifford held out to her. 'It's alright, Mr Moore, I appreciate you being sensitive on my account.'

'I don't!' the barmaid hissed as she marched over to deal with a man tapping a coin pointedly against his empty glass further down the bar.

'Ah, ta, Mr Clifford.' Alvan nodded as he accepted his pint.

Clifford raised his own glass. 'To absent friends and family.'

Eleanor grimaced at the sip of debatable quality gin. 'I popped into your mother's shop this morning, Mr Moore. Forgive my directness, but I was rather concerned. Your mother, err, seemed to be struggling a little with something.'

Alvan spun round making Eleanor rock backwards. How had she missed the similarity of those piercing blue eyes? The same as his father's, except the last time she had seen those, they had been blank and lifeless.

Alvan's tone seemed to hold a lifetime of tired resignation. 'When isn't my mother struggling with something? That's more likely the question, m'lady.'

'Well, some people have a more delicate set of sensibilities, I suppose. Perhaps it's not always so easy to live with though.'

'No, it isn't, and it wasn't all the years growing up.'

The barmaid reappeared and laid her hand on his arm. 'Alvie, luv, you don't have to talk about any of this with… them.' She glared at Eleanor.

'Leave it, Beth. Just passing the time. There's no harm in it.'

'Well it don't seem like that to me,' she hissed. 'Folk like them don't just happen into places like this.' Her head jerked to the other end of the bar. 'Alright, alright. I'm coming!'

Eleanor let the awkward silence hang in the air between her and Alvan. He cocked his head.

'Maybe Beth's right.'

'Really? Keeping secrets can do a lot of damage, I find. Especially when the news finally gets out, and it's all over the town. That can be very hard to live with.'

He laughed harshly. 'As if I didn't know!' He stopped his pint halfway to his lips, a frown on his face. 'She… she told you, didn't she, m'lady?'

Eleanor nodded.

'My blasted mother! See what I mean about her? Spends an hour bending my ear about me not saying a word, not to Beth, not to anyone. Then you turn up and she tells you the lot.' He slapped the bar, then took a long swig of his drink. 'I swear one day…' He tailed off and stared at the ceiling.

'I am sorry, I didn't mean to throw any salt into an open wound.'

He waved a hand but then spun round on his stool. 'Do you know what I'd love to do, m'lady? March over there and just let it all out. She lied to me all those years, then acted like it wasn't anything she could have done different. Well, maybe I should show her what that feels like.'

Eleanor caught the corner of Clifford's eye. 'And how do you think she would take that?'

'What should I care?'

She tried to get the conversation back on track and softened her voice. 'My sincere condolences, by the way. And apologies for not starting with them. But once you'd learned Mr Canning was your father, wasn't it awkward? You must have run into each other in the area on occasions?'

Alvan gave her a devilish grin. 'Yeah, and every time we did, we had a fierce old row.'

She leaned forward to speak just as the barmaid bowled past with a full tray of dirty glasses. She plonked the tray down next to Eleanor, who she clearly felt was too close to the man she had laid claim to.

'Leave off, Beth,' Alvan growled. She stomped off muttering.

Eleanor waited until she was at the other end of the bar and then turned back to Alvan. 'So, did you know your father was on heart tablets?'

He nodded. 'Wasn't much surprise when he… died. He was stubborn, m'lady… like me.'

'I can see why you were angry with your father, Alvan. It must have been hard finding out he lived so close but chose not to be a part of your life.'

He ran his hand round the back of his neck. 'Makes you think there's something… wrong with you. Your own father not giving a damn. Only I know the truth now. Oh, excuse the language, m'lady.'

'That's alright.'

'Pretty stupid of them both. Mum thought she could get away without anyone knowing for sure she'd gone with him. Course folk were going to guess, look at me!' He ran his arm over his body, then pointed to his eyes. 'You ever seen anyone look more like their dad than I do? No wonder the rumours never stopped.'

'Alvan.' This time Eleanor slid off her stool. 'I'm sorry for your troubles with your father. At least he left you some money.'

He glanced up at her, then away. 'I see my mother told you that as well.' He shook his head slowly, clearly still in shock. 'I still can't believe he left me… anything. I mean, it weren't like he ever said sorry for leaving me to grow with just her at home. And he still owed people as far as I know.'

'Anyone in particular?'

'Alvan Moore!' the barmaid screamed. 'If you're gonna go parading your fancy bit round the place, you can sling your hook, right now!'

CHAPTER 27

After the Nest, the Winsomes Tea Rooms were an oasis of calm amid the vanilla wallpaper softly lit by cream wall sconces and a sprinkling of tasteful chandeliers. It seemed the owner was too fastidious to allow the crassness of Christmas to intrude into the tea rooms, for it was conspicuously absent of seasonal decorations except for a sprinkle of discreetly placed tinsel. Being lunchtime, the delicate chink of fine, bone-china cups set delicately back down on their matching rosebud-patterned saucers mingled with the hum of civilised conversation. Eleanor's presence was met with many a whispered, 'Ooh, that's Lady Swift!' as she weaved between the tables, following the petite, rather nervous waitress.

Once seated in the otherwise empty, short-raised section at the far end of the building, known as the gallery, Eleanor sat back in her ivory button-backed chair. She felt in her pockets and hurrahed as she pulled out her notebook with a flourish.

Clifford arched an eyebrow. 'Traditionally, we have taken a table here to aid discretion while discussing an investigation, my lady.'

'It's fine, no one comes up here unless downstairs is full, because you can't hear the gossip from the next-door tables. Now, let's tackle this in reverse order for a change. We'll do Miss Moore in a moment. So, what did you make of Alvan's story?'

'My immediate impression was that he shared all of his father's most unfortunate characteristics.'

'Except physically. There's not much that's unfortunate there. Those eyes could melt a nun trapped in a glacier.'

'My lady?'

'I just meant that I can see why Canning did so well with the ladies, if all the stories are true. Not my type, but I can imagine in his day, Canning was quite the fox women would have howled at the moon over.'

'I will have to bow to you on that one, my lady.' He ran his finger along his starched white collar. 'If I may return to his son? To my mind, his animosity to his mother seemed misplaced compared to his father's abandonment of him.'

'But she did lie to him all the years he was growing up about Canning being his father.'

'Quite so, my lady. But I found his anger at his mother, rather than his father, disquieting, or implausible.'

She tapped her chin with her pen. 'You know, you're right. Maybe he was trying to play down his anger at Canning. If he is the murderer, then he probably has guessed that we're investigating his father's death and at least suspect foul play. But I didn't sense that he was lying when he said he didn't know he would benefit from Canning's will until his mother told him.'

'Although for a man whose tongue was loosened with alcohol, he was very calm about it. And soberly quiet in coming forth with any reason his father gave for cutting him, and his mother, out of his life.'

'I must say, you ordering him a fifth pint may have been going a bit too far to get the information we needed. He'll wake up later with a horribly thick head.'

'I regret to offer a contradictory view, my lady. Aside from the fact that I ordered him a substantial luncheon to accompany his last pint, Mr Moore is a man extremely capable and practised at holding his drink.'

'Which means he was probably more sober than he pretended.' She paused and sighed. 'Actually, forget all about Alvan or the case, you have to rave over this fruit cake first. It is divine.'

Clifford ate a morsel and nodded. 'Very good, indeed. Now to return to the case?' She took another bite and waved him on with her other hand. 'I found it difficult, my lady, to believe his readiness to admit to a lady, and one he does not know, his feelings about his father refusing to acknowledge him. And in a public bar, of all places.'

'Hmm. I do agree with you. And you know what else didn't feel right? He was really quite pleasant with the barmaid until she interrupted when he was in the middle of telling us how much he blamed his mother, not Canning. Then he positively snarled at her.'

'I too noticed the momentary personality shift, my lady.'

'So either he is an excellent mood actor or that is going to be one fiery household if those two end up together.'

In her notebook, Eleanor drew a doodle of a flame next to Alvan's name and wrote 'lying about being angry with his father?'. She looked up. 'Oh yes, more tea please and two of those lemon custard fellows in the pastry shells, they look sublime.' The waitress who had come to check on them nodded and looked at Clifford who shook his head.

Eleanor leaned back in her seat. 'Now on to Miss Moore. If Alvan was telling the truth about how he feels towards his mother, maybe Miss Moore blamed Canning for abandoning her and turning her son against her? Two very strong motives for murder. I mean, is Miss Moore really the doting mother, blissfully unaware of how her son feels about her or—'

'Or is she acutely aware and has now just lost her last hope of getting him back? Because his father has left him enough money, we presume, for him to be independent and really fly the nest?'

'Although that might mean that she didn't have a motive to murder Canning.'

'Unless she had no knowledge about his will when she poisoned him.' Clifford folded his napkin into a perfect square. 'Of course, there is the possibility that we might need to have a joint first place at the top of the list.'

'Of course! Alvan and Miss Moore could have been in on Canning's murder together.'

'Indeed, both enraged by Mr Canning's treatment of them over the years.'

Eleanor hastily scribbled in her notebook. 'I would say even without Miss Moore and Alvan having any knowledge of Canning's recent will, they are both at the top of our suspect list for sure. They both had the means, motive and opportunity.'

'My lady.' Clifford clicked his fingers. 'There is yet one more possibility.'

She groaned and held up the untidy, ink-covered page. 'There can't be, I've run out of room.'

'My apologies, but next to the rose you have drawn for Miss Moore, you might just have room to redraw the small round spectacles you drew previously.'

'Ah, Miss Moore and Doctor Browning! Or all three might have planned it!' She stared at the page, her eyes unfocussed for a moment. 'Hang on, what about Doctor Browning's insinuation that the reverend was romantically involved with Miss Moore, not him?'

'Not to forget, my lady, his assertion that the reverend was seen with Mr Canning's bag not half an hour before the race.'

Eleanor wrote these details down and stared at the page again. She groaned. 'My head is positively spinning.'

Clifford arched one brow and gestured to the near-empty cake stand. 'Rather than the case, my lady, perhaps it is a side effect of the mountain of sugar consumed, do you suppose?'

Back at the Hall, once Eleanor had extracted a very excited Gladstone from the folds of her skirt and accepted his gift of a leather slipper, she picked up the telephone. Clifford hovered behind her. 'Chipstone 452 please.' She tapped her foot impatiently.

Clifford caught her eye. 'I do believe the nurses prioritise the patients over the telephone, my lady.'

'Well then, they must have filled all the beds and be piling more sick people up in the corridors. This is interminable.' In truth her show of impatience was just her way of hiding her nerves. *What if the news isn't good, Ellie?* 'Oh, hello, Chipstone Hospital?... Yes, wonderful, thank you. May I inquire after the Reverend Gaskell and Mrs Fontaine?... Me? Lady Swift... Gracious, do thank him for that.' She stared at Clifford's reflection in the mirror. 'The nurse said that the doctor asked to speak with me if I called. Odd?'

'Perhaps not so much. You did mention we are possibly the closest thing either of them have to family, my lady.'

She winced. 'Why does that feel like a bit of a bold claim, right now? I mean, you've known them both for years and I... well, I've only just arrived so that was something of a fib really, wasn't it?'

'Yes, but one made with very positive intentions.'

She held her finger up as a tired male voice came down the receiver.

'Indeed it is Lady Swift, Doctor. Thank you for speaking with me. How are they doing?'

His words were muffled by the rustling of papers.

'Waiting for stabilisation, you say... Monitoring...' Her hand flew to her chest. 'Gracious, Doctor, I so hoped you'd tell me they were sitting up sipping tea. Well, maybe not tea... oh I see, a very long way off that possibly... yes, yes I understand, it is your job to paint the bleakest picture, just in case... Oh, this isn't just in case, rather in this case. Oh, Doctor, please do everything you possibly can, even though I know you already are... yes, yes, silly thing for me to say, my apologies. Is there anything I can do? ... No?... Well, thank you, Doctor. I do hope you get a break soon.'

She slowly placed the handset back on its cradle.

'Not the news we wished to hear, I take it, my lady?'

She sighed. 'The doctor said the best he can say is that neither of them have deteriorated any further.'

Clifford shook his head. 'The situation is far graver than I had hoped. And the case more baffling. We have established a plethora of motives for any or all of our suspects to want to kill Mr Canning. However, we have established absolutely none for any of them wanting to kill the reverend and Mrs Fontaine. We have conjectured that one, or both of them, may have seen something, but then, as you rightly pointed out, why did neither of them speak up? It is hardly likely that they would have seen Mr Canning murdered and then said nothing about it.'

Eleanor groaned. 'Where is that brandy? Please come and join me.' She turned towards the snug but stopped. 'I have a most peculiar desire, Clifford.'

'Ice cream and carrots? Ginger cake and sardines? Mrs Trotman will be happy to oblige.'

'Neither, thank you. I wish with all my heart and soul that the inspector was here. I'm too worried this time. It feels like the case has completely gotten away from us. If only—'

She was interrupted by the jangling of the telephone. Clifford stepped over to answer it, passing her a paper bag of mint humbugs from his pocket as he did. She popped one in her mouth. 'I'm not here, whoever it is,' she whispered.

'Henley Hall. Ah, good afternoon, Chief Inspector.'

CHAPTER 28

Ten minutes later, she was still staring at the telephone when Gladstone broke her reverie by shoving his wet nose into her hand. His stumpy tail batted the back of her legs. She knelt on the rose-coloured Wilton runner and snuggled her face into his soft, wrinkled forehead.

'Hello, old friend,' she whispered. 'What is going on in my head, do you suppose? Every time I see Lancelot, I can't stop wishing the day would never end, even though he's terribly fatuous at times. But then, when the inspector calls...' She sighed and hit her hand against her temple. 'The brain is definitely too full to think about matters of the heart though, my soppy chum. We've got a murder to solve.' She rose wearily and turned to see Clifford approaching with a silver tray on which sat a decanter of sherry.

'A reviver? Top idea, Clifford!'

He gave his customary half bow but didn't continue on along the hallway, instead he stood waiting patiently.

'Alright.' She took a deep breath. 'As you know, Fry took samples of anything he thought Canning might have drunk or eaten just before the race and sent it up to the inspector to have analysed.'

Clifford nodded.

'Well, the first thing they analysed was the washing-up water Polly used to clean the glasses after the guests had had their Christmas mead. As we know, Mrs Trotman served Canning his glass of mead herself.'

Clifford nodded again.

'Well, they found digitalis in the washing-up water and the inspector is coming down as soon as his other case, and the snow, allows.'

Clifford's brow furrowed. 'Are you sure, my lady? In the washing-up water?'

She nodded. 'Joseph told Polly to tip it into a barrel rather than waste it and he'd use it as and when he needed to water the greenhouse plants. Of course, being winter he's only growing stuff in the heated greenhouses. Fry took samples from there, among other places.' She sighed. 'This is all getting very complicated, Clifford. I think we both know the time has come to tackle the manner in which Uncle Byron so unfortunately died in February. Maybe, as we said before, it will shed some light on what's happening now.'

'Hence the decanter of Dutch courage, my lady.'

'Perfect. Where to?'

'The left tower sitting room, adjacent to his late lordship's study.'

Having previously dismissed this as yet one more space she'd never need, Eleanor now looked round with fresh eyes. The oak panelling was the lightest she had seen and gave the room a delightful honey glow, making it cosy, even without the fire crackling in the grate. Three watercolour portraits of Gladstone hung in the spaces between the floor-to-ceiling windows, adding more homeliness, especially when she spotted her uncle's signature at the bottom of each.

Gladstone had, in fact, paused in the doorway, uncharacteristically dispirited. He padded over to the nearest of the three deep-buttoned Chesterfield armchairs and gave a soft whine as he laid his head on the seat, his tail hanging limply.

'Missing your master?' she muttered, stroking his back.

Clifford pulled a matching footstool out from behind the chair and shuffled the bulldog to one side. 'One moment, Master Gladstone.' He patted the leather top and the bulldog sprung forwards clumsily, getting only his front legs on.

'Watch your back, Clifford,' Eleanor said as he helped the dog's scrabbling hind legs up to join the rest of his body. He pulled off one of his white gloves and ran his hand under Gladstone's chin.

'There, back where you used to sit.' He gestured to one of the other two armchairs and she joined him and Gladstone.

He poured them both a sherry. Eleanor took a sip and relaxed. 'That is divine. What's not to love about the richest fruits, aged for years in seasoned barrels? Fabulous cheese and savoury biscuit selection, too.' She put down her glass. 'Perhaps we should pretend we didn't know Uncle Byron personally? Might make it a tad easier. Mind you' – she fiddled with the buttons on her cardigan – 'I didn't know him as you did.'

Clifford nodded. 'You have a great many unanswered questions about his lordship. Perhaps now is the time for me to answer some of them.'

She smiled. 'Without being too indiscreet, of course. I greatly appreciate your loyalty to him. And to save telling me again, I'll summarise what you've already told me.' She furrowed her brow. 'Let's see. To start, you and he were in the army together. You were his batman, and you were stationed in India a lot of the time. He was sympathetic to Indian self-rule, which must have been a tad awkward. Oh, and you told me of many of the wonderful things he did for the people in the area.' She frowned, trying to remember what else Clifford had told her. 'Oh, yes, he really was quite the inventor, and eccentric! He was a great fan of western movies, and as a result he insisted you call him Tex when it was just the two of you. I still haven't found out his nickname for you, but don't fret, that isn't one of my questions today.'

'Nor for tomorrow, I hope.'

She shook her head. 'But I'll pop it in my diary for a future date. Hang on, though, I also remember you telling me he was a fan of Charlie Chaplin.'

'Indeed. His lordship and I were fortunate enough to meet Mr Chaplin. Once in America and once here in England. Anyway, I digress. I believe I also explained why, when your parents disappeared, his lordship did not arrange for you to live at the Hall but rather chose to send you to boarding school?' He sighed. 'Now I confess, I have only told you part of his reasons, for which, my lady, I sincerely apologise.'

'Not necessary. I know you would have had good justification for doing so. Go on.'

'His lordship's work, and his private activities too, regrettably made him a fair number of enemies. Too many for him to feel it was safe to have a young girl at the Hall for anything other than short periods of time.'

'He really did look after me, even if from a distance. I realise that now. I still have no idea what his work actually was though.'

Clifford ran his finger along his collar. 'In April 1919, after the terrible events in Amritsar, your lordship resigned his commission in the army. With a heavy heart I might add. But he could no longer go against his increasing sympathy for Indian self-rule. He was far too principled a gentleman for that.'

'I remember reading about that horrible Amritsar business in South Africa. What did he do then?'

'He continued to speak out on the subject in public. Inevitably, his stance made him unpopular with some powerful people in the Government.'

'Ah!' She nodded slowly. 'And then?'

'As the question of Indian self-rule became more heated with the actions of Mr Gandhi, his lordship's views were seen in influential quarters as anything from an embarrassment to a threat.'

'And you think the powers that be decided to… silence that threat?'

'It is one possibility, my lady. But there is another…'

CHAPTER 29

Clifford refilled their sherry and waited until Eleanor had finished her biscuit and cheese.

'My lady, you have yourself borne witness to the unusual people his lordship sometimes associated with.'

'Like that giant chap we recently had locked up in the cellar for a short while? Hands like ham and an incredible appetite for Mrs Trotman's cooking. Oh, what was his name?'

'Ambrose Cooper.'

'That's the fellow.'

'Indeed, people like Mr Cooper. His lordship developed something of a reputation amongst the less law-abiding classes for helping the innocent victims they preyed on when the police were unable, or unwilling, to intervene. And this sometimes included minor felons who had tried to make it onto the straight and narrow, but were forced back into crime.'

'Like Ambrose Cooper.'

'Exactly, my lady.'

'So Uncle Byron helped victims of, what… criminal gangs?'

Clifford nodded.

She nodded back. 'Okay, criminal gangs. And he also helped minor gang members escape the influence of these gangs and helped them tread the virtuous path once again?'

'Exactly. And those he helped would gratefully return the favour when he needed to assist other victims. There are many such gangs in this part of the country. One reason is the large amount of smuggling. Contraband goods are brought up from the Thames Estuary and distributed by these criminal organisations throughout the area.'

'Right. So Uncle Byron made a whole raft of enemies among the powerful and the bad. We've got that far.'

He nodded. 'Which is the other possibility. That one of these criminal gangs killed his lordship.' He paused and frowned. 'However, I still do not believe that either of these groups could have caused his lordship's death. I and the ladies were always alert for unknown callers at the Hall and Silas religiously patrolled the grounds, as he does now.'

Eleanor raised her glass and eyebrows. 'And yet someone was able to get into one of the garages a while back and tamper with the Rolls?'

'That is true, although that is not the same as entering the main house and tampering with his lordship's heart pills.'

'Which he kept in his bedside drawer, I imagine?'

'No, my lady. Inside a brass globe he used as a bookend, to fortify his daily resolve to always be healthy enough to travel.'

'So even if someone had managed to break in, which I trust your view of that being highly unlikely, they would never have known to look in there for his tablets.'

'Indeed not.'

'But surely that means…'

She looked up at him and he nodded slowly.

'That the person who murdered his lordship was known to him.'

'And…' She hesitated to say what was in her mind.

Clifford cleared his throat. 'And had a knowledge of not only where his lordship's bedroom was but also probably where he kept his heart pills.'

She swallowed hard. 'Which was only the ladies, Joseph, Silas and…'

'And myself.' She silently thanked him for saving her from saying it. 'But you know already that I was most thoroughly investigated.'

She blushed. 'And by myself too. Sorry about that. So moving on, you and I both know categorically that it wasn't you or any other member of the staff.'

'I would insist on going to the hangman myself if the judge's gavel pronounced one of the other staff guilty. It is an impossible consideration that they would have hurt his lordship.'

'So how do we proceed from here? We both still believe Uncle Byron's and Canning's deaths are too similar to be coincidental, yes?'

'Absolutely. And both took place at Henley Hall. And all of our suspects are visitors, regular or otherwise to the Hall.'

'Really?' She flipped back to the list on the first page of her notebook. 'Canning, well he's not a suspect for his own murder obviously.'

'No, but when his lordship was alive, he called regularly and, as you are aware, still did up to the time of his death. Even in the summer months, the kitchen range and the hot water system use a great deal of fuel.'

'But he wouldn't have come in, would he?'

'True. But it is possible Mr Canning had an accomplice.'

Eleanor tried to digest all of this. 'But how would Canning have known where Uncle Byron kept his heart tablets?'

'He would not, my lady, but it might not be hard to learn the information from someone who did know, either deliberately or in a chance conversation.'

'True. Who else came to the Hall?'

'Doctor Browning.'

'He was Uncle Byron's doctor? Of course, he must have been. I never thought about it before.'

'The doctor attended his lordship in bed on a few occasions due to a significant illness.' He paled. 'And on one of those, I distinctly remember him asking me to pass his lordship's tablets to him.'

'Which you would have done, after opening their hiding place up first.'

'But the globe was not a hiding place. It was just a quirk of his lordship's.' He stared down at his hands.

'Clifford, it's alright. Even if we find out it was the doctor, it couldn't possibly have been your fault. He could easily have given Uncle Byron an extra strong dose by sending you off for a glass of water and taking one from his pocket.'

He nodded. 'Of course. Also Reverend Gaskell and Mrs Fontaine were frequent visitors. The vicar more so in terms of meeting with his lordship. Mrs Fontaine would of course meet with the ladies in the kitchen.'

'What would the reverend be doing in uncle's bedroom though?'

'Several things. He would always call and share a toddy when his lordship was unwell. And more recently, they realised they shared a great passion for Dostoevsky.'

'And they would go and peruse Uncle Byron's shelves in his bedroom.'

'Indeed. Of course, the library held most of his books, but some of his favourite authors he'd keep in his bedroom.'

She scratched her nose thoughtfully. 'That just leaves the Moores. I know Miss Moore did all the floral displays for Uncle Byron. Would she have wandered around placing them as I asked her to do for the Christmas Eve lunch?'

'Indeed, she did. Even those upstairs, although they were only ordered when married guests were staying, of course.'

'Of course.' Eleanor nodded, having no idea why that should be, but deciding it wasn't important at the moment. 'So there's a chance she saw something. The globe not put back together properly, or she might have overheard one of the ladies talking about it?' She frowned. 'But Alvan doesn't call at the Hall.'

'Not any more, my lady. Not since you took over.'

'Because?'

'Because despite a great many similarities with his lordship, you do not share his love of gentleman's relish and pickled herring.'

'Ugh! I certainly don't.' She rubbed her chin. 'So, even though our suspects had the opportunity, some much greater than others granted, what possible motive could any of them have had for killing Uncle Byron?'

Clifford sighed. 'I am quite unable to imagine a motive at this juncture for any of our suspects.'

She accepted the top up of sherry he offered. 'You know, with the reverend and Mrs Fontaine also falling victim to the poisoner, Doctor Browning is a strong contender for the position of Poisoner General. Even if we haven't uncovered a motive for him killing Uncle Byron yet, he's still the number one suspect in my mind.' She frowned. 'But it's hard to imagine our serial poisoner being a doctor.'

'Unfortunately, my lady, it is not as unusual as one might imagine. Doctor Thomas Cream, the infamous Lambeth Poisoner, for instance, shows that those who have power to yield life and death, sometimes yield death.'

Eleanor pictured the stooped doctor with his watery grey eyes sitting at her uncle's bedside, passing him a pill… She shivered. 'You knew Uncle Byron better than me, Clifford. Assuming none of our suspects are actually insane, there must be a reason one of them wanted him dead?'

Clifford drained his glass. A look crossed his face that she had only seen once before when he believed someone had been trifling with her heart. 'Whatever the reason, for the murderer's safety, I shall have to ask Chief Inspector Seldon to lock me up when we find out who it was.'

Eleanor frowned. 'You know, in all this… fright with the reverend and Mrs Fontaine, we've entirely forgotten about our mysterious bearded man who argued with Canning, knocked him over in the race and then—'

'Vanished?'

CHAPTER 30

Eleanor woke with a start to the jangling bell of the telephone out in the hall. With a grunt, she untangled herself from the thick woollen blanket that had magically wrapped itself around her. The soporific effect of the glowing fire and the soothing sherry had lulled her into a deep sleep. She rolled her neck in a circle and groaned.

Oh, you feel like an old woman, Ellie. And you not thirty 'til March next! She glanced at the mantel clock. Seven fifteen! *You must have been asleep for a couple of hours, Ellie.*

While she was stretching, Clifford appeared in the doorway. 'Who was it? Not the inspector again with more bad news, I hope?'

Clifford shook his head. 'No, my lady, Constable Fry.'

'Oh!' Eleanor tried to clear her foggy brain. 'Let me guess, the murderer walked into Little Buckford Police Station and gave a full confession!'

'Yes, my lady.'

Her laugh died on her lips as she looked into his eyes. 'Clifford, why if it's true, do I feel a horrible sense of dread?'

The signature blue lamp of Chipstone Police Station threw a patch of cold, stern light into the evening darkness as Clifford parked the Rolls. She was up the steps first, with Mrs Butters and Mrs Trotman rushing behind and Clifford bringing up the rear.

They burst into the reception area. Eleanor headed straight for the fresh-faced constable on the front desk.

'Oh, Constable Lowe, it's you. Where is Sergeant Brice, please? It's urgent.'

'Good evening, Lady Swift. 'Fraid I have to tell you that he's right caught up at the moment, interviewing a prisoner.'

She forced herself to remain calm. 'Tell me, Constable, how many prisoners do you have in the cells this evening?'

'Oh, just the one, m'lady. It's been a slow week what with one thing and another.' He glanced over his shoulder and lowered his voice. 'Sergeant Brice is always on about us all not doing our jobs properly, but I ask myself, why can't it just be that everyone's been behaving this week? 'Tis Christmas and all.'

'Yes, it is. Now please interrupt the sergeant. He's probably scaring the wits out of his one prisoner right at this moment.'

Lowe looked down at the desk and ran a finger over the open notebook headed Lost and Found, apparently intended to disguise a single sheet of handwritten notes underneath. 'I've been told to erm... ask you to wait patiently, m'lady.'

'Oh, please, I—'

'No matter how many times you ask, m'lady.'

'Now look here—'

'Or how many times you insist, m'lady.'

'But you don't understand—'

'Or how many good reasons you' – he peered at the sheet of paper and coloured – 'er, dream up, m'lady.'

Eleanor couldn't help but smile at the young constable's discomfort. 'So Sergeant Brice had the time and wherewithal to prepare all those scenarios ahead of my arrival, did he?'

'No, Lady Swift. I did.' DCI Seldon's deep voice reverberated down the stairwell. His smart leather shoes appeared, followed by his long, grey-suited legs, blue wool overcoat, broad shoulders and then that head of tousled chestnut curls framing his brown eyes.

'Inspector. Good evening. I didn't realise you'd arrived already.' She smiled awkwardly, wishing they didn't always have to meet on opposite sides of an argument.

'And I didn't realise you would bring a full deposition with you.' He looked past her at her three staff standing by the door.

'Perhaps not, but it seems you gave Constable Lowe a comprehensive list of instructions in my regard, nonetheless?'

'Yes. But it also seems I omitted the most obvious one.' He shot Lowe a stern look. 'Which was not to read the blasted list out!'

'Sorry, sir,' the constable said. 'Shall I, err, sort some tea for the visitors, sir?'

Eleanor held up a hand. 'Most kind, but there's no need. We should be in and out in a trice. Just came to give a quick explanation to sort out the misunderstanding, collect Polly and be off. Constable Fry told me that she ran into his house with some silly tale about poisoning Mr Canning. Apparently Sergeant Brice was there and for some unfathomable reason, arrested her and brought her here despite Constable Fry's insistence that he ring Henley Hall first.'

Seldon held her gaze. 'Constable Lowe, tea will in fact be required. A large pot, I have a feeling this is going to be a long evening.'

The young policeman bolted off.

Eleanor froze. 'Inspector, you can't possibly think… you've met Polly.' She stumbled to get her words out fast enough. 'She slopped tea all over your suit once, she's—'

'A suspect, Lady Swift. The main suspect, to be precise. And as you well know, it is a detective's job to act on facts and evidence, not conjecture or hunches.' He grunted. 'Despite what you may have read in those penny dreadful so-called police crime novels the general population seem to devour.'

She had the good grace to blush, being an avid reader of such books herself. Out of the corner of her eye, she saw Clifford lead the ladies to the four wooden chairs in a line against the far wall, which served as a waiting room.

'Inspector, I know how much you believe in police procedures, truly I do. And you're a remarkable policeman. Genuinely, that has never been in question. But this is a fifteen-year-old girl we are talking about.'

'No, Lady Swift, this is a dead man we are talking about. A man who I believe you were correct in thinking was murdered by the way.' She noted he didn't blush as she had. 'And now two more possible cases of deliberate poisoning.'

She sighed. 'May I at least see Polly? I can't imagine how terrified she is.'

The interview room was harshly lit by a single bare bulb that made her blink on entering. Brice lurked in one corner, while Seldon stood behind a worn wooden table. On the other side sat her lady's maid on a hard, wooden chair.

'Polly!' Eleanor instinctively rushed forward. But Brice blocked her path. The young girl looked up at Eleanor with red-rimmed eyes and muttered. 'So sorry, your ladyship.'

Seldon gave Eleanor a pointed stare and held his finger to his lips. He cleared his throat. 'Miss Patton, you have been read your rights, which I hope you understand. You are in a grave situation but you have the right, and the opportunity now, to tell us the full truth.'

It was obvious to Eleanor that despite his obsession with protocol, the inspector was making an effort to speak gently to ease her distress.

Polly let out a quiet sob. 'I am telling the truth, sir, I promise. I k-k-killed him.' She dissolved into hysterical sobs that had the two policemen staring at each other helplessly. Seldon ran his hand round the back of his neck and nodded to Eleanor who ran round to comfort the girl.

Seldon poured a glass of water that he held out to Eleanor to give to Polly. Once the young girl had taken a few hesitant sips, he tried again. 'Miss Patton, did you mean to kill Mr Canning?'

The girl's eyes were saucer-wide as a fresh barrel of tears fell from them. 'Oh no, sir! Never, sir!'

Seldon rubbed his temples. 'Miss Patton, please explain in a few sentences what you think happened that resulted in Mr Canning now being dead.'

This seemed to be too many words for Polly to process. Seldon sighed and gestured to Eleanor to translate with a helpless wave of his hand.

'Polly?' Eleanor held the girl gently by the shoulders. 'Why is Mr Canning dead, do you think?'

'Because… because I poisoned him with the washing-up water, your ladyship. I got it wrong like I always do.' She swallowed hard. 'Mrs Trotman said to change it just afore I couldn't see the bottom of the bowl 'cos it were all dirty, but I got all caught up and forgot. And now it's too late because I poisoned him with dirty water. I-I killed him, your ladyship.'

Eleanor sighed with relief. So that was it! 'No, you didn't Polly. You didn't kill Mr Canning.'

Polly shook her head, tears running down her cheeks. 'But I heard you. On the telephone, your ladyship. I wasn't earwigging, I promise, but you said it so loud. That… that the police had found poison in the washing-up water. And I'm the only one who ever does the washing-up. 'Tis my job, so it had to be my fault.'

'Oh, Polly!' Eleanor looked up at Seldon, who stood, eyes closed, pinching the bridge of his nose.

He opened his eyes and glared at Brice. 'Release the priso—release Miss Patton. And don't go anywhere, Brice. I'll want a word with you later.' He strode from the room.

Eleanor hugged Polly as they followed him out, Brice standing to one side looking as if his mind was uncomfortably preoccupied with his upcoming meeting with his boss.

In the reception room Eleanor gave Polly up to Mrs Butters' and Mrs Trotman's hugs. She turned to find Seldon.

'Inspector, I'm so grateful.'

He held up a hand and cleared his throat. 'Lady Swift, I have to ask you, who made the Christmas mead that Mr Canning drank at your lunch for the villagers?'

Eleanor stared at him in confusion.

'Lady Swift? I repeat my question.'

'I did.' Mrs Trotman stepped forward. 'I did, sir. And I served him his mead as well.'

Seldon turned to the cook. 'In that case, Mrs Trotman, I am taking you into custody on suspicion of poisoning Mr Canning.'

Eleanor gasped. 'What! You can't be serious, Inspector?'

'Lady Swift, it now seems clear that Mr Canning died from digitalis poisoning. We have found traces of digitalis in the washing-up water that was used to clean the glasses your guests drank their Christmas mead from. This suggests to me the poison was in the mead. However, none of your other guests have shown any symptoms of poisoning. Therefore the poison must have been administered to Mr Canning's glass only. And as Mrs Trotman by her own admission not only made the mead and served Mr Canning...'

He left the obvious conclusion unspoken. To her dismay, Eleanor found herself in agreement with the inspector. *Who else could have administered the poison?* She shook her head. *This is madness, Ellie! You know Mrs Trotman is innocent.*

'Inspector, there must be another explanation. Maybe… I…'

Seldon nodded to Brice to take the cook's arm and lead her away. Mrs Trotman's lips were set in a thin line and the look she gave the sergeant made him hastily decide she was perfectly capable of walking to the cells unaided.

Eleanor's mind raced as she desperately tried to find another explanation before her cook was led away. 'Maybe… maybe the digitalis was added to the washing-up water afterwards!'

Seldon grunted. 'In that case, Lady Swift, there would have been no digitalis in the Christmas mead itself and Mr Canning would not have been poisoned.'

She groaned. *Of course he wouldn't have been!* She turned to her cook who was waiting silently with a stoic expression on her face. 'Mrs Trotman, don't be concerned. I will move heaven and earth and wilfully obtuse inspectors to get you out of here, I give you my word.'

Mrs Trotman nodded. 'Thank you, my lady, but you have no need to worry about me.' She cocked an eye at Brice and Seldon and smiled grimly. 'They won't find me so easy to browbeat as young Polly, I'll warrant.'

Eleanor turned back to Seldon. 'Inspector, this is ridiculous. What possible motive would Mrs Trotman have for poisoning Mr Canning?'

'That,' Seldon said, as Brice unlocked one of the cells and ushered the cook in, 'is what we shall have to spend this evening finding out.'

CHAPTER 31

'Doctor, I can't tell you how heartened I am with your news.'

It was the following morning and with only three days to go before New Year's Eve, Eleanor had driven to the Chipstone cottage hospital straight after a hurried breakfast. She hoped to hear that the reverend and Mrs Fontaine might be back at the vicarage in time to see the new year in along, she hoped, with her cook.

'That's as may be, Lady Swift, but I still cannot stress enough though that it is early days. Either patient could regress, although I am optimistic that will not happen. Neither of them seems to have ingested as much of the poison as I'd feared at the outset.' He paused and shook his head. 'Your Inspector Seldon informed me that it now seems the reverend and his housekeeper were deliberately poisoned. A bad business.' He looked at his notes. 'Anyway, either they drank very little, or your poisoner misjudged the amount needed to kill them both.'

Eleanor winced at his words. 'Well either way, it's wonderful news.' She and the doctor were standing in the hospital's reception area. She looked him up and down. 'Have you been relieved from duty at all since we were last here?'

He smiled wanly. 'If you've been a doctor as many years as I have, it is automatic that sleep comes last, if at all.'

'Well, you have my utmost respect. I am a nightmare if I miss even a night's sleep.' She caught Clifford nodding out of the corner of her eye.

*

The men's ward was little more than a large room with three metal beds either side, each separated by two rails holding thin, white cotton partition curtains, most tied back. The floor shone to sterile perfection, the smell of iodine and coal tar hanging heavily in the air.

'Lady Swift, my dear,' came a weak voice from between the gap in two curtains.

'Reverend?' Eleanor stepped forward, nodding to the nurse to ask if it was alright for her to enter.

'Dear, dear lady. And Mr Clifford too, simply marvellous. How are you both?'

'Gracious, Reverend.' She held his hand as she perched on the counterpane of his woollen blanket and starched white sheets. She bit her lip at the sight of his ghostly thin face, his greying hair seeming so much whiter since she'd seen him last. 'It is for us to ask how you are.'

He smiled weakly. 'Eternally in the debt of yourselves and these amazing medical people. And in increasing moments of lucidity, of my old friend, Jeremiah, chapter seventeen, verse fourteen: "Heal me, O LORD, and I shall be healed; save me, and I shall be saved: for thou art my praise."'

She smiled. 'We've been so worried about you, Reverend. How do you really feel?'

'Grateful, foremost. But perhaps it would be untruthful were I to pretend that I'm not rather weak and sore from my throat to my stomach. But those most disturbing red and yellow flashes I kept seeing have subsided. If you hadn't come when you did, poor Mrs Fontaine and myself might now be with our Maker.' He chuckled weakly. 'Which is a day I will heartily relish, when the time is finally right.'

'Which it isn't for a great many years yet.'

He looked up at the ceiling. 'I trust in His plan for me, dear lady. But between you and me, I'm rather enjoying my time in our delightful little community, among St Winifred's loyal flock.'

Eleanor took a deep breath. 'Reverend, please forgive me being so direct but we need to ask you some questions.'

'Of course you do, dear lady. Perhaps I might have some of my own answered along the way.' He tried to plump the pillow behind his back but this brought on a ferocious coughing fit. Eleanor called the nurse in hurriedly, as Clifford held a cup of water to the vicar's lips.

With the patient comfortable again, the nurse pulled Eleanor to one side. 'Begging your pardon, m'lady, but it might be best if your visit is not too long. His body is working so hard to recover, he really hasn't the energy for much conversation and certainly not any shocks or bad news.'

'Of course, of course,' Eleanor said. 'We'll be quick.' She turned back to the vicar who now seemed to have recovered. 'Can you tell us what you'd been doing just before you collapsed?'

'Of course. Mrs Fontaine and I had finished our various tasks early, and she suggested we have a cup of tea as it was still a while before you were due to arrive. Mrs Fontaine and I are the same in that respect, we can both drink tea all day long. Anyway, Mrs Fontaine made it as usual and I thought it had a peculiar tang to it. She poured herself one to try. She agreed it was a little tart and said she'd pour the rest away even though she hates waste, like me.' He blinked hard. 'And the rest is as blurry as my vision seemed to go.'

Mindful of the nurse's caution not to wear out the patient, Eleanor tried to pick her words carefully. 'Reverend, are you aware that Conrad Canning had similar symptoms to yours and Mrs Fontaine's when he died?'

'Goodness, no,' he said breathlessly.

Clifford put his hand on the vicar's shoulder. 'Reverend, we know you are very tired. We have just two more questions. Do you feel strong enough? We can come back another time.'

'Mr Clifford, if you and Lady Swift think it is important enough to ask me now, the Lord will give me sufficient strength.'

Eleanor hesitated. 'It's a little hard to broach, but why didn't you tell us before that you had rowed with Mr Canning?'

'Shame, dear lady. Plain and simple. I should have found another way rather than rowing with him in public.'

'Another way to do what?'

'Make him love his son. And treat the woman who bore his child with decency.' He looked down at his hands. 'Forgiveness can be difficult, even as a vicar sometimes. I watched that lady struggle for so long. And his son always looked like the lost orphan child no one wanted.'

The vicar's words reminded her of Doctor Browning's hint that the reverend might have been the one who had been romantically involved with Miss Moore. She dismissed asking him such a loaded question when he was in a frail state. 'It's alright. We know you mean Miss Moore and Alvan. But you've borne that secret for a great many years. That in itself must have been hard.'

He nodded. 'I failed because I tried to change their fate but that was not mine to change. It was Mr Canning's. His choice.'

'One last question, can you remember what it was you handed Mr Canning just before the race started?'

'A peace offering.'

Eleanor looked confused.

'My dear lady, please do not think badly of me, but I found a bag left in the changing rooms. I peeked inside to see who's it might be. There was a wrapped portion of Mrs Trotman's superb yule log and a few clothes. It could have been anybody's. But then when I looked at it again, I realised it was an old sailor's shore bag. I'd seen Mr Canning with a similar bag earlier. I toyed with the idea of leaving it somewhere and not caring if he got it back.' He hung his head. 'I'm not proud to say those words, I can tell you.'

'But you did give it back to him. Two different people saw you.'

'Then they probably saw me add to my shame and engage in fierce words with him. My peace offering was met with some invective, which shouldn't have caught me by surprise, but it did. Only minutes later he was up to it again with Mr Wraith as they took their places on the start line. I always had a romantic notion that comrades at sea had each other's backs, not throats. But perhaps it was different when they were both on dry land.'

'Mr Wraith?'

'Hubert Wraith. Enormous man with an enormous beard. Tattoos, similar to Mr Canning's. It seems you can't be a sailor without at least one. A resident of Chipstone. I know him a little from the tavern on Pinkers Row. Mrs Fontaine enjoys the market day pies they serve. It has become something of a regular tradition if the weather is nice enough for her to sit outside, away from too much inappropriate male chatter, of course.'

'Did you hear what Mr Canning and Mr Wraith were rowing about?'

'Not a word, I'm afraid.'

'Thank you, Reverend.' Eleanor offered him another sip of water. 'We greatly appreciate your honesty and your stamina in answering more questions than we promised we'd ask. Now, you need to rest so we can all welcome you back home sooner rather than later. I shall call in on Mrs Fontaine before we leave. But can we drop anything round for you or perhaps contact any family?'

'No, thank you. Mine are all long gone and happily residing in Heaven. And Mrs Fontaine's, well, it's best you don't ask her. She puts on a brave face but I know it is very hard on her. Such a good

Samaritan, she goes to visit her family every Wednesday despite their less than Christian behaviour towards her. Such a shame.'

After leaving Clifford to wait in the Rolls, a nurse ushered Eleanor into the women's ward and to Mrs Fontaine's bed. She looked frail. But certainly better than the vicar.

'I am a lucky woman,' the vicar's housekeeper said to Eleanor after they'd exchanged greetings. 'Very lucky. But tell me, please, how is the reverend? They will not let me see him and I have been so worried.' Her hand trembled as she held it out to Eleanor.

'He is doing well enough. He chatted with Clifford and myself and asked me not to tire you out.'

To her dismay, Mrs Fontaine's eyes filled with tears. 'Oh dear, he is fine, vraiment?'

Eleanor nodded. 'Really. Wearing yourself out worrying about him won't help you. Or him.'

'This I know, but how can I help but to worry about the man who has always been nothing but kind to me? Lady Swift, you don't know my story but he helped me when I imagined myself lost. Mais, excusez-moi! I have not thanked you. And Mr Clifford too. It might have been a very different story but for your actions, non?'

'We were just happy to have been in the right place at the right time.' Eleanor hesitated. 'I… I just need to ask you a couple of questions, Mrs Fontaine. The reverend said you both thought the tea tasted peculiar and, well, he doesn't remember too much after that.'

Mrs Fontaine nodded. 'I never say, but he make this comment many times since the war. He is right, nothing is the same now. The food or the drink is not the same quality as before the rationing.'

'So you didn't think there was anything wrong with it?'

'Not especially. It was a little, how you say, sour? Bitter? But I was going out to make the fresh pot because the reverend was expecting you. Lady Swift, I don't know what happened but I remember dropping the tray. Then I wake up in here.'

'Mrs Fontaine, what did the doctor tell you made you ill?'

The woman's eyes widened. 'He said we had drunk something, something poisonous. But how can this be so?'

Eleanor rose. 'I should leave. I don't want to tire you out. Can you just tell me if you noticed anyone unusual around the vicarage any time lately? A different visitor perhaps? A new tradesman?'

Mrs Fontaine shook her head slowly. 'Lady Swift, Reverend Gaskell is a vicar who takes the duties very seriously. The house, it was always open to whoever had reason to see him.'

Or who had reason to poison him, Ellie.

CHAPTER 32

In a short, unmade-up road of tumbledown cottages, Eleanor counted again.

'Dash it! It's no good. No matter how hard I try to find it, there is no number thirteen. Look, there are only twelve houses here. Six on this side and six on that.' She sighed in exasperation. 'This is a wild goose chase. We left the hospital an hour ago. We should be at the police station right this minute, forcing them to release Mrs Trotman. They've no evidence at all. It's all circumstantial.'

Clifford nodded. 'I agree, my lady. They will have to release Mrs Trotman soon unless they can find more evidence. Or a strong motive for Mrs Trotman killing Mr Canning. And as neither of those two events are likely to occur, th—'

'Wrong, Clifford!'

He stopped and looked at her in obvious surprise. 'I beg your pardon, my lady?'

'Think about it, Clifford. The killer is not only smart but ruthless, as shown by him attempting to kill again. Now, we both know Mrs Trotman is as innocent of Canning's murder as you or I. Agreed?'

'Agreed, my lady.'

'So I don't understand how he did it, but the killer has framed Mrs Trotman for Canning's murder. Somehow, he made sure the poison was in Canning's mead only, knowing that she would serve it to him. The only explanation I can come up with is that the killer planned to use Mrs Trotman as the fall guy, or gal in this case, from the very beginning.'

Clifford nodded again slowly, understanding dawning in his eyes. 'And you think that as the killer has proven himself to be so meticulous—'

'And ruthless.'

'That he may very well have arranged more false evidence of Mrs Trotman's guilt which the police have yet to uncover?'

She nodded grimly. 'And if I am right, it will only be a matter of time before they do. The only other scenario I can envisage is that the killer will wait to see if the false evidence he's already planted is sufficient to damn Mrs Trotman or not.'

'And if not and she is released?'

'Then he'll act.'

'Then, my lady, I believe, wild goose chase or not, we should proceed with our present course of action. It is the best lead we have at the moment. And as to there being no number thirteen…' He pointed to a ramshackle brick lean-to attached to number twelve. 'Perhaps our error is in expecting number thirteen to be a house like the others?'

'Well done.' Eleanor examined the dilapidated structure. 'Gracious, that does seem rather cramped for the giant of a man I remember Wraith to be. I shall devote a full hour to counting all my blessings tonight, Clifford.'

'As should the gentleman we have come to see. Many returning soldiers or sailors were less fortunate after the war than those who found a dwelling that offers at least a modicum of protection from the elements.'

She stamped her feet and looked up at the snow that had started falling again in earnest. 'Well, at least it must be a sight warmer inside.'

'What do you want?' Hubert Wraith scowled between his dark mop of hair and bushy beard, both equally unkempt.

Eleanor smiled sweetly. 'Good day to you too, Mr Wraith.'

'I'm busy.'

Clifford stepped forward. 'As are we, Mr Wraith, so we will be quick.'

Wraith eyed them suspiciously. 'About what? 'Cos if something went missing at the lunch you put on, it's a damn cheek coming round here accusing me.'

Clifford held up a warning finger at the man's choice of language.

Eleanor decided it was time for the direct approach. 'We're not accusing you of anything, Mr Wraith. We just want some information. About Mr Canning.'

Wraith's eyes darkened. 'Now, why would I want to talk about that blackguard? He was no friend of mine.'

'We know. That's why we're here.'

Wraith stared at her in surprise and then shrugged. 'Better come in than you standing there, letting out the last of my heat.'

Eleanor stepped over the rolled-up blanket that served as a draught excluder and into the room. Where the last of Wraith's heat was hiding, she had no idea, because she had been wrong – it was marginally warmer outside than in.

She tried not to stare at the threadbare armchair facing a barely flickering fire. The only other furniture was a worn wooden table and a tatty chair butted up against a cracked sink. At the far end, an iron bed frame poked out behind a short wall, which she dreaded might also house the bathroom, if there was one. Of Christmas cheer, or the upcoming New Year's Eve, there was not a trace.

'Ever been down on your luck, Lady Swift?' Wraith said caustically, watching her look around.

'I have actually.' She held his stare. 'Ever been halfway over a mountain range with the snow and night closing in, with no prospect of food or shelter and not another human being within a hundred square miles?'

Wraith frowned but then let out a raucous laugh. 'No, but I've experienced much the same on the seas. You're a strange kind of lady, I must say.'

She waved a hand. 'Say away.'

Aware that Clifford was standing defensively close to her, she smiled to let him know she felt safe enough. He took a small step back.

'Mr Wraith, I heard that you and Mr Canning were at sea together.'

'That was years back. I haven't seen a lot of him since. Not that he's changed at all. Once a rogue and a cheat, always one, I say.'

'Did he cheat a lot then? Cards was it? Mind, I never thought you'd have many hours to play cards while away sailing the oceans. Ships are awfully complicated things, aren't they?'

'Not when they're in your blood, they're not. Once you have been aboard a number of years, you still feel the motion of the waves even back on dry land.'

Eleanor pointed to the one decoration in the place, a newspaper cutting with a half page photograph of a three-masted clipper. 'Do you miss the sea, Mr Wraith?'

'Sometimes. Don't miss the storms, the maggots in the meat, nor the infected fingers least once a month.' He turned his hands over to reveal a host of white-scarred lesions. 'But that first breath of sea air in the early morning when I'm down the coast, that 'tis almost enough to make me go back.'

'From the years I sailed abroad with my parents as a child, I've also experienced that early morning salty fug that pulls you outside still in your pyjamas.' She looked wistful. 'It's quite magical.'

Wraith nodded, his clenched jaw relaxing. He leaned against the wall with his hands in his pockets.

Not wanting to lose the short amount of ground she'd made, Eleanor tried to choose her words carefully. 'You must have seen some amazing sights. And had some incredible adventures.'

'Some good memories, alright.'

'But sadly, none of Mr Canning?'

'Not one.' He scowled. 'I should have known better after that last voyage we was on together.'

'Perhaps that's what you were arguing about at the Christmas Eve luncheon, Mr Wraith?' Clifford said.

'Wild horses, Mr Clifford,' Hubert said darkly, 'even they couldn't drag it out of me. 'Twas between him and me. Nobody's business that, not even the lady's here.'

This is going nowhere, Ellie! We don't have time for this.

'Mr Wraith, were you by any chance arguing with Mr Canning over the small fortune you believe he swindled you out of when you were partners in smuggling?'

It was a complete shot in the dark, but the look on Wraith's face told her she had scored an unexpected bullseye. Clifford appeared unmoved, but she could see in his eyes he was impressed. He cleared his throat.

'It seems, Mr Wraith, that we don't need wild horses to drag the truth out of you. Your face betrays you well enough.'

For a moment, Eleanor thought Wraith would attack her. She wished she'd brought her umbrella. She'd learned the rudiments of Bartitsu, a form of self-defence practised by Sherlock Holmes, among others. It was amazing how effective a tightly rolled-up umbrella was against a surprised opponent. Clifford had also stepped forward to be at her side.

Wraith's expression, however, changed from one of fury, to one of defeated amusement. He shook his head and shrugged. 'It seems you've got it all worked out.' His eyes flicked back and forth between Clifford and Eleanor. 'What I can't work out is, if you're so clued up on my past dealings with that rogue Canning, what you want? Although I'm not saying it's true,' he added hurriedly. 'I ain't admitting nothing.'

She regarded him for a moment without speaking. *Let him sweat a minute, Ellie.* 'What we want, Mr Wraith, is to find out who killed Mr Canning.'

He leaned back on the wall and laughed. 'And why would a lady like yourself be interested in that?'

She thought of telling him about their suspicions concerning the connection with her uncle's death. But one glance at Clifford, who was shaking his head almost imperceptibly, showed her he'd guessed her thoughts and heartily disapproved.

She smiled thinly. 'You didn't seem very surprised that he had been murdered?'

He shrugged. 'News is all over town. Anyway, he was such a double-crossing cur, it was only a matter of time before someone took the law into their own hands.'

'And was that someone you?'

He heaved himself off the wall again and loomed over her. Clifford went to step between them, but Eleanor waved him back.

'I asked, Mr Wraith, if you killed Mr Canning?' She held his gaze.

For a moment he said nothing. Then he folded his arms.

'Is there something else you wanted? Otherwise, you best be going.'

'One last question. You wouldn't know what the small key Mr Canning always carried with him was for, would you?'

Wraith's jaw clenched. 'Nope.' She could see the struggle in his eyes as he tried to feign disinterest. He failed. 'What… what sort of lock is it for?'

'Well, that's what we were hoping you might tell us. But no matter.' She turned to go.

He blocked the doorway, moving with unexpected speed for one so huge. Eleanor saw Clifford's hand go to his pocket. *Has he come armed?*

'I'll take a look at that key, if you don't mind?' He held out a meaty palm.

She patted her pockets. 'Silly me, I seem to have forgotten to bring it with me.'

CHAPTER 33

Eleanor pulled her wool hat further down over her ears and pushed her hands into her coat pockets, wishing they had brought her uncle's hand warmers. They were walking back to the Rolls, Clifford having insisted it was left in a more salubrious part of Chipstone. Like Wraith's, few houses here showed much sign of Christmas cheer, the odd window sporting a festive display that looked as if it had been made in the reign of Queen Victoria. The pavements were lethal, ice-covered skating rinks. She checked behind her to make sure Wraith wasn't following them. He wasn't.

She turned to Clifford.

'And I thought Canning was difficult!'

Clifford waited until she had safely navigated a frozen puddle the width of the road before replying.

'Perhaps Mr Wraith's brusqueness was partly due to him feeling defensive?'

'Really? He's twice my height and three times as wide.'

'And a hundred times poorer.'

'Ah, yes. Good point. Poor chap is only just scraping along, isn't he? That can't be at all easy.' For the second time that day, she stared at the snowy sky and sent her uncle a heartfelt thank you for ensuring she would never want again. She resolved to continue finding ways to help those less fortunate than her as soon as they'd caught the murderer.

Clifford cut into her thoughts. 'However, my lady, there was obviously bad blood between him and Mr Canning.'

'Which he freely admitted to. Odd, if he is the murderer, wouldn't you say?'

'Usually, yes, but in a small community like this, it is hard to hide a long-standing grudge.'

'True, although the reverend managed it, didn't he?'

'Indeed, until the start of the race, that is.'

She nodded. 'I suppose the reverend pointing a pistol at Canning at the start line rather gave the game away?'

'Without a doubt, my lady.' He paused. 'If I might, however, leave the matter in hand and congratulate you on your masterful guess concerning the argument Wraith and Mr Canning had at the Hall. And the dangling of the proverbial carrot of the key.'

'I know. He couldn't help himself, could he? He desperately wants that key. Maybe the chest in Canning's cellar is indeed a treasure chest which Wraith is convinced he was due half, or all of?'

'That would certainly be sufficient to cause bad blood. And we now know for sure he was a partner in Mr Canning's smuggling.'

'But again, I don't mean to highlight Wraith's size, but he could have flattened Canning with a single slap of one of those hefty bear paws of his. Why wouldn't he have just extracted his share with physical menaces?'

'In my experience, guile almost always defeats brawn. Mr Canning appears to have been particularly shrewd and I would say he passed a good deal of that onto his son, Mr Moore.'

Eleanor pulled up short. 'Wait though, Canning has left everything to Miss Moore and Alvan. The solicitor called it "a tidy sum".' She frowned. 'It does paint a peculiar image.'

Clifford frowned in return. 'Might I ask what is peculiar about that image?'

'Oh you know, it suggests perfectly ordered piles of money, each wrapped with paper bands exactly aligned and with the picture and the banker's signature all the same way round.'

'What other way is there to store money, my lady?' Clifford's question was tinged with horror.

'Oops, never mind. What I meant was that if Canning's chest is full of money, the solicitor wouldn't know how much is in it because we have the key. The "tidy sum" he referred to obviously can't be inside the chest we found.'

'Bravo, my lady! So is that "tidy sum" the Moores have inherited the money Mr Wraith believes is owed to him? Or did Mr Canning amass a second fortune through his nefarious activities?'

'And is that second fortune hidden in the chest our key unlocks, I wonder?'

'Unless...' Clifford stopped and turned to her. 'Mr Wraith is after the contents because they would be most damaging to him.'

She frowned. 'You think maybe Wraith wants to get hold of the key to destroy the contents? Seems unlikely. What on earth could be in there that would embarrass a man like him? And I don't mean that unfairly. I just mean he doesn't look like the sort of person who gives a fig what people say. Or think.'

'Perhaps, my lady, the contents might send him to prison. Or to the gallows?'

She gasped. 'Do you think it might be evidence of his career as a serial poisoner? Perhaps even evidence showing he was responsible... for Uncle Byron's death?'

They were so deep in conversation they almost missed Sergeant Brice waving to them on the top step of the police station as they drew level.

'Lady Swift, Mr Clifford? A moment of your time, please!'

As Brice ushered them into a room that seemed to be a cross between a makeshift office and a chair store, Eleanor noticed a young auburn-haired woman. Standing in the reception area in a plain navy dress, she was staring at Clifford intently. Once in the room, she dismissed the woman from her mind.

'Whatever is it, Sergeant?'

'First things first, Lady Swift, if I might, please, since this is now a murder investigation and' – he puffed his chest out – 'Chief Inspector Seldon has put me in charge.' He cleared his throat. 'Partly on account of his being called away, granted, but nevertheless, I am in charge and as such, I shall be expecting your full cooperation.'

'Why would you expect anything less, Sergeant?'

'Because, well, because you have gotten involved in these things afore, Lady Swift, and it hasn't always gone that smoothly from where us police have been standing.'

She hid a smile. 'Well, rest assured, you have my full support. I am quite sure you are the man for the job. So, why did you call us in?'

The policeman's face switched from proud to stern, a look that he needed to practise more, she felt. 'The samples. From the vicarage.'

'Yes?'

'The expert, er, johnnies in Oxford found,' he said, surreptitiously reading from a scribbled note on the desk, '"dried foxglove leaves and berries in the tea and residue on the sides of the caddy."'

Eleanor stared at Clifford. 'Bullseye,' she muttered. 'Sorry, Sergeant, what did you say?'

'Not what, Lady Swift, who. Your Mrs Trotman. She's obviously been up to her tricks again. Chief Inspect—'

Eleanor snorted. She was normally a kindly person but not when someone came after her staff. 'Mrs Trotman? Sergeant, you and the inspector have failed to find a shred of evidence she was the poisoner. And do you know why?' She stepped closer, Brice shrinking back against the desk. 'Because there isn't any! Good day.'

As Clifford started the Rolls, Eleanor's anger erupted. 'Clifford, this is intolerable! If they hadn't moved Mrs Trotman to Oxford, I'd have knocked Brice out and let her out myself! I could scream.'

'I agree, my lady.' He swung the Rolls in a wide arc and headed off in the opposite direction from Henley Hall.

'Clifford? We haven't got time to be—'

'Forgive my contradiction.' He turned right. 'But we absolutely need to. Ah, there she is.'

He drew alongside a narrow alleyway where the woman Eleanor had seen in the navy dress in the police station's reception was waiting for them.

'Jump in,' Clifford said in a low voice.

Breathless and clearly nervous, the woman slid into the back of the car.

Clifford nodded to her and turned back to Eleanor. 'My lady, this is Miss Abigail, Mr Sandford's niece.'

Eleanor's eyes widened. Abigail worked at Chipstone Police Station and had helped Eleanor and Clifford solve several cases by passing on information to her uncle, the Langham's butler, who then passed it on to Clifford. They had, however, never met until now.

'Oh, Abigail. Lovely to meet you finally and thank you for your help in the, err, previous matters.'

'My pleasure, Lady Swift. Please forgive me for risking us being seen together, but it's urgent.'

She caught up. 'Ah! You were signalling to Clifford in the police station.' She stopped, registering the woman's words. 'What is so urgent?'

The young woman glanced furtively out of the back of the car. 'They're coming, m'lady!'

CHAPTER 34

Clifford half-turned to reply and then spun back round as the Rolls slid sideways. He calmly corrected the slide and cleared his throat. 'I'm sorry, my lady, but if we are to arrive at all, I dare not proceed any faster. There are patches of black ice and the road surface is like a skating rink. The Rolls is a fine vehicle, but even it is at the mercy of its tyres. And I do believe they are at the limit of their grip. If not beyond.' The car slid sideways again, emphasising his point.

This time his efforts to correct the skid failed, and they were gently stopped by a hedge.

Eleanor groaned. They had hastily thanked Abigail and dropped her at the next corner. From there they'd made good progress until they reached the end of Chipstone High Street. From that point on, the driving conditions had deteriorated rapidly. Now, half an hour later, they were less than halfway back to the Hall and it seemed – she poked her head out of the window – stuck in a ditch. She pulled out her watch. Two-ten. It would be dark in less than two hours. She glanced at the swirling, grey sky. *More like an hour, Ellie.*

If they weren't in such a hurry, she'd have marvelled at the beauty of the winter wonderland around her. The sky had merged with the land, making it seem as if the snowflakes were materialising out of nowhere above her, before they vanished into the white carpet at her feet. In the distance clumps of beech trees sprouted from pristine fields of white, their snow-capped tops fading into the smudged grey-white sky.

After fifteen minutes, using a snow shovel and two metal rails Clifford had had the foresight to place in the boot when the bad weather had first arrived, they were on their way again. Eleanor constantly turned and searched the road behind them expecting any minute to see a police car bearing down on them, Seldon furiously waving a search warrant out of the window.

She ran over what Abigail had told her. She'd overheard Brice on the phone with Seldon and had caught the words 'search warrant' and 'Henley Hall'. Having been snubbed by Seldon, Eleanor figured Brice had only called them in as they passed to show that he was still theoretically in charge of the case. Whatever the reason, it had given Abigail the chance to alert them to Seldon's impending arrival at Henley Hall.

The car performed a series of snake-like manoeuvres and somehow Clifford avoided another altercation with a ditch. He glanced at her. 'Take heart, my lady. Chief Inspector Seldon obviously does not trust Sergeant Brice to carry out the search. Therefore, he must be coming from Oxford with his men. It is very possible he may, himself, be in a ditch at this very moment.'

Eleanor laughed grimly. 'Well, let's hope it's a deep one.'

Having abandoned the car halfway down Henley Hall's drive, Clifford and Eleanor struggled through the rapidly accumulating snow.

Finally reaching the entrance, they stumbled into the hallway. 'Mrs Butters! Polly!'

Silence.

'If I might suggest, my lady?' Clifford marched back to the top step and pulled on the doorbell repeatedly.

'Goodness gracious,' Mrs Butters' voice floated down from upstairs. 'No patience, some people.' She appeared behind the bannisters, balancing a pile of neatly folded sheets across her arms. 'Oh, my lady, 'tis you!'

'Mrs Butters, quick, please. Just drop the sheets, get the others and meet us in the kitchen. Immediately.'

It was a sombre crew who assembled by the range. Joseph, having dashed in from the vegetable greenhouse was breathing heavily, while Mrs Butters' face was cherry red, having fetched Polly, who stood trembling, breathless with nerves. Meanwhile, Gladstone lay with his head hanging over the edge of his bed clearly sensing the anxiety in the room.

'Whatever has happened, my lady?' Mrs Butters asked.

'It hasn't yet, but it's about to, any minute. Inspector Seldon is on his way here.'

'And I'm guessing he's not coming for tea.'

'But that's just it, he is. Poisoned tea!'

Mrs Butters stared at Eleanor and then swivelled to Clifford for clarity.

'It appears Chief Inspector Seldon is of the notion there may be dried foxglove leaves and berries here at Henley Hall. The same as used to poison Reverend Gaskell and Mrs Fontaine.' He glanced at Eleanor. 'We believe he will find them.'

There was a collective gasp from the cook and the gardener. Polly looked at both of them in confusion.

Clifford nodded. 'We believe the false evidence has already been planted somewhere in the Hall in order to further incriminate Mrs Trotman.'

Mrs Butters opened her mouth, but Eleanor raised her hand. 'We don't know how. Or who. What we do know is we need to move fast. If they find such evidence' – she looked at Mrs Butters – 'it might not be so easy to secure Mrs Trotman's release.' *If at all, Ellie.*

She clapped her hands. 'Now, we assume the poisoner wants the police to find the evidence somewhere that makes it seem likely

Mrs Trotman hid it there. So start in the kitchen, the pantry, places like that. And, of course, Mrs Trotman's bedroom.' She smiled apologetically at her housekeeper.

Mrs Butters shook her head. 'Begging your pardon, my lady, but I don't see how anyone could have—'

Eleanor took the housekeeper by her shoulders. 'Neither do I. But neither can I work out how Canning was poisoned by drinking Christmas mead that Mrs Trotman made and served him, and yet I know she is not the one who poisoned him.'

Mrs Butters nodded vigorously. 'Point taken, my lady. Joseph, you do the pantry and kitchen. I'll do Trotters' room and then help you. Polly, you look in every packet or in anything that has a lid like a canister, a jar, the cake tins. Anything you've ever seen Mrs Trotman pick up or use. And look really hard. Dig to the very bottom with your fingers. All the rules are out of the window, search everywhere, you got that? And you understand what you're searching for?'

'Y-es, Mrs Butters.'

The housekeeper laid a hand on the young girl. 'Listen, Polly, just show Mr Clifford or the mistress anything you find, alright? Even if you're not sure.'

Polly nodded and scurried to the Welsh dresser. She began ripping the tops off the neat line of decorative tin caddies, their lids clattering onto the wide central shelf.

'Good girl.'

Eleanor's eyes darted around. 'Where else, Clifford? The Hall is so enormous.'

'My lady, if someone has planted the poison here, then it has most likely been planted amongst the comestibles or Mrs Trotman's possessions as you said, though we cannot be sure. In the meantime, I will contact Silas and tell him to slow the police down. Although' – he looked out of the window at a wall of white – 'I wonder if the inspector and his troops will make it here at all.'

*

Spurred on by the thought of heavy police boots pounding through the back door at any moment, Eleanor flew out into the hall and down the long, oak-panelled corridor that led to the conservatory, another place that seemed likely the killer might have hidden the evidence. Her heart sank at the enormity of the task. It was used to dry and then store herbs from the garden, hence somewhere where the killer might have hidden foxgloves. She stared at the drying racks hung from the ceiling, bunches of herbs tied to each rail, and the wooden drawers lining one wall where the herbs were kept once dried.

Yanking two drawers open at a time, she cried out. 'I don't know what dried foxglove looks like!'

'Distinctively olive green,' Clifford said as he entered the conservatory by the garden door.

'Everything in here is green! That doesn't help at all.'

'My lady, think of the precise colour of your favourite twill trousers and matching cardigan.'

'Oh, that green.'

'With flecks of magenta from the flowers.'

Frantically, they searched. But to no avail. Ignoring Clifford's concerned look, Eleanor dragged the wooden stool from the corner and scrambled onto it to reach the drying racks, wobbling dangerously as she stretched forward.

Clifford stepped over. He took hold of a chain she hadn't seen and lowered the rack to elbow height.

'Ah!'

'Perhaps a broken leg won't help at this juncture, my lady?'

Ten minutes of hopeless searching later, Eleanor threw her head back and stared at the ceiling. 'Nothing!'

He looked up from the last basket and nodded. 'Equally nothing!' Grabbing the broom leaning against the workbench, he started off on a brisk turn of the floor.

'This is no time for tidying up!'

'Nor for leaving the room in the obvious state of having been searched prior to the police's arrival.'

She nodded. 'Good point. We—'

A shrill shriek split the air. *Oh no, they must be here.*

But in the corridor, instead of Seldon and his men, they were met by Polly skidding down to meet them. She trembled as she held out an intricately painted, rectangular bone-china tea caddy.

'Very sorry, Mr Clifford, but Mrs Butters did say no rules. I would never have touched it otherwise. Not seeing as I broke the last one. But this don't smell like the special guest tea does.'

He lifted the lid and shook the contents at an angle. Eleanor leaned forward and took a sniff. 'Smells just like the stuff we found in the vicarage! Polly, I do believe you have saved the day.'

Clifford bestowed a rare and precious smile on her. 'Well done, Polly.'

'Now.' Eleanor looked around her, patting Polly on the shoulder as she did so. 'Where the devil can we hide it?'

CHAPTER 35

'It's like the great baker in the sky has taken a sheet of white marzipan, my lady, and carefully laid it out over the countryside.'

Eleanor and her housekeeper were on the lookout for any signs of the police arriving. The light was fading fast, however, and all they could see out of the window was snow, and more snow. The wind had risen further and was piling it in great drifts, the drive barely distinguishable from the formal lawns on either side in the gloom.

The telephone bell interrupted their vigil. A moment later Clifford appeared. 'Chief Inspector Seldon for you, my lady.' There was a twinkle in his eye.

'Is he stuck in a ditch by any chance?' Eleanor whispered in case her words carried out into the hall.

'I do not believe the chief inspector imparted that information. The line, I admit, is very bad. I fear the snow may soon bring down the phone cables. He did, however, sound a little... fraught.'

As she put the telephone to her ear, she made out the faint sound of singing on the other end. 'Inspector? Are you there?'

Seldon's deep voice came down the line. 'Yes. Hello? Lady Swift?'

She smiled. He didn't sound fraught to her. More furious. She couldn't help herself. 'Lovely weather we're having. How's it in Oxford?'

She was sure she heard a muffled curse. 'The weather, Lady Swift, is anything but lovely. And I am not in Oxford.' There was a pause and crackling on the line before he came back on. 'In fact, I am in a public house somewhere between Oxford and Henley Hall.'

'That's nice for you to have some time off, Inspector. Are you having a sing-song with some friends?' She was sure that was another curse, hastily covered up with a cough. 'No, Lady Swift, I am stuck in this place due to the weather. I…' Somewhere between a grunt and a sigh came down the line. She could picture him running his hand through his chestnut curls. 'Lady Swift, regrettably this is not a social call. I was on my way to Henley Hall… with a search warrant.'

Eleanor counted to three before replying. 'A search what, Inspector? The line's very bad.'

'A search warrant. For searching Henley Hall to ascertain if there are any poisonous berries, leaves or other toxic substances on the premises. However, due to the weather it seems I and my men will be spending the afternoon, if not the night, in this—'

Whatever it was was lost on Eleanor as the singing increased in volume, drowning out his words. She heard what sounded like a shouted command and a few seconds later, the singing dropped back to its previous level.

'Inspector? Are you still there?'

'Yes, unfortunately I'm still here.' There was a pause. 'Lady Swift, I have no choice but to delay the search of Henley Hall until the weather improves. I must ask you not to touch any toxic substances that you might come across in the meantime. Please leave them exactly where you find them. Is that understood?'

She crossed her fingers. 'Of course, Inspector, I wouldn't dream of it.'

'I wish I could have a little more confidence in that statement,' she heard him mutter.

It obviously hadn't been intended for her ears, but it made her bristle. She really did respect the inspector, but this was her staff – no, her family – he was trying to find evidence against, even if it was out of a sense of duty. 'And I wish I could have a little more confidence in the police recognising when someone is obviously being framed! First you arrest a fifteen-year-old girl and then a fifty-year-old cook. Who are you going to arrest next?' *Ellie, do you always have to go and start a fight?* She bit her lip.

After a brief pause and more crackling on the line, the inspector's voice came back. 'I'm sorry, Lady Swift. I am merely doing my duty. Now, if you'll excuse me, I have to help dig a couple of police cars out of the car park or I'm here for the night. And if that happens, I think there may be more murders committed if those blasted singers don't stop.'

Despite herself this made Eleanor smile. 'Inspector. Before you go, do you have a minute?' *Ellie, why did you ask him that? What are you going to say?* She didn't know. She just didn't want to end one more conversation at loggerheads with him.

'I do, Lady Swift, but I am not sure this line will stay up. I also fear I won't be able to find my car to dig it out if I delay much longer.'

His reply made her relax a little more. 'You've just apologised to me, Inspector, so I wanted to… to apologise. And to thank you.'

He grunted.

She took that as her cue to continue. 'First, I wanted to thank you for releasing Polly. And I understand you were only doing your job in detaining Mrs Trotman. And…' She hesitated. 'Look, I'm not very good at apologising, but I'm sorry for being a royal pain. Even though you must admit, I have been a great help in several cases in the end.' She hurried on. 'But I do realise that you find me as infuriating as I find you.' *Ellie!* She sighed. 'I'm sorry, Inspector. I'd rather hoped my apology would come out better, and more politely, than that. And, perhaps just a bit more ladylike.'

Was that a grunt or a laugh? She wasn't sure. Either way, the inspector when he spoke again sounded as if he was a trifle less furious, or fraught, than before. 'Thank you, I think that is possibly the best apology I've ever received, although you spectacularly omitted to actually say the word "sorry".'

'But I do mean it. I...' She bit her lip again. 'I don't want to fight with you every time we meet. Or talk.'

'Neither do I. I'm a policeman, I'm supposed to be the one to break up fights, not engage in them.'

'And I'm supposed to be a lady, I'm not supposed to be the one to start them, but somehow I seem to.'

She wondered if the line had finally died, but then his voice returned. 'Lady Swift, I confess I am in a quandary. In fact two.'

She laughed. 'Inspector, I hope I am not the cause of either?'

'Actually, you are.'

Her heart beat faster. She tried to sound casual. 'Well, if I am the cause, how can I help you solve them?'

'Lady Swift, officially I am telling you not to investigate this case, but these are very unusual circumstances. So, unofficially... I am asking you to.'

She gasped. 'Inspector?'

'Lady Swift, this is strictly between us, but I simply cannot let a murderer escape justice because of some damned snow! Excuse the language. On the other hand, I cannot allow you to place yourself in any danger. However, if you were to discreetly investigate, you may turn up something that, when the snow clears sufficiently, leads to the criminal's arrest. And, perhaps, to proving Mrs Trotman's innocence. I also know that Mr Clifford will be a voice of caution and reason.'

Eleanor could hardly believe the inspector's words, but she knew that he was passionate about justice and, as he said, could not countenance letting a criminal walk free.

'Alright, Inspector, just between us, I'll discreetly see what I can do. And I promise I'll take heed of Clifford's cautionary advice.'

Seldon grunted. 'I hope so, Lady Swift. I would rather all the criminals in England went free than you placed yourself in danger.' Before she could reply he cleared his throat loudly. 'But if we could have less friction between us when we meet next time that would be a splendid start. And seeing as we only seem to meet when there has been a suspicious death, you've left me in a second quandary.'

She frowned. 'Which is, Inspector?'

'That of hoping there will be more suspicious deaths in the area. Goodbye.'

The line went dead.

She put the receiver down and called out. 'Panic over! The police aren't coming!' She looked back down at the telephone and smiled.

CHAPTER 36

'So, we are cut off.'

Clifford nodded. 'Indeed, my lady. Henley Hall and the village, Silas informs me, are completely snowed in.'

It was the following morning, and with only two days before New Year's Eve, Eleanor was keenly aware that unless they had a breakthrough in the case soon, one member of Henley Hall staff would be spending it behind bars. She tried hard to concentrate.

'Golly, that's not a common occurrence, is it?'

'Not at all. It will be only the second time in all my years here.'

Mrs Butters nodded. Polly looked at her and nodded solemnly as well.

Eleanor rubbed her temples. 'Well, we can't just sit here and wait for it to clear. We've got a murderer to catch. Mrs Trotman can't celebrate the new year in jail!'

Clifford coughed. 'May I suggest, my lady, that first we move the poisonous berries and seeds to somewhere even the chief inspector, if he ever were to arrive, could not find them?'

She nodded. 'Good shout, Clifford.'

'Thank you. Did you, by any chance, hide them behind the section of wainscoting where you used to secrete your sweets stolen from the pantry during your rare childhood visits?'

'No, I didn't think of that in the rush.' She blinked. 'But how on earth did you find that out all those years ago? I thought at the time, I'd managed to keep that a secret.'

'You had, my lady, until the mouse population inexplicably exploded.' He rose. 'Where should I look for them, instead?'

'Oh, I hid them in the bottom of my underthings drawer.'

He shot back into his seat and cleared his throat. 'Then they will be safe enough, I'm sure.' He pulled on his collar.

She hid a smile. 'I didn't have time to be very creative and I figured it's better to find out now whether the inspector is the gentleman he purports to be.'

She swore she saw the corner of his lips twitch. He cleared his throat again. 'As I said, I am sure they will be fine where they are. Now, if I might return us to the case?'

She nodded and opened her notebook at her updated suspect page:

Main suspects

Dr Browning. Motive: Canning tried to get him struck off medical register believing he killed his mother.

Reverend Gaskell. Motive: Canning enraged him with his treatment of Miss Moore, one of his parishioners.

Miss Moore. Motive: Revenge for abandoning her and her son, Alvan. Also, if she knew she was a beneficiary of Canning's will then she had two motives.

Alvan Moore. Motive: Revenge for abandoning him and his mother. Also, if he knew he was a beneficiary of Canning's will then he had two motives.

Hubert Wraith. Motive: confessed to rowing with Canning. Suspiciously interested in the key we found.

'Well, we can cross the reverend and Mrs Fontaine off our list to start with.' She shook her head, remembering how frail they still looked in the hospital. 'That narrows it down a bit.'

She tapped her pen on Hubert Wraith's name. 'We know now his motive for possibly killing Canning was because he believed

Canning had swindled him out of his share of the fortune Canning amassed from their smuggling together. But how would he have planted the poison in the Hall?'

Clifford rubbed his chin. 'We do know that whoever planted the poisoned tea was here inside of the last three weeks.'

'We do?'

'Yes, because even though the formal tea service is rarely used, as you are not in the habit of holding formal events.' He pursed his lips. 'Out of deference to Lord and Lady Fenwick-Langham, I employed it when they came at the beginning of the month to invite you for Christmas luncheon. And I feel that it would have been almost impossible to plant the poison without being seen on the day of the Henley Hall Christmas Eve luncheon with guests and staff everywhere.'

'I agree. Top-notch thinking, Clifford. Well we can rule out Wraith then. As far as I know, he'd never called at the Hall at all until the Christmas Eve lunch.'

'I agree, my lady. To my knowledge, Mr Wraith has never set foot on these premises before.'

'Right!' She boldly crossed Wraith's name through. As Clifford went to speak, she held up a hand. 'I know what you are going to say, but we simply don't have time to check and double-check everything. We need to whittle down our list to the most likely suspect, or suspects, and act.' She turned back to her list. 'Now, that leaves us with three main suspects. Let us therefore start with Doctor Browning. Ignoring the Christmas Eve luncheon as you say, Clifford, when do we all agree he was last here?'

Polly raised her hand. 'Not since I was poorly, your ladyship. I remember that was November end as I was worried I would be too laid up to help with the Christmas prep… prep… Christmas things.'

The housekeeper nodded. 'He's not been here since. Mr Clifford's accounts would show otherwise.'

Clifford nodded.

'Indeed. Excellent point, Mrs Butters.' Eleanor crossed Doctor Browning's name through. She ignored Clifford's slight tut of disapproval. 'Now, what of Mr Moore? To my knowledge he's not been up to the Hall.'

'Not to disagree, my lady, but he has,' Mrs Butters said.

Eleanor stiffened. 'Really?'

'Yes, my lady. I found him at the back door. I think it was Tuesday last, having been sent by Miss Moore to collect the vases and fancy bowls for the Christmas arrangements. Or so he said.'

Clifford frowned. 'I had the conversation with Miss Moore that she would call herself on the Wednesday to collect them.'

Mrs Butters shrugged. 'He said she'd told him to collect them early as she'd realised she was going to be extra busy on the Wednesday. Mind, I'd told her the day afore that everything was boxed up ready in the storeroom so perhaps it's something and nothing.'

Eleanor's thoughts were whirling. 'Was he left alone at all, Mrs Butters?'

'No, not for a minute. Oh, except...'

'Except?' Eleanor and Clifford chorused.

'Well, maybe it was my mistake because the note she'd given him said fifteen vases and whatnot but I'd only packed fourteen.'

'So you went off to get the last one?'

Mrs Butters nodded. 'From the hall table on the second landing, my lady.'

'So Mr Moore might have had a chance to plant the poison?'

Mrs Butters shook her head. 'Begging your pardon, but Alvan Moore had never set foot outside this kitchen afore the special lunch. It would have taken him too long to find the butler's pantry, search for the tea caddy and switch the tea.'

Clifford nodded. 'I am inclined to agree. However, we cannot rule out the possibility. His mother knows the house and could have informed him of the layout.'

Eleanor's eyes narrowed. 'Miss Moore might have colluded with her son then. Or planted the poison herself. And speaking of Miss Moore, the next on our list, I remember that she was here less than three weeks ago when I invited her here to discuss the flower arrangements.'

'Of course, Miss Moore was also here on the morning of the Christmas Eve lunch,' Mrs Butters said. 'I remember 'cos she ran into Mr Canning.'

Eleanor and Clifford straightened like two puppets yanked by their strings.

'Were they in the kitchen, Mrs Butters?'

She nodded. 'Yes, my lady. You know Mr Canning, if he didn't get a cuppa he was even more grumpy than ever. Seeing as it was so cold, I didn't make him take it out on his wagon like I do in the better months. Miss Moore must have come to get more water for the flower arrangements.'

'You mean you weren't in here with them?'

'No, I went to get more milk from the cellar and Trotters was checking a delivery out front. You could have cut the atmosphere with Joseph's axe when I returned, I tell you.'

'Were they arguing?'

'Folk can't argue if they're not speaking to each other. There must have been some cross words just afore though, 'cos just as I came in, Mr Canning marched out the back door and slammed it hard enough to need new hinges.'

Clifford tapped his forefinger on the table. 'And how did Miss Moore seem to you? Was she upset?'

'No, more sad. Not to be indiscreet, but it reminded me of those rumours about the two of them all those years ago, if you'll pardon me for mentioning it, Mr Clifford.'

Eleanor looked down at her list. 'So it seems Miss Moore and her son are our chief suspects at the moment, whether they were working alone, or together. And it seems we might have been hasty in assuming the berries and leaves couldn't have been planted the day of the Christmas Eve luncheon. Certainly if, like Miss Moore, the poisoner was here before the guests arrived, it might have been feasible.'

The back door opened as Joseph pulled his boots off and stepped inside in his thick woollen socks. 'Morning, m'lady.'

'Morning, Joseph,' Eleanor said. 'And how are you? You must be frozen.'

He grinned as he rubbed his hands. 'I'm looking forward to that stove you so kindly thought of getting put in the shed and no mistake. Reckon I'll be the luckiest gardener in the county.'

Eleanor again recalled Canning's words to her on the morning before the lunch. 'People say I bring a sack of trouble.' *Talk about an understatement, Ellie!*

Joseph was still talking. 'Lucky that the vicar and his housekeeper got back before the worst of the snow, though.'

The hairs on the back of Eleanor's neck stood on end. 'What!?'

'That's right, my lady. I saw them early this morning when you could just about get back from the village afore the snow turned extra fierce. Apparently, they came back first thing. A couple of nurses helped them up the steps to the vicarage, but they was walking, just 'bout.'

Clifford scanned her face. 'Something is troubling you, my lady?'

Eleanor looked around the table, her face ashen. 'Whoever it is, the killer has already struck once.' She glanced at Clifford. 'Possibly twice if you include Uncle Byron. He's also unsuccessfully tried to kill who we assume are two witnesses, even if those witnesses don't realise they saw something. With half the county snowed under and Little Buckford unreachable by any outside help, what would you do in his shoes?'

Clifford nodded slowly. 'I would finish the job I started.'

CHAPTER 37

Eleanor gestured for Clifford to join her out in the hallway. He came over and cleared his throat. 'Why am I overcome by a strong sense of apprehension, do you suppose, my lady?'

She shrugged. 'Because you know what I'm going to say. The phone lines are down since last night so we can't call Constable Fry and the inspector's probably still stuck somewhere in Oxfordshire. That only leaves us.'

He shook his head. 'I cannot countenance you being in danger again, my lady. And I believe you promised the chief inspector that you would investigate the case discreetly and listen to my cautionary advice. I can, however, instruct Silas to proceed immediately to the vicarage.'

She tilted her head. 'And who will protect the ladies then, Clifford? The killer has already breached the Hall's security and left poison here. Suppose he were to again? Without Silas, the ladies are sitting ducks.'

She raised her hand as he went to reply. 'I don't like this any more than you do. But what if, as we speculated, we were the poisoner's intended victims, not the reverend and Mrs Fontaine? Then they almost died because of our actions. Okay, we were trying to catch a murderer, but nonetheless, I feel responsible.' She looked him in the eye. 'And whatever I promised the inspector, I am not going to sit here and have their deaths on my conscience if the killer does try again and succeeds.'

After a moment or two, he nodded. 'I agree, my lady, if' – he reached into his inside jacket pocket and pulled out the pen she had given him on Boxing Day morning, tapping the inscription – 'you promise me, on his lordship's memory, you'll let discretion be the better part of valour. Although, I fear, in agreeing to this plan, discretion may already have fled in disarray.'

'I promise.' She hoped the tremble in the pit of her stomach wouldn't betray her. 'But we need to move. And fast. We'll have to continue talking about the case on the way. There's just no time.'

Fifteen minutes later they were both suitably dressed against the elements. Clifford held a canvas bag with sturdy leather straps. 'Two hot flasks, a bag of biscuits, two torches, blankets, snow goggles, folding shovel, small tent and spare boot laces, my lady.'

Despite the gravity of the situation she had to smile at his thoroughness. She waved the book of poisons she had grabbed from the library. 'I'm not usually superstitious but this felt like a good talisman to go with my notebook. And I did remember a pen.' A thought struck her. 'Why didn't you bring the skis in from the boot room, though? I know I'm horribly rusty but they've got to be the quickest way, surely?'

'Too dangerous, my lady. With the snow drifting, it is too hard to tell how close obstacles are underneath. And the way down to the village is steep and tortuous as you know.' He clicked his fingers. 'One moment.' He strode off and returned with what looked like four heavy-duty tennis rackets with cut down handles. He also had four ski poles tucked under one arm.

'Snowshoes, my lady.'

'Ever tested them?' she said dubiously.

'Indeed, your late uncle was meticulous in testing his equipment.'

'Right then, let's go.' On hearing these words, Gladstone lumbered out of his bed and climbed up her leg. 'Oh, no, I didn't mean you, Gladstone old chum, you can't come with us.' She cupped his wrinkled jowls. 'You need to stay and protect the ladies.' She looked up at Clifford. 'Although it's a shame Uncle Byron didn't make a set for him.'

'He did, in fact, my lady. But Master Gladstone never took to them. He rather favours navigating the snow by sliding on his stomach, as you are aware.'

'Plenty to cushion you there, my friend,' she whispered to the bulldog.

Clifford swung the bag onto his back. 'I have warned the ladies to be extra vigilant and Silas, with Joseph's help, is patrolling the immediate grounds.'

She straightened up and grabbed her ski poles. 'Here goes then.'

Outside, the sun shone in an almost cloudless blue sky. Giant icicles hung from the guttering along the front of the house, while snow covered the roof, except for the two steeply tiled roofs of the needle-like towers that flanked the main entrance. A cruel arctic wind, however, forced them to keep their heads down as it whipped stinging, frozen snow into their eyes. Ten minutes after setting off, they reached the second field beyond Henley Hall's grounds.

Eleanor paused, breathing hard. 'I'm sure you were right about not taking the road, Clifford, but even in these snowshoes, this is quite an effort.'

He stopped and nodded. 'True, but if, by any chance, the killer double guesses our intentions, then he will be watching the road into the village from the Hall. By going across country, we can reach the vicarage without alerting anyone.'

'I agree, but I've only used snowshoes once or twice before. I seem to remember you lift your knees higher than usual, flick your heels upwards and plant both poles in front of you.' She adjusted the straps. 'Right-oh, let's have another go!'

They continued, stumbling over buried tussocks and at one point tumbling full tilt over a snow-covered cattle trough.

As they entered the thickly covered beech woods, it was eerily silent, the snow deadening all sound. Hidden just out of sight under the snow, the tree roots proved a lethal tripping and slipping hazard.

Eleanor pulled herself upright for the umpteenth time. 'This would be such a fun adventure if we weren't trying to stop a rampant poisoner and prove Mrs Trotman's innocence.'

Clifford nodded. 'Indeed. Mrs Trotman's ordeal is far from over. She will soon be standing trial unless we can—'

Eleanor stopped dead. 'Say that again, Clifford.'

He stopped as well and looked at her in confusion. 'I said, my lady, that Mrs Trotman will have the ordeal of standing trial if we are unable—'

'That's it! Oh how did we miss that! Trial by ordeal!' She rammed her ski poles into the snow. 'Clifford, Canning wasn't poisoned wi—'

'Not poisoned, my lady? I must disagree. He—'

'Clifford, Canning was poisoned, yes, but not with digitalis.'

Confusion showed on her butler's normally inscrutable face. 'I am sorry, my lady, I fear I am not following you. At all.'

Slow down, Ellie. 'Okay, I know I'm not always crystal clear, so I'll try to explain it as if you were talking to me.'

'It would be a help.'

Despite the knot in her stomach, she smiled at his remark. 'Right. The riddle we simply couldn't solve was this: how did the poisoner actually poison Canning? I mean, the mechanics of it. If he'd put the poison in all the Christmas mead, then all the guests would have been poisoned. If he'd put it into the jug Mrs Trotman poured Canning's drink from, anyone else Mrs Trotman served from that jug would equally have been poisoned.'

Clifford nodded. 'Which means the poison must have been in Mr Canning's glass only.'

'And the only person who could have made sure that was the case, was the person who poured Canning's glass.'

'Mrs Trotman,' they chorused.

'But,' Clifford added, 'we know she didn't poison Canning.'

It was Eleanor's turn to nod. 'Exactly, so there was no digitalis in Canning's glass! I remember clutching at straws and suggesting exactly that when Seldon arrested Mrs Trotman. And he rightly replied that in that case Canning wouldn't have been poisoned. And he's right. Unless, that is—'

Clifford stiffened. 'He was actually poisoned later on with a completely different poison?'

'Exactly! The digitalis was just a distraction from the actual poison used. Like a magician will tell you to look over there, while deftly switching cards over here. The killer spiked the washing-up water with digitalis as an insurance policy in case Canning was discovered to have been murdered. In that instance the police would test the last thing he ate or drank, and on finding digitalis in the washing-up water, which matched Canning's symptoms and the digitalis in his blood as he took heart tablets, would look no further. All they would then need to do would be to work out how it got into the water.'

Clifford nodded slowly. 'And as Mrs Trotman served Mr Canning the glass of her homemade Christmas mead and Polly then washed-up the glass in the same water—'

'Why look any further for another explanation?'

'Or another guilty party?'

She nodded grimly. 'The poisoner has had us, and the police, running around trying to work out what he drank twenty minutes to half an hour or so before the race—'

'Whereas, we should all have been... what, my lady?'

Eleanor pointed to Clifford's sack. 'The book of poisons, please.'

A minute later, Eleanor stabbed at a page with her thick-gloved finger. 'Tanghin seeds! That's it. I remember hearing of it on my

travels. It's only found on Madagascar and the surrounding islands.'
She read on. '"The symptoms of Tanghin poisoning are notably
similar to digitalis poisoning. The nut of the tagena tree contains
cerberin, which is related to the toxin found in foxglove. This causes
the heart to fibrillate (an uncoordinated spasmodic contraction that
fails to pump blood), and in many cases, completely stop beating."'

She looked up. 'So Tanghin poisoning makes it look as if the
victim had a heart attack. And if poison is suspected, digitalis is
the natural assumption because no one is looking for an obscure
tropical poison. I doubt if the coroner even knows Tanghin seeds
exist.' She carried on reading.

'"The Tanghin seeds were used by the ancient rulers of Madagascar as a form of 'trial by ordeal'."' She looked up again. 'That's
why when you mentioned what an ordeal it would be for Mrs
Trotman to stand trial, it jogged my memory. The Tanghin tree is
also called the Ordeal Tree.' She read further. '"The rulers forced
the accused to eat the Tanghin seeds. If the accused died, he was
guilty, if he survived, innocent. The rulers abused the system to get
rid of their enemies by making sure they gave them a large enough
dose that they always died."'

She read the next line slowly. '"The poison is made by grinding
the seeds into a kind of paste, resembling ground almonds."' Eleanor
whistled. 'So the killer couldn't have put that in the Christmas mead
Mrs Trotman served him. He'd have to have put it in something
Canning ate.'

'Mrs Trotman's yule log, perhaps?'

She nodded slowly. 'It could be. But again, a lot of other guests
ate the yule log, so the killer must have poisoned just Canning's slice.'

Clifford was deep in thought. 'And the time it takes for the
victim to show major symptoms of Tanghin poisoning, my lady?'

She scanned down the page. '"The main difference with digitalis
poisoning is… that whereas the worst effects of digitalis poisoning

take twenty to thirty minutes on average to manifest, the main symptoms of Tanghin poisoning take only a few minutes.' She snapped the book shut. 'So if the poison was in the yule log, Canning must have eaten it immediately before the start of the race. He must have felt awful, but somehow kept going.' She looked at Clifford. 'Do you suppose…?'

He nodded. 'Given Mr Canning's character, even though poisoned he kept going out of—'

'Sheer bloody mindedness in order to beat his old partner, Wraith?'

'I would have put it differently, but yes.'

She took a deep breath. 'We've not a moment to lose. Let's get going.'

They put the book back and continued making painfully slow progress towards the village. As they came to the edge of the woods, Eleanor slapped her forehead. 'Oh, Clifford, Miss Moore is a botanist. She used to work at Kew Gardens. I bet they have a Tanghin tree there. That means she might have been able to get hold of some seeds.'

Clifford nodded. 'And Mr Canning sailed the South Seas which means Mr Wraith may well have been on some of the same voyages along the East Coast of Africa. Less plausible, perhaps, but Mr Wraith could have a contact still at sea who could have provided him with the seeds.'

'How on earth do you know Canning sailed there?'

'When Doctor Browning gave Mr Canning his cursory examination at the end of the race, he pulled down the deceased's vest which revealed a turtle tattoo. The navy's honour for crossing the equator, my lady. I noticed when we visited Mr Wraith, he had the same tattoo on his forearm.'

'Wraith could have gone to Madagascar with, or without, Canning then. But how would Doctor Browning have known about the seeds? And, more pertinently, how would he have got hold of them?'

'Medical training might cover some of the less common poisons, but it seems unlikely given that it seems cases of Tanghin poisoning rarely occur outside of Madagascar and the surrounding islands. It is also difficult to see how he would have obtained those specific seeds.'

'Also, remember, Wraith and Doctor Browning haven't visited the Hall in the last three weeks, so that still makes Miss Moore with her links to Kew Gardens, or her son, Alvan, the most likely suspects.'

'I agree, my lady, Miss Moore—'

'The bag!'

He frowned. 'Bag, my lady?'

As the realisation sunk in, Eleanor felt sick in the very pit of her stomach. 'Mr Canning's sailor's bag—'

'That the reverend went to great pains to hand back to him?'

She nodded. 'Contained a portion of Mrs Trotman's yule log.'

Clifford's frown deepened. Then understanding dawned. 'You mean, perhaps the reverend never found Canning's bag?'

She nodded again. 'Maybe he didn't find it at all. Maybe he stole it, laced Canning's slice of yule log with Tanghin seeds and then returned it before the race started?'

Clifford shook his head. 'And then he poisoned himself and Mrs Fontaine with just enough digitalis to make it look like Mrs Trotman was "up to her old tricks again" as Sergeant Brice put it.'

'Having already planted the berries and seeds at the Hall for the police to find after, I imagine, he had given them an anonymous tip off.' She groaned. 'And the reverend was in Madagascar! On the missions.'

As they struggled on the last leg into the village, the frown on Eleanor's face deepened.

*

The remains of an army of snowmen who had been relegated to snowball-throwing practice were the only sign of life as they reached the village green. A couple of forlorn ducks walked up and down the frozen pond quacking in disgust, while a moorhen sulked among the reeds. A few footprints in the snow led towards the high street, the only sign that anyone else was out and about.

Eleanor shook her head again. 'We've gone over this already, Clifford.'

He rubbed his hands over his eyes. 'But, my lady, you promised—'

'I know. And I promised the inspector. But no one is going to attack me just because I turn up on the doorstep. I can easily stall for the few minutes it will take you to find Fry and get back. It's perfectly plausible that I wanted to welcome the reverend and Mrs Fontaine home and offer any help I can.'

But when she finally reached the door of the vicarage, her speech to Clifford felt less convincing. She let out a long breath. *Last time you were here, Ellie, you found two near-dead friends. Now you know one of them never was a friend, but a killer. What on earth will you encounter this time?* She shook her head and whispered, 'Too late to back out now.' She lifted the knocker and let it drop.

CHAPTER 38

'Lady Swift, what a surprise, but welcome, welcome!' The vicar hobbled over to her, a look in his eyes that seemed somewhere between confusion and apprehension. He looked over her shoulder. 'But gracious, did Mr Clifford leave you to walk here?'

Eleanor laughed as she kicked off the snow from her boots on the boot scraper. She'd removed her snowshoes at the gate. 'The roads are unmanageable, Reverend, and your driveway is rather slippery. He walked me here, but he had some urgent matters to take care of. I'm meeting him later.'

Reverend Gaskell closed the door behind her and took both her hands in his.

Stay calm, Ellie. Breathe.

'You seem remarkably well... recovered, Reverend. I hope you don't mind my calling unannounced, but the telephone lines are down and I was surprised, and delighted, when I heard that you had been allowed back to the vicarage so soon.'

Taking her arm, he led her down the hallway, steadying himself with his other hand. 'The doctor at the hospital is a wonderful man who understood we would recuperate faster in the familiarity of home. Also, unfortunately, they had another localised outbreak of influenza and desperately needed the beds. And the police are looking into the unfortunate matter you and Mr Clifford saved us from, which is most comforting.'

His face bore an expression Eleanor couldn't fathom. She smiled as he continued, 'I admit, however, I was itching to be back to conduct this evening's service.'

She shook her head. 'Out of the question, surely? You must need to rest and, besides, St Winifred's will be freezing.'

'Merci, Lady Swift,' Mrs Fontaine said as she appeared from the kitchen. 'I have been trying to say this all day. Only those who live in the centre of the village will make it to the church, anyway. How you and Mr Clifford made it here I cannot imagine. But maybe now you listen, Reverend?'

He looked from one to the other. 'I see I am to be chided by both of you, in which case I shall have no choice but to gracefully surrender.'

'About the time too,' Mrs Fontaine said, folding her arms.

Eleanor smiled at the look of genuine concern on the house-keeper's face. 'And how are you?'

'Better than the reverend, Lady Swift. And less of the stubborn mule too.'

The vicar seemed to lose a little more of his good humour. 'It was King David's mule who bore Solomon to Gihon. They are much maligned creatures, actually, Mrs Fontaine.'

Eleanor looked between the drawn faces in front of her. 'I have to say you two remind me of Clifford and myself. We find ourselves squabbling over the smallest of things on occasions, especially when we are exhausted.'

She watched as the vicar seemed to check himself. 'Mrs Fontaine, I am sorry if I have been waspish, perhaps I'm more tired than I realised.'

'Et moi, Reverend.'

'You must both be.' Eleanor nodded towards the sitting room. 'Why don't we sit by the fire and you have a rest? I would love to hear some of your tales that inspired this.' She pointed to the painting of the wooden building flanked by the baobab trees. 'You must tell me all about it.'

In the sitting room, Eleanor was drawn up short by the fireplace. However, it wasn't the fireplace itself that had caught her attention, but a small drawing in a plain wooden frame sitting at one corner. She'd never noticed it before. The drawing looked medieval and was of a man's head. Surrounding the man's head was a halo.

The vicar paused in taking his seat. 'Ah, I see you have spotted my namesake.'

'Namesake, Reverend?'

'Yes. It is a fifteenth-century drawing of Saint Gideon. I bear the same forename. It inspires me to try and emulate such a man of faith as much as I am able.' He chuckled weakly. 'Not that I consider myself a saint, dear lady.'

Not even a saint with a past, Ellie?

Mrs Fontaine put her head round the door. 'Lady Swift, will you take tea? I—'

He interrupted her. 'Rest assured, it is an entirely fresh box, dear lady. In a new caddy kindly brought round by our churchwarden's wife. I decanted the tea in there myself earlier while Mrs Fontaine was laying the fires.'

Smile, Ellie! 'That would be lovely.'

While the housekeeper went to make the tea, the vicar stood up and with an effort put another couple of logs on the fire. Eleanor wanted to intervene and help, but at the same time she wanted to see just how miraculous his recovery was.

The glow from the now crackling fire highlighted the vicar's taut and drawn face. Gone was the jovial figure Eleanor had seen shepherd his flock with a gentle, caring hand. She realised just how little she really knew of the man sitting in front of her. Apparently he'd returned to Little Buckford about eight or nine years ago, but no one knew that much about him before that.

'So where were you based for the majority of your years abroad, Reverend? What was it ten, no eleven years ago now?' Aware that the vicar's housekeeper had returned with a tray, she cleared a space on the low table between their two armchairs.

The vicar leaned back. 'Eleven, so Mrs Fontaine often reminds me. And we were based in Madagascar. Although I believe the natives may have taught me more than I can claim to have given them in return.'

'Travelling really is quite the eye opener, isn't it?' She chose her words carefully. 'I always loved the idea of continuing some customs I witnessed abroad. But somehow, here I am in sleepy Buckinghamshire getting more and more immersed in a very English way of life.'

'Some customs do not travel well beyond their original borders,' the vicar said quietly.

'And yet some do.' She held his gaze.

Mrs Fontaine appeared at Eleanor's side. 'A mat, Lady Swift. To go under your saucer.'

'Thank you. And how did you enjoy Madagascar, Mrs Fontaine?'

'Me?' The housekeeper looked surprised. 'Fine enough, merci, but I prefer civilisation, if you can call Little Buckford civilisation.' She glanced at the vicar and then back to Eleanor. 'You have been having the history lesson of how I met the reverend, non? It is quite the dull story. I should switch to talking of the scenery, it is better. Here is your tea, Lady Swift. And yours, Reverend.'

'Actually.' Eleanor leant forward quickly. 'May I swap cups?' She reached out to take the reverend's tea. 'This one looks much more the colour I prefer.'

He flinched. 'Really, dear lady? Maybe Mrs Fontaine could make you another? Perhaps stronger?'

'No need, thank you. This looks perfect.' She pulled the cup from his grasp with difficulty. *He may still be recovering, Ellie, but there's nothing wrong with his grip.* She smiled at both of them. 'Now, do you mind if I take our conversation briefly back to poor Mr Canning? Reverend, what did you say was in the kit bag when you looked to see whose it was?'

The vicar was still frowning at her swapping cups. 'Gracious, do we need to discuss such things just now?'

'The bag, Reverend?' She kept her eyes on his. 'Unless it's a problem to answer, of course?'

He shook his head angrily. 'Why should it be a problem, except for the fact that we could have some respite from all this recent unpleasantness?' He reached for his tea and lifted the cup to his lips.

'Non!' Mrs Fontaine screamed, dashing the cup from his hand.

CHAPTER 39

'What on earth?' The vicar looked from his housekeeper to Eleanor in confusion.

Eleanor stood up. *Where's Clifford with Fry, Ellie? They should be here by now.*

'Lady Swift?' the vicar stuttered. 'What on earth is going on?'

'It's quite simple, Reverend, Mrs Fontaine saved you from being poisoned again. Only this time you wouldn't have recovered.'

He stared at the empty cup at the end of the arc of tea on the rug, then at his housekeeper.

'Nonsense!' Mrs Fontaine snapped, recovering herself swiftly. 'Lady Swift, I am sorry, but I think you sticking your nose in too many cases that should be left to the police has made you, how you say, over suspicious.'

'You do?'

'Oui, I do.' Mrs Fontaine moved to the vicar's side. 'Upsetting the reverend with more talk of poison is not the kind thing to do. He has come home to rest and recover his health. You should go. Now!'

'Lady Swift!' The vicar eyes were saucer-wide. 'You can't possibly be suggesting that Mrs Fontaine was… behind us being poisoned?'

'I'm not suggesting she was, Reverend. I'm telling you she was.'

'But we nearly died.' He half rose and then sunk onto the arm of his chair. 'My dear lady, I fear you have taken leave of your senses.'

Mrs Fontaine's eyes darted to Eleanor's, containing a flash of triumph. 'I suggest, Lady Swift, you return to your fancy manor house and stop trying to make trouble. Accusations are dangerous things.'

Eleanor ignored her and moved in front of the door leading to the hallway. 'I'm sorry, Reverend, but Mrs Fontaine is not the woman you believe she is. The tea she knocked from your hand was intended for me. As was the poison she laced it with. She has used the cover of being a vicar's housekeeper to surround herself with respectability and I was about to ruin all that.' She shook her head. 'You see, Reverend, my mother told me that every sinner has a past. And you yourself told me every sinner has a chance to put that past right. You believed Mr Canning chose not to do so before he died, but you were wrong. He made a will just before Christmas.'

The Reverend shook his head. 'I don't understand. Even if he had done such a thing, he had nothing to leave.'

Mrs Fontaine uttered a cry of rage. 'He did! My money to those worthless—' She clamped a hand over her mouth, horrified by her admission. The vicar stared at her dumbfounded.

Eleanor nodded grimly at the woman. 'I think you mean to those he believed he'd wronged, Miss Moore and her son.' She turned back to the vicar who sat, mouth agape. 'You see, Reverend, the rumours about Mr Canning having a fortune hidden away were true.'

The vicar looked from one to the other. 'So… so the stories about Mr Canning amassing a fortune through smuggling were right?'

Eleanor nodded. 'And Mrs Fontaine was the go-between in his smuggling operations.'

A glimmer of understanding showed in the vicar's eyes. 'The "family" she's been visiting every week for years…'

'Doesn't exist, I think you'll find. I believe she used it as cover so she could meet the shipments that Canning brought at night via the Thames, hidden in Canning's coal barge.' She silently thanked Sandford for that information at the Langham Christmas lunch.

'She then arranged for the contraband goods to be distributed via criminal gangs throughout the area.'

Mrs Fontaine scowled at her, shaking with rage. 'Non! You cannot prove any of this!'

Eleanor was on a knife-edge, but she had to see this through for Canning's sake. And Uncle Byron's. *Where are those blasted reinforcements, Ellie? This woman has killed, and attempted to kill, who really knows how many times?*

She swallowed hard. 'Can't I? Let's start with Mr Canning who you poisoned at the Christmas Eve lunch at Henley Hall with Tanghin seeds hidden in his yule log.'

The housekeeper's defiant air evaporated in an instant. She stared at Eleanor as if she were the devil. 'How... how can you know this?' she whispered.

The vicar started. His jaw hung open as he stared at his house-keeper.

Eleanor needed to keep talking. 'I remember you saying you studied under a pâtissière, so it would have been easy for you to copy Mrs Trotman's yule log. You also volunteered to help Mrs Butters on the food table so when it was Canning's turn to be served, you could make sure he got the slice of poisoned log you'd made earlier. And when the reverend mentioned being in Madagascar ten years ago, I recall you saying at the Women's Institute that you'd been with him for eleven years, so I realised you must have met the reverend and become his housekeeper there. The island, after all, is run by the French, so that made perfect sense. Which also meant you could have known about the Tanghin seeds. And, obviously, during and after the war rationing was widespread and we were all encouraged by the government to forage for wild food. So, a trained French cook would have soon learned which wild plants were edible and safe, and which, like foxgloves, were poisonous.'

The vicar's eyes widened as he stared at the woman he had trusted for over ten years.

Eleanor read the question in his eyes. 'Mrs Fontaine realised that…' She blushed. 'That we believed you poisoned Canning.' The reverend's disbelieving gaze switched to her. She hurried on, omitting to mention that Mrs Fontaine had been right. 'She was desperate. To throw suspicion off you, and herself, she planted foxglove berries and leaves in Henley Hall. And then, when she knew I was coming around, put just enough poison in your tea to make you ill, but no more. She also made sure she took some herself.'

'No!' The reverend looked utterly devastated. 'She… she can't have! I… I trusted her…' He tailed off, shaking his head.

Eleanor nodded sadly. 'To start with, Clifford and I fell for it, but then the doctor mentioned you both seemed to have consumed much less poison than he'd first thought.' She turned back to Mrs Fontaine. 'I finally worked it out when I remembered you mentioning a French woman wearing the trousers wasn't so unusual. It was something about the way you said it. Full of pride, as if you yourself were an example. That's when I realised later that in your mind you were in charge of the smuggling operation, not Canning. And that's why you insisted the money he amassed should have been yours.'

'It was!' Mrs Fontaine's voice shook with anger. 'Canning just brought the goods to me. I was the one who did everything else. The one who took the money and the most risks. Without me Canning would have made nothing! That money was mine by right!'

'So you snuck around and found out he'd made a will leaving all the money you thought was rightfully yours to Miss Moore and Alvan?'

She spat. 'I did not need to sneak about to learn it! He was happy to scream the news at me when I challenge him one more time for my money. He told me I would get nothing, never, because he was going to do right by those he should have. Stupid fool. I knew if he was out of the way, I could have got the money. There are people who would help me.' She gave a reptilian smile. 'But he beat me to it. I did not realise he made the will already. He deserved what he got.'

The vicar turned his gaze on his housekeeper. 'I... can't believe it.' He shook his head slowly. 'Poor Mr Canning.'

'Poor Canning, nothing!' Mrs Fontaine shouted. 'Reverend, you saw how he treated people. He lied, cheated and stole whenever he could.' Her eyes flashed. 'He stole from me, so I stole from him.'

'You stole his life and his future!' Eleanor said quietly. 'That's not a fair exchange, whether or not he truly owed you that money.' She felt a wave of sadness. 'Only you didn't in the end.' At the housekeeper's confused look, she continued. 'I finally understood, struggling through the snow to get here. Canning realised how bad his health was getting. He'd been warned by his doctor. He told me on Christmas Eve that he would prove everyone wrong who said he'd never do a good deed before he died.' She looked at Mrs Fontaine with contempt in her eyes. 'You killed Canning, but it was all in vain. The joke, if you can call it that, was on you.'

The housekeeper started to shake. 'What do you mean?' she whispered.

Eleanor addressed the vicar who had collapsed back into his chair. 'What I couldn't figure out was why Canning changed his will rather than just giving Miss Moore and Alvan the money. After all, he never spent any and lived as poor as a church mouse. But you see, Canning was fiercely proud. False pride you might call it, Reverend, but proud nonetheless. He wanted to put his wrongs right, but he couldn't bring himself to admit he'd behaved badly all those years. And I unexpectedly gave him the chance he needed by inviting him to the Henley Hall Christmas Eve lunch. Straight afterwards he made a will leaving everything to the two people he'd wronged and—'

'Dear lord!' The vicar stared at Eleanor. 'And then he ran in your race…'

Eleanor nodded. 'Believing his heart would give up before he finished the course.' She turned to the now catatonic housekeeper. 'Canning never intended to live beyond that day. He'd lived life on his own uncompromising terms his entire life and he intended to leave the same way.' She shook her head, looking into the woman's eyes. 'Everything you did, including poisoning Reverend Gaskell, the man you truly loved, was a complete waste of—'

With amazing speed Mrs Fontaine hurled the teapot at Eleanor's head. Eleanor ducked, the pot sailing past her ear and smashing against the door. By then Mrs Fontaine was in the kitchen heading for the garden. She wrenched the door open to be met by Clifford, shotgun in hand, advancing forward. She sprinted back into the sitting room and across to the French windows where Constable Fry's looming form, truncheon at the ready, stopped her dead.

She spun back around, her eyes like a trapped animal. With an unholy scream, she grabbed the letter knife from the mantelpiece and launched herself at Eleanor.

CHAPTER 40

Eleanor couldn't believe Langham Manor looked even more splendid on New Year's Eve than it had on Christmas Day. With the decorations still up and giant gold paper lanterns and rows of flickering candles lining the corridor to the ballroom, she felt transported to a fairy-tale kingdom.

With the party in full swing and the orchestra playing Strauss' 'Viennese Waltz', the weight of the hideous events that had started on Christmas Eve began to lift as Lancelot waltzed her around the ballroom. Her visit to Miss Moore that morning had helped…

'Miss Moore, please forgive me turning up announced.' Eleanor stood on the doorstep of Canning's old house.

'Lady Swift, what a surprise.' Miss Moore smoothed out her floral-print apron. 'Forgive the state of me, I thought I would come and make a start on scrubbing the house before Alvan and I move in. Please come in.'

Eleanor stepped over the threshold into the small hallway she'd stood in a few days before.

'I realise it's New Year's Eve morning, but this couldn't wait.' She reached into her bag. 'I believe this is yours.'

'A… key?' Miss Moore took it and looked at her with puzzlement.

Eleanor took a deep breath. 'Mr Canning had that key about his person when he fell at the end of the race. It fits a very… special kind of lock. As Mr Canning left you all his possessions' – *and we know now she's not his killer, Ellie* – 'I wanted to make sure you got this as well.'

Miss Moore shook her head. 'There's nothing this would fit. Alvan and I have been in every room.'

'Even the cellar? I believe many of these houses have one.'

Turning the chest over on the kitchen table, Eleanor exposed the hidden lock with studied surprise. 'Lucky guess! My late uncle had one similar.'

She shrugged, hoping the explanation was vaguely plausible. Fortunately, Miss Moore's curiosity was too piqued to think of anything except running her fingers over the trunk. Despite her own burning curiosity, Eleanor's conscience pricked her.

'Oh gracious, how insensitive of me. I should leave you to look inside on your own.'

Miss Moore looked up. 'No, please stay. You were the only one who believed there was any good in Conrad. And the only one who sought justice for him. And… and I don't want to be alone at this moment.'

'Of course,' Eleanor said quietly.

Having unlocked it, Miss Moore's hands trembled as she placed them either side of the chest's lid.

Eleanor bit her lip, suddenly fearing it might be empty or worse. *Oh, Ellie, despite everything, maybe you were wrong about Canning. Please, please let it not be something awful.*

As Miss Moore lifted the top, they both held their breath and stared inside.

An oblong of red silk, edged in matching velvet filled the top.

'What?' Miss Moore breathed, gingerly reaching to lift it. As she did so, she turned to Eleanor. 'Oh, m'lady! Letters?'

'Many, many letters.' Eleanor smiled as her heart skipped for the other woman. 'All addressed to you.'

Miss Moore lifted a few of the letters out of the case and turned them over in her hand. 'But he never sent them. Why would he have written all of these… he barely spoke to me in all these years.' She paled. 'I'm too nervous to open one.'

Eleanor put her arm round the woman's shoulder. 'Given that the letters are lying in hundreds of dried rose petals, I think you'll be delighted with what he wrote to you, and over a great many years by the look of it.' The realisation that Canning had in fact written Miss Moore a love letter each night in bed and then trudged down to the cold, dark cellar to hide it in the chest which he locked tightly back up before returning to bed, brought a lump to her throat.

'Miss Moore, he might not have been able to say it to you in person but I shall leave you to read just how much he truly loved you.'

'Sherlock? Where have you gone?'

Eleanor blinked. 'I'm sorry, I… I was just remembering something. Something I learned earlier today.' She shook her head.

'That's better, Sherlock.' Lancelot pulled her closer as they glided across the crowded marble ballroom floor.

It wasn't the champagne but the feel of his hand through the emerald organza panel of her evening gown that was making her lightheaded. *Ellie, remember your promise to yourself when you left Miss Moore. Don't make Canning's mistake. You have to follow your heart.*

His blue-grey eyes were locked onto hers. 'I think we need to twirl out into the hall where the mistletoe is,' he murmured.

'Goggles?'

'Yes, darling fruit.'

'I think we need to slow down.'

'Not a chance, old girl. We're keeping up with all the other twirlers, look around you.'

She bit her lip. 'I meant our relationship. You and I. Maybe not slow down. Maybe…'

'What?' His arms tightened around her. 'Sherlock, no more torture. I've told you what you do to me.'

'As have I. And you will always be the cat's pyjamas, I promise, but my head is all over the place. I've got confused and I just think—'

'Too much,' he said, stroking her cheek. He said nothing more for a moment and then sighed. 'Seldon?'

She blushed. 'I… I don't know. I just know I need some space… and time to think clearly.'

He searched her eyes. 'I can see there is no point in trying to change your mind. If that is what the lady wants, that is what she shall have. Promise me one thing, though? However this ends, we'll still remain friends.'

'I promise.'

'Then, Lady Swift, let me dance you to the champagne table one more time as I resign myself to you being the most exquisite and peculiar fish that might end up getting away.' He nuzzled her ear as he whispered, 'I am, however, going to twirl you the long way round, just to have you in my arms a few precious minutes longer.'

CHAPTER 41

Breathless and flushed, she somehow made it to the end of the ballroom. Lord and Lady Langham were seated at a table with the Dowager Countess, her niece Cora, and Viscount and Viscountess Littleton who seemed to still be finding each other's company a chore.

Eleanor looked back at the dance floor and paused as she watched Baron Ashley twirl his petite English rose of a wife, their faces alight with love. She nodded to herself. *You'll never know if you don't try, Ellie.*

Lady Langham cut into her thoughts. 'Eleanor, dear. Do come and join us.'

Lord Langham stood up and clapped Lancelot on the back. 'Take a pew, my boy.' He placed his arm around his son's shoulder.

'Lancelot, why don't you sit next to Cora?' the countess said wickedly.

Lancelot slid into the chair next to Eleanor but had the good grace to throw Cora an apologetic smile.

'Augusta, Harold, what a wonderful party. It is absolutely perfect.' Eleanor reached out and patted both their arms.

'My dear girl.' Lady Langham hung onto her hand. 'It is only the beginning of the rest and relaxation you need. Fancy Clifford letting you get mixed up in such nastiness again. I have to say I am extremely surprised at him.'

Eleanor laughed. 'He did put his foot down on more than one occasion, but he eventually bowed to my stubborn insistence. He really is entirely above reproach.'

Lord Langham nodded to his wife. 'Think about it, light of my life. This mere slip of a girl is, in reality, a headstrong rhino in disguise and well you know it.'

'I do,' Lady Langham said.

'Not much of a disguise.' Lancelot winked at Eleanor.

'Anyway, it's all over now. Finished and done with, as am I with investigating nasty matters.'

Lord Langham waved his empty champagne flute at a passing footman. 'Eleanor old thing, we've heard that tosh before.'

'Harold, dear,' his wife chided.

'But we have. It's not the girl's fault though. Trouble attracts trouble so they say.' He chuckled and ruffled Lancelot's hair.

Lady Langham tutted. 'Eleanor, I for one am so relieved to hear you say that. To think what might have happened. Oh gracious!' She fanned her face.

Cora leaned forward. 'Lady Swift, I was told you were in the most terrible danger.'

Eleanor blushed. 'It was a little... fraught at one point.'

'But, there was something about the killer having a knife!' Cora's eyes were popping out of her head.

Eleanor realised the rest of the table were waiting to hear the end of her tale. Even Lady Langham seemed perched on the edge of her seat.

'Well, I really have Uncle Byron to thank for saving me.' *Even in death, he's looking out for you, Ellie.* 'He was quite the brilliant inventor. You see, I left my snowshoes at the gate but the ski poles were collapsible – Uncle Byron's design. So I'd hidden one up my sleeve as I had a feeling it might get a little trickier than I'd planned. Anyway.' She ran her hand through her curls. 'With a tad of Bartitsu, a form of martial arts, and a lot of unladylike yelling, I managed to disarm her.'

'Her!' the viscount shuddered.

Eleanor nodded. 'And then Clifford and Constable Fry took over.'

Cora looked faint. Her aunt took a swig of the whisky beside her. 'What'll happen to the terrible creature now?'

Eleanor blushed and avoided Lancelot's gaze. 'Inspector Seldon said there is enough evidence to charge her with killing poor Mr Canning and poisoning the reverend. Would you excuse me just a moment?' Lancelot rose with her, but she gently shook him off.

Lord Langham slapped the table. 'Eleanor, old thing, it's only a few minutes to midnight. There's no time for wandering off.'

'I'll be back in a jiffy.'

Out in the garden she shivered as she leaned against the stone balustrade of the rear terrace. *Take a deep breath, Ellie.* She could not shake the memory of her last conversation with Mrs Fontaine. With Little Buckford still cut off, Constable Fry had locked the prisoner in his one-room gaol at the village police house until the roads were cleared. Out of deference to Eleanor's help in solving the case, he'd let her see Mrs Fontaine to ask the question that would burn in her, and Clifford's, mind forever if she didn't.

'Why should I tell you?' Mrs Fontaine said carelessly.

'No reason at all, unless, like Canning, you want to put one part of your past right while you still can.' Eleanor's voice shook as she asked again. 'Although a different poison was used it seems to be your modus operandi. Did you kill my uncle?'

Just when Eleanor thought she would never reply, Mrs Fontaine shrugged. 'You'll never prove it, mais, oui, I did. He interfered with the business of one of my… distributors and they asked me to… deal with him.'

Eleanor clenched her fists. 'Who was it? What is his name?'

The woman shrugged again. 'I cannot remember, I have such a poor memory. But' – she flashed Eleanor the same reptilian smile she had in the vicarage – 'I will not forget you, Lady Swift.'

Eleanor shivered, but she needed one last answer. 'Did Canning know you killed my uncle?'

Mrs Fontaine laughed mockingly. 'Non! He was a fool. If I had told him, he would have stopped me.'

Out in the snow-covered Langham Manor garden, Eleanor shivered again at the memory. She knew she would have to deal with the pain and support Clifford as he dealt with his own grief. Like her though, he had taken some comfort in knowing the truth. And one day, together, they would find the person who had ordered her uncle's death.

The sound of a gong inside the ballroom reminded her that that fight was for another day. She was here to celebrate the new year with friends. Hurrying inside, her elbows were grabbed by Lord Langham on one side and his wife on the other. With the hundred-strong guests all having linked arms, they started counting down the last seconds of 1920…

With her farewells and happy new years said, Eleanor fell into the Rolls at the bottom of the grand steps. As the car cleared the end of the drive, Clifford gestured to the glovebox. 'I took the liberty of bringing fortifications, my lady.'

She smiled as she pulled out a brandy miniature and crystal glass from the case. 'What made you think I might need this?'

'Perhaps a difficult conversation with a certain gentleman?'

'Oh, Clifford, am I really that open a book?'

'Only to those anxious to read,' he said with a rare smile.

She took a sip of warming brandy and tilted her head. 'Do you know the only thing I want now?'

He nodded. 'Yes, my lady. And we will be there in time.'

*

'Oh, my lady, 'tis ten minutes to midnight.' Mrs Butters winked at Eleanor as she and Clifford stepped in through the front door of Henley Hall. Mrs Trotman and Polly came hurrying out from the kitchen, followed by an over-excited bulldog.

'I wanted to be back in time and we made it.' Eleanor pointed at the tall grandfather clock. 'To the green drawing room, ladies. We've only a few minutes!'

As the rest of the staff skittered off, Eleanor whispered to Clifford, 'How many clocks are there here at the Hall?'

'Forty-three, my lady.'

'And you set all of them back an hour just so I could go to the Langham's ball and Polly could still experience a proper New Year's Eve celebration?'

'In truth, Polly does not read the time too well and normally only consults the three grandfather clocks at the Hall. However, I did not wish to risk her being disillusioned. Now, shall we do justice to the last minutes of the old year? Again?'

In the cosiest of the drawing rooms, Eleanor was over the moon to see the three ladies had been joined by Joseph. Gladstone bowled past her into the centre of the group, not sure what all the excitement was about, but determined to join in.

'No chance Silas might appear?' Eleanor asked Clifford.

'Regrettably not, my lady.'

'More parsnip perry and chestnut liqueur for us then,' Mrs Trotman chuckled as Clifford uncorked the first of the bottles on the walnut table. 'I have to confess, at one point I fair thought I'd be celebrating the new year in jail. I can never thank you enough, m'lady.' She removed a starched white cloth from a silver salver. 'I've made your late uncle's favourite, Stilton cheese straws with onion relish and apple chutney. I hope that's alright.'

Eleanor looked up at the full-length portrait of her uncle, overcome with a sense of calm, of peace. Uncle Byron truly was still at the Hall, she could sense him beaming down at her. Clifford nodded at her. He'd felt it too.

'Cheese straws, your formidable home-bottled concoctions, and, more importantly, all the staff back at the Hall for the new year? No, Mrs Trotman, it is not alright.' Eleanor linked arms with Polly and Clifford. The others followed suit until they were one connected circle. 'It is in fact, perfect!'

She led the countdown, and as forty-three clocks struck midnight in unison and Gladstone woofed his heart out, Henley Hall echoed to the sounds of 'Auld Lang Syne' and Eleanor truly felt she was home.

A LETTER FROM VERITY

Dear reader,

I want to say a huge thank you for choosing to read *Murder in the Snow*. If you did enjoy it, and want to keep up to date with all my latest releases, just sign up at the following link. Your email address will never be shared and you can unsubscribe at any time.

www.bookouture.com/verity-bright

I hope you loved *Murder in the Snow* and if you did I would be very grateful if you could write a review. I'd love to hear what you think, and it makes such a difference helping new readers to discover one of my books for the first time.

I love hearing from my readers – you can get in touch on my Facebook page, through Twitter, Goodreads or my website.

Thanks,
Verity

@BrightVerity

veritybrightauthor

veritybright.com

ACKNOWLEDGEMENTS

To all the amazing staff at Bookouture who have worked as hard as I have to make sure *Murder in the Snow* was as good as it could be. And to all the fabulous readers who have followed Ellie, Clifford and Gladstone's adventures at Henley Hall.